FINAL CIRCUIT

ALSO BY BARBARA HINSKE
DEADLY PARCEL ("WHO'S THERE?!" BOOK 1)

Guiding Emily

Rosemont Series

Coming to Rosemont

Weaving the Strands

Uncovering Secrets

Drawing Close

Bringing Them Home

Shelving Doubts

Novellas

The Night Train

The Christmas Club (adapted for The Hallmark Channel, 2019)

Available at Amazon in print, audio, and for Kindle.

UPCOMING IN 2020

The seventh novel in the Rosemont Series

CONNECT WITH BARBARA HINSKE ONLINE

Sign up for her newsletter at **barbarahinske.com** to receive a Free Gift, plus Inside Scoops and Bedtime Stories.

Search for **Barbara Hinske on YouTube** to tour inside her historic home, plus learn tips and tricks for busy women!

Find photos of fictional Rosemont, Westbury, adorable dogs, and things related to her books at **Pinterest.com/BarbaraHinske**.

Facebook.com/BHinske

Twitter.com/BarbaraHinske

Instagram/barbarahinskeauthor

bhinske@gmail.com

FINAL CIRCUIT

"WHO'S THERE?!" BOOK 2

BARBARA HINSKE

Casa Del Northern Publishing
Phoenix, Arizona

Copyright © 2020 Barbara Hinske.
Cover by Elizabeth Mackey, Copyright © 2020.
All rights reserved.

ISBN: 978-0-9962747-9-1
Library of Congress Control Number: 2020906863

Casa del Northern Publishing
Phoenix, Arizona

DEDICATION

To my remarkably supportive husband, Brian Willis, who is my rock
and the wind in my sails. Always.

CHAPTER 1

Olivia Osgoode turned up the collar of her heavy woolen coat against the icy wind that skimmed the concrete block wall of the parking garage. She glanced around her. She was truly isolated. She should have paid to park in the underground garage down the block instead of this shabby municipal parking structure that rose six stories, like a blemish on the face of downtown. Her grandmother had raised her to be thrifty and Olivia's penny-pinching ways were firmly set, now that she was in her late twenties. If she'd thought about the fact that she'd be returning to the garage after the end of normal business hours—alone—she'd have spent the money on the other garage.

She pushed the button to summon the elevator. The last rays of afternoon sunshine failed to penetrate the elevator lobby of the garage. The sole fluorescent bulb flickered, scattering shadows into the corners. The elevator arrived and she hurried in, pushing the button for the top floor.

The heavy metal doors crept together. Olivia steadied herself for the chug of the car as the motor engaged, but the elevator sat motionless. She stabbed at the button for her floor. The elevator didn't move. A frisson of fear ran up her spine. *How long will I be trapped before help arrives?* She rubbed her hands together. It wasn't much warmer in the elevator than it had been in the garage.

She located a red button on the control panel and bent over to read the words that had been worn off by frequent use: *Call Help.* She pushed the button but no alarm sounded and the dented speaker grill next to the button remained silent. *Will I be here until people arrive for work in the morning?* She racked her brain—how cold was it predicted to be that night? *Will I freeze to death while I wait?*

Olivia shook her head to clear her thoughts. *Stop letting your imagination run away with you.* She leaned into the button for her floor, then jabbed it three times in succession. The motor shuddered and the elevator began its sluggish ascent. Olivia moaned softly and fished a crumpled tissue out of her coat pocket to dab at the tears that came so easily since her grandmother's death.

The elevator lurched to a stop at her floor. She stepped out and the doors closed behind her. She shielded her eyes from the glare of the setting sun with one hand and hoisted her purse onto her shoulder with the other. A movement at the far end of the garage caught her attention. She froze and stared in disbelief.

Silhouetted against the crimson sky along the outside row of parking spaces, a tall figure in a black jacket leaned over the open trunk of a dark sedan, his face obscured by a ski mask. He struggled under the weight of the large object he carried.

Olivia blinked hard against the blinding light and focused. He was carrying a woman wearing a black skirt and low heels. A scarf draped across the woman's body provided a slash of crimson against her inky clothing and white hair. Her head dangled at a precarious angle. The woman was dead.

Olivia heard herself scream. The sound reverberated in the concrete structure. Bile rose in her throat.

The figure lifted his masked face to hers. He stood no more than two hundred feet from her.

Olivia stumbled backwards until the closed elevator doors stopped her escape. *No!* She pressed against the unyielding metal surface. *I've got to get out of here!* She jerked herself around and fumbled for the button to summon the elevator. She punched at it frantically and watched the readout over the door as the elevator worked its way back to her, floor by floor. *Come on! For God's sake, come on!*

She whipped her head over her shoulder and forced herself to look at the man as he threw the body into the trunk and slammed the lid. The victim's head and one foot caught on the opening of the trunk and the lid sprang back up after hitting them with a sickening thud. He abandoned the body and began to run toward Olivia.

She tried to scream for help but this time no sound emerged. The elevator was still two floors away. *It's not going to make it in time!* She swung to her right and saw the door next to the elevator marked

"Stairs." She lunged at the handle and tugged, but the door wouldn't open. *Shit, shit, shit!*

The man was coming fast.

Olivia thrust herself back to the elevator as the doors began to part. She flung herself into the elevator and searched for the Close Door button. *Focus!* she screamed internally as she looked at the symbols for Open Door and Close Door. *Which is the right one? The arrows pointing toward each other?* That had to be it.

Her hand shook as she reached out to push the button. She couldn't make a mistake. If she hit the wrong one he would capture her. And kill her. *I have to do this.*

Olivia took a deep breath to steady herself. She pushed the button and the elevator doors started to close. She looked up to stare in horror at the man running toward her. He'd covered half of the distance between them and was picking up speed as the elevator doors made their steady progress toward each other. Her heart hammered in her chest and she flattened herself against the back of the elevator.

The man dove toward her as the doors shut. He grunted as his torso hit the ground outside the elevator. He thrust one gloved hand into the opening and curled his fingers around the edge of the door. The doors stopped moving toward each other.

Oh, my God, he's going to open the doors! Olivia's breath caught in her throat. If she didn't do something—now—she would be his. She bounded toward the door, her eyes fastened on his hand as he tried to force the doors open. She brought the heel of her right foot up and lashed out at him, kicking viciously at his fingertips. Her heel connected firmly with his gloved hand but he held on. She brought her foot back and struck again. She hit her mark and lost her balance, sprawling on the floor of the elevator. She tilted her head back and stared into the dark eyes behind the killer's mask. Olivia recoiled at the malice that glittered there.

He lost his grip and his wrist hit the metal threshold of the elevator. She tore her eyes from his and crawled to the control panel, leaning into the Close Door button. His hand slid out of sight and the doors closed.

The elevator shook as the masked man pounded on the closed door. Olivia propelled herself, crablike, into the far corner of the elevator and drew into a ball, hugging herself. She held her breath, expecting the doors to reopen, but the motor engaged. The elevator began its descent. Olivia bent forward as another wave of nausea washed over her. For one frightening moment, she thought she might pass out. She swallowed hard. *Don't give in. Keep your wits about you.* She wasn't safe yet. He could be waiting when she got out of the elevator. She needed to call the police.

Olivia tried to pull herself into a standing position but her legs were too shaky to support her. She crawled to her purse and retrieved her cell phone. She sat cross-legged on the filthy floor and brought the phone's screen into view. A guttural moan escaped her lips. She had no cell service in the elevator. She flung the phone back into her purse. *Now what?*

The elevator bounced to a stop on the first floor and the doors began to part. Olivia forced herself to her feet, placing one hand on the opening to steady herself. She reached for the Close Door button with her other hand. *What if he's out there, waiting for me?*

She leaned out of the elevator and quickly looked right and left, sweeping her eyes over the shadowy scene in front of her. Everything was still. She could see most of the first floor of the garage from her vantage point. The only vehicles remaining were an SUV and a minivan. There were no dark sedans in sight. The first floor of the garage was deserted and the masked man was nowhere to be seen.

Olivia gulped in a deep breath. She couldn't stay where she was. She had to get out of there and call for help. She propelled herself from the elevator, swiveling her head wildly, searching for the killer as she ran. She stumbled, almost sprawling on the ground, but managed to keep her feet under her. She rounded the corner and ran out of the garage, darting across the street mid-block. A van screeched to a halt, narrowly avoiding her, and the driver laid on his horn. Olivia ignored him and raced to the double glass doors of the office building where she had been meeting with the lawyer for her grandmother's estate less than fifteen minutes earlier. She'd be safe with him. Howard Asher would call the police; he'd know what to do.

Olivia tugged at the heavy doors of the building. They didn't yield. She checked her watch; it was almost six thirty. The doors were locked. People had been streaming out of the building when she'd arrived at five thirty for her appointment with Mr. Asher. She thought he'd been kind to agree to wait for her when she'd telephoned to say that she'd be an hour late—now she was sorry that he hadn't insisted she reschedule.

She had been ready to leave work for her appointment when she'd taken the call from the father of the teen that had died in a tragic car accident over the weekend. She'd spent over an hour with him, discussing the details of the funeral that would be held at Hilton Mortuary the next morning. What the grieving man had really needed was the sympathetic ear of a compassionate listener. Olivia hadn't had the heart to hurry him off the phone so she could attend to her own business.

Now, here she was, standing on a deserted sidewalk with a killer on the loose, looking for her. She wouldn't find a safe haven at Asher Law, PLC. *I've got to call the police.*

She turned to the street, searching for any sign of the masked man. A streetlight further down the block was out, leaving the entrance to the next building in deep shadow. She narrowed her eyes, straining to detect any movement in the darkness. Her hands shook as she tried to punch 9-1-1 into her phone.

CHAPTER 2

The man ignored the telltale pain in his knee and ran full tilt toward the elevator. He was twenty feet from the opening when the doors slowly began to shut. With an extra spurt of effort, he closed the gap and dove for the opening. He landed on his stomach and managed to curl the gloved fingers of his right hand around the door.

The woman stared at him from the back of the elevator, her mouth grotesquely open as if she were screaming. He heard nothing but the whistling of the wind. He watched her lash out at his hand with her foot once and then again; felt the pain as she hit her mark. He lost his grip on the door and his wrist struck the metal threshold as the doors shut.

He propelled himself to his feet and pounded on the metal doors as the elevator slipped to the floor below. The sound of his hands pummeling the outer elevator doors echoed through the thin twilight. The elevator kept going.

He struck the doors one last time before he gave up. Now he'd done it. *Damn it!* He'd been seen. He raced to his car, pushing himself on his throbbing knee as pain seared through his right hand. He cursed under his breath as he dislodged the dead woman's foot from the metal support that held the trunk open and shoved her head back into the lightless space. He ripped his ski mask from his head and tore off his jacket, throwing them on top of the woman's sightless eyes as he slammed the lid shut. He flung himself into the driver's seat and pushed the ignition button with his right thumb. The fingers of his right hand curled into a tight ball. He brought his injured hand to the steering wheel and inhaled sharply as he flexed his fingers and grasped the steering wheel. *Thank God.* If he was able to do this, she probably hadn't broken anything.

He sped down the ramp to the first floor and approached the exit onto the main street but veered off at the last minute, opting to exit through the service vehicle entrance from the alley on the other side of the parking structure. He inched the nose of his sedan into the alley and let out his breath in a rush. The alley was deserted.

The man drove slowly up the alley, turned right, and then left onto the main street that ran in front of the garage. Two blocks down and across the street, he observed the woman from the elevator standing on the sidewalk. She was poking at something in her hand—presumably her phone.

Today's my lucky day. He'd gotten away with killing the old lady. He would be more careful next time; return to his tried-and-true method of helping his victims into the future they all longed for. A small dose of any of the easy-to-obtain date-rape drugs, followed by suffocation with a pillow, was all it took.

Stick to the plan, he reiterated to himself. *When you resumed this a year ago, you promised yourself you'd be more careful.*

Olivia's hands shook as she punched the digits 9-1-1 into her phone and brought it to her ear. She continued to swivel her head from right to left, searching for any sign of the masked man in the thin blue light from the street lamps.

Someone rapped soundly on the glass door behind her. Olivia jumped and lost her grip on her phone, swiping at it frantically before it tumbled to the ground. She turned to see a tall, familiar looking man nodding to her as he unlocked the door and stepped onto the pavement.

He bent and picked up her phone, holding it out to her.

It was Thomas Hilton, her boss' identical twin brother. She took the phone from him, bringing it to her side. Olivia ran her eyes over him while she gulped air to steady herself. Both were tall men with full heads of graying hair that gave them a distinguished and dapper air. Sam sported an additional thirty pounds on his brother and was handsome in a comforting, reliable family-man way while Tom's sleek and toned frame suggested a suave and sexy man of the world. They'd recently celebrated their fiftieth birthday. Sam managed the family-owned funeral home where she'd been employed since graduating from high school. She'd seen Tom when he'd attended occasional meetings at the mortuary but he didn't work there.

"Are you all right, miss?"

"No," Olivia managed to croak. "I… I… I've just seen a murder."

"What?"

"In…" Olivia burst into tears.

"What's all this?" he asked, placing his hands on each of her arms and turning her toward him.

Olivia looked into his eyes. "There's a dead woman in the parking garage."

"I'm sorry," he said. "I didn't get that."

Olivia repeated herself, forming her words slowly and distinctly. The cleft lip and palate that she'd been born with, which had been so inexpertly repaired when she was a small child, interfered with her speech at the best of times. These were not the best of times; she knew she had been unintelligible when she'd just spoken to him.

"There..is..a..dead..woman..in..the..parking..garage."

"What are you talking about?"

"I got off the elevator on the top floor and he was there. With her."

Tom bent down and moved closer to her, staring at her lips.

"A..man..put..a body..in..the..trunk..of a car." She took a deep breath. "On the top floor of the garage," she added slowly.

He rocked back on his heels but kept his eyes locked on her face. "Go on."

"A big person—maybe your size—wearing a ski mask. He was carrying a woman in his arms." Olivia disengaged herself from his steadying hands and demonstrated the stance of the man holding the body.

Tom gasped. "How do you know she was dead?"

"Her head was hanging at a crazy angle."

"Good God," he said.

Olivia shook uncontrollably. "It was horrible. I thought he was going to get me and kill me, too."

Tom put his arm around her shoulders and she sagged against him. He looked into her face. "Did he see you?"

Olivia nodded and spoke in short, jerky sentences. "He came at me. He was running across the garage. I got back in the elevator." She choked on a sob. "I was trapped in the elevator and watched as he almost made it before the doors shut. He got one hand in the opening and I was scared the doors wouldn't close. I kicked his hand free. He pounded on the doors after they closed."

"That must have been terrifying. Do you know who he is?"

Olivia shook her head. "I have no idea. He was wearing a ski mask."

Tom nodded. "Why did you come here?"

"My grandmother's lawyer works in this building. I just left from an appointment with him and I hoped he was still here. I'm trying to call the police, but I keep losing cell service."

Tom rubbed his hand along her arm. "You're shivering. It's cold out here. Come with me and we'll place the call from my office."

CHAPTER 3

Tom held Olivia securely to him as he escorted her to his office. Even through her thick coat, he could feel her body tremble. He steered Olivia to a leather sofa that ran along the back wall of his office. She sank into its deep cushions. He leaned over her and looked into her eyes. He patted her hand and straightened.

"Let me get you some water before you make that call," he said as he moved to the small refrigerator in the corner of his office.

Olivia nodded. "Thank you, Mr. Hilton."

He spun to face her. "Do we know each other?"

"I work at the funeral home." Her eyes searched his face for a spark of recognition. "I'm the bookkeeper… Olivia Osgoode."

He turned sharply away from her. She worked for Sam? He didn't recall seeing her there on any of his visits, however infrequent, to the family business where he'd worked as a teenager and that was now run by his twin brother. He was still a minority owner. He really should pay more attention to it—his share of the profits represented a lot of money over the years.

Tom retrieved the bottle of cold water from his refrigerator and held it out to her.

She took it from him with a weak smile of thanks.

Tom reached into his pocket for his cell phone with his left hand. He punched in the emergency numbers and shifted the phone to his right hand.

"This is Tom Hilton," he said with great authority into the phone. "I'm here with a woman who says she's seen a man carrying a dead body in the Jefferson Street parking garage."

Tom paused as he listened to the 9-1-1 operator's response.

"Olivia Osgoode. She's with me in my office and she's nearly hysterical." He glanced across his desk to where Olivia sat, gripping the water bottle.

"No. I haven't seen any of this myself. I placed the call because she's not able to talk right now." He paced as he gave them his address. "The building is locked but we'll come downstairs to wait for you."

Tom hung up his phone. "They're dispatching officers now." He nodded to the unopened water bottle that she was clutching. "Would you like something stronger? To calm your nerves?"

Olivia shook her head vehemently.

"What do you remember about this man?"

Olivia leaned forward and cradled her head in one hand. "I don't know," she moaned. "I don't remember anything, really. Just that he was wearing a ski mask and holding a dead body." She turned her chin up to face him. "He was about your size."

"I'm just over six feet. That describes a lot of men."

"I know. He could be almost anybody."

Officer Byron Tucker pulled into the flow of traffic and checked the clock on the dashboard of his car. He'd get home on time for once; he and his daughter would have dinner together before she started her homework. His radio crackled and he listened intently to the message relayed by the dispatcher: a dead body in a downtown parking garage. He hesitated for a millisecond. Suspected homicides were rare in Marquette—he had to respond. Missie would understand; she always did. He checked his mirrors, turned on the flashing red lights, and responded to the call.

Olivia swayed slightly from side to side, taking deep breaths to calm herself, while Tom hovered by the glass doors in the lobby. "They should be here any minute now."

Olivia nodded mutely.

Byron Tucker parked in front of the building, alongside two patrol cars, and joined his fellow officers on the curb. Tall and solid, he had the imposing build of a weightlifter. As the senior officer, he took charge.

"I'll question the witness." He pointed to the other two officers. "Secure the garage. There are vehicular entry points here," he gestured to the garage across the street, "and along the alley. You'll need to find the stairwells. If memory serves, they're next to the elevators. At least it's a freestanding structure so we don't have to deal with access to adjacent buildings. Make sure no one enters or exits."

The officers nodded.

"Call in backup to search the garage, floor by floor. They'll need to work in pairs. I'll see what the witness has to say and we'll take it from there."

The officers crossed the street to the garage. Byron approached the building as the familiar vehicle of Senior Detective Fred Novak pulled up. The detective rolled down his window and motioned Byron over to the car.

"I heard the call come in. What've we got?"

"Tom Hilton placed the call."

"Local financial planner?"

"That's the guy. Said he's with a woman who saw a man carrying a dead body in the garage." He gestured with his head to the structure across the street. "We're securing it and I'm on my way to question the witness."

"We don't see many homicides around here." Detective Novak put his car into park and got out. "Let's talk to her together. I'll question her and you can run a background on her as soon as we get her name and info."

They walked to the door. Tom opened it and motioned them into the lobby.

"You're Tom Hilton?" Detective Novak asked. "You called in a suspected dead body in the parking garage across the street?"

Tom gestured toward Olivia. "She saw a man in the parking garage. Says he was carrying a dead body."

Detective Novak turned to Olivia. "You're the witness?"

Olivia swallowed hard and nodded.

"Did you see any of this?" he asked Tom.

"No. I was leaving the building after work—I have an office here—and came across Olivia. She was obviously in great distress, so I asked if I could help her."

"Do you frequently work late?" Detective Novak asked.

"Two or three times a week."

"So you were in your office the whole time?"

"Yes, I was."

"What did she say to you?"

"Just what I told the police dispatcher—that she'd seen a man carrying a dead woman's body in the parking garage. I told her that we had to call the police. She was too shaky to do it, so I helped her."

The officers turned to Olivia. Novak flipped to a new page in his notebook. "Can you tell us your name and address, please?"

Olivia lowered her chin to the ground and whispered her shaky response.

Detective Novak looked at Olivia over the top of his glasses. "Let me read that back to you. I'm not sure I've got it."

Tom listened attentively. He was familiar with the stretch of rural road where she lived. He made a mental note of the address. He'd drive her home and make sure she got inside safely. She was part of the *Hilton Mortuary family*—it was the least he could do.

Byron slipped out the door to his patrol car and entered her name and address in his computer. Olivia Osgoode owned the property that corresponded to the address she just gave them and had no criminal record whatsoever—not so much as a parking ticket. A seven-year-old Corolla was registered in her name. He made a note of the VIN and license plate number and rejoined the group in the lobby.

Detective Novak ran his hand over his thinning hair. "Let's run through this again."

Olivia brought her hand to cover her mouth in the habitual gesture that she employed to hide her deformity. She began her story, focusing on forming each word distinctly. Detective Novak stepped closer to her, interrupting her frequently to ask her to repeat herself.

Olivia's voice cracked on her fifth recitation of the description of the woman's head as it dangled from her body in the man's arms. Tom put his arm around Olivia's shoulders. She leaned into him.

"I'm sorry to keep asking you to repeat yourself, ma'am," Detective Novak said. "We need to be clear on the details." He glanced at Byron and raised an eyebrow.

Byron inclined his head slightly.

"Why don't you drink some of your water." Detective Novak gestured to the bottle she was holding, twisting and untwisting the cap. "I'm going to confer with my colleague and I'll be right back."

Olivia sank deeper into Tom. The sensation of being supported by a man's arms was unfamiliar to her.

Detective Novak and Byron stepped to the doors and looked out into the night.

"I'm not trying to be difficult. She has a serious speech impediment. I can't understand her. Can you?" Detective Novak asked.

"I can," Byron responded. "Why don't you direct the search of the garage? Here's the license plate of her car." He tore off the sheet from his notepad and handed it to the detective. "It's a white Corolla and should be on the sixth floor... with the sedan in question, if it's still there. I'll finish up with her."

Detective Novak nodded. "Good. I'm making it worse for her." He turned to glance back at Olivia. "She's an odd one. Do you think we're going to find anything? I'm not sure she's telling the truth."

Byron followed Detective Novak's gaze.

"Don't you think her story sounds a little far-fetched?" Novak asked.

"It may be far-fetched, but I've been observing her. She's telling the truth. There was a body in that garage. Whether it's still there, now, is another story."

"Dead bodies—or missing persons—have a way of turning up. Someone will report something. Whether we find one in that garage or not, we'll know soon enough if Olivia Osgoode is telling the truth."

CHAPTER 4

Byron turned back to Olivia as Detective Novak exited through the glass doors. She stood in profile. Her blond hair was corralled into a bun and she wore sensible black shoes, a black turtleneck, and a shapeless black coat. From this vantage point, she looked to be in her mid-forties. He'd been watching her as she spoke to Detective Novak—been looking into those violet eyes set in a flawless complexion. She wore no makeup to cover up any signs of aging. He tapped the end of his pen against his teeth. Although her attire was that of a middle-aged woman, she couldn't be any older than her late twenties or early thirties.

Byron cleared his throat.

Olivia and Tom spun to face him. She made no move to separate herself from Tom.

"Are you done, here, Officer? Olivia's had enough. She'd like to go home."

"I understand, ma'am," Byron said, directing his comment to Olivia. "I'm sure this is very hard on you. We'll let you go just as soon as we can."

"She's given her statement," Tom said. "It doesn't sound to me like she saw anything that will be useful."

"Detective Novak is supervising the search of the garage. When they're done, we'll need to take Olivia over there to go over what she saw."

Olivia moaned softly.

Tom tightened his arm around her shoulders. "Surely that can wait until morning."

"This is a murder investigation, sir. We need to gather information now." Byron fixed Tom with an icy stare.

Tom shrugged.

Byron addressed Olivia. "While we're waiting for the results of the search, I'd like to go over your statement. Confirm a few details."

Olivia tipped her face up to look at Byron. At six foot four with his massive frame, he was physically intimidating—the kind of man she instinctively shied away from. There was a softness around his large brown eyes, however, that telegraphed kindness. She straightened and exhaled slowly. "Sure. I'll do my best."

"Let's back up a bit," Byron began. "Can you tell me why you were in the parking garage?"

"I had an appointment with an attorney in this building," she replied. "Howard Asher."

Tom drew back from Olivia slightly and looked at her intently. Howard Asher was a prominent estate planning attorney and many of Tom's clients had been referred to him by the attorney.

"What was the nature of your business with Mr. Asher?"

"He's my grandmother's—my late grandmother's—attorney," she replied. A sob escaped her lips.

Byron stopped making notes, his pen suspended over the paper. "I'm sorry for your loss," he said. "How long ago did she die?"

"Three months, one week, and four days ago," Olivia replied quietly.

Byron paused as Olivia fumbled in the pocket of her coat and pulled out a tissue to dab at her eyes.

"Do you need to take a break?" Byron asked.

Olivia cleared her throat and forced herself to answer. "I'm fine; I'd like to continue."

"You had business with Mr. Asher regarding your grandmother's estate?" Byron asked.

Olivia nodded her head yes. "I inherited her house."

"How long was your appointment?"

"I'd guess I was there about half an hour."

"And you parked in the garage?"

"Yes. On the top floor."

"Did you go directly to your car after your appointment? Did you stop anywhere else first?

"No. I went straight there."

"Now we're back to the events we've already talked about. I'd like to clarify a few points. You say the man was putting the body into the trunk of a car. A dark sedan?"

Olivia nodded.

"Can you give me the make and model of the car?"

"I don't know. I'm not a car person and it was on the other side of the garage." She shook her head. "And I was looking into the setting sun. All I know is that it was dark—black or gray. And four-door. I know that describes a lot of cars. I can't give you any other details."

Detective Novak broke away from the group of officers clustered at the elevator bank as Byron and Olivia crossed the street and stepped onto the sidewalk skirting the garage. Tom followed closely behind.

"We've completed our sweep of the garage," the detective said, pausing and looking directly at Olivia.

"Did you find the car with the body?" she asked.

Detective Novak shook his head. "Unfortunately, no. The garage was practically empty. There were no dark sedans. The only vehicles remaining were your Corolla, an SUV, a minivan, and a handful of light-colored sedans. Are you positive it was a dark car?"

Olivia nodded.

"Then we didn't find anything. No body, no car, no masked man."

Olivia recoiled from his gaze.

"Are you sure you remember seeing these things?" Detective Novak asked.

Olivia felt a flush creep up her neck. "Of course I remember seeing them. I'm telling you the truth. He's gotten away." She squared her shoulders. "You let him get away."

Byron stepped between Olivia and the detective. "It's entirely possible that the perpetrator moved his car to another location before we arrived. He—or she—would have had time." He gestured to the officers standing nearby. "We may have recovered evidence—fibers, tire treads, fingerprints—from the elevator door. I'd like you to walk us through everything you saw."

Olivia nodded and stared at her shoes, swallowing hard.

"I know this will be scary, but I'll be right here with you," Byron said, taking her arm and steering Olivia to the elevator.

Tom stepped in line behind them.

"I'm sorry, sir," Detective Novak put out an arm to block Tom. "Police only."

"But I'm with her," Tom sputtered.

"We've got it from here."

Tom took a reluctant step back. "Olivia," he called. "Would you like a ride home when this is over?"

Olivia looked over her shoulder at him.

"You're pretty shook up. I don't think you should be behind the wheel tonight," Tom said.

Olivia nodded. "I'd appreciate it." She gestured to the upper level of the parking garage. "I don't know how long I'm going to be. Don't you have to get home?"

"Absolutely not," he lied. "I was going to work late tonight anyway. Catch up on paperwork." He was actually supposed to escort his wife to the annual charity ball held by the hospital auxiliary. She was the chairwoman of this year's event and might be annoyed at him for not showing up. In reality, she'd be so busy hobnobbing with her society set that she probably wouldn't notice his absence. It was more important to make sure that Olivia was taken care of.

"I'll bring her to your building when we're done," Byron said.

Tom retreated across the street.

Byron motioned to one of the uniformed officers to join them. He summoned the elevator. "You said you parked on the top floor and didn't access any of the others?"

Olivia nodded as the three of them stepped into the elevator. "Except the ground floor when I left."

"You arrived after the end of the work day. Why did you go up to the top floor? Weren't there spots below?"

"I wanted to see the view from the sixth floor. I never get to see the city from up high." She shrugged. "I know that sounds silly."

"You'd be surprised at the number of people who do that," Byron said as the elevator bumped to a stop at the sixth floor. He looked into her eyes. "When this door opens, I'd like you to reenact what happened. What you saw and what you did."

Olivia's lip quivered.

"I know this is frightening, but we're right here with you. And it's crucial to our investigation."

The doors opened slowly and Olivia stepped out of the elevator. Byron placed a steadying hand on her elbow as she reenacted the terrifying events of only an hour earlier. Although she was clearly shaken up, her account was cogent and detailed. Olivia Osgoode was smart, articulate, and truthful. He was sure of it.

When she'd run through her recitation several times and answered numerous questions, Byron gestured to her car that was now the sole vehicle remaining on the floor. "Do you want to get anything out of your car before we leave?"

"I don't need anything. Are we done here?" Olivia asked, releasing a deep breath.

Byron nodded. "This has been very helpful. Thank you."

Olivia pointed to her car with a hand that trembled. "Maybe I should just drive home."

"I agree with Tom Hilton. You're in no condition to drive tonight. You can leave your car here overnight. It'll be perfectly safe."

"I guess you're right," Olivia said as the other officer summoned the elevator. "Tom said he'd give me a ride."

"Do you know this guy?" he asked Olivia as they stepped onto the elevator.

She brushed a strand of hair that had escaped its confinement in the bun off her forehead. "I work for his brother—his identical twin brother. That's why I know who he is. He's not really a stranger or anything."

Detective Novak extended his hand to Tom. "Thank you for seeing Ms. Osgoode home," he said as they shook.

"Least I could do," Tom replied.

"Thank you for your statement," Detective Novak inclined his head toward Olivia.

Olivia covered her mouth with her hand in the characteristic gesture. "You're welcome."

Byron bent slightly to catch Olivia's eye. "Will you be alright tonight? Is there someone you'd like to call to be with you?"

Olivia shook her head no. "I'll be fine."

"If you think of anything else, please call me," Byron said, handing her a card with his phone number.

Olivia nodded again. Tom put his hand in the small of her back and steered her toward his car in its reserved parking spot behind the building.

Byron stood with Detective Novak and watched the patrol cars pull away from the curb.

"Find anything promising in there?" he asked his superior.

"Hard to say. We didn't get much. A few fibers. No fingerprints." He faced Byron. "I'm not convinced anything really happened back there." He gestured to the parking garage with his head.

"Why do you say that?"

"Olivia Osgoode doesn't strike me as a reliable witness."

"I don't read her as the type to make up stories. She wasn't doing this for attention."

"Maybe. She's also grief stricken over her grandmother's recent death. You know how unreliable people's memories can be even when their mental state is sound." The detective shook his head from side to side. "She doesn't seem mentally stable to me. Not too smart, either."

"She has a speech impediment, Fred, not a learning disability. She has a cleft palate and it affects the way she talks."

"I'm not so sure." He shrugged. "Let's see if a body turns up or if anyone is reported missing."

CHAPTER 5

Olivia fastened her seatbelt in Tom's BMW sedan. She looked over her shoulder to locate Tom and found him at the back of the car. He glanced into the car and their eyes met. An involuntary shiver ran down Olivia's spine. His sedan was dark gray—could this be the car she had seen in the parking garage? *Could Tom be the killer?* She swallowed hard. *What's wrong with me?* This is Sam's twin brother—he's part of the Hilton Mortuary family. He was the kind man that had helped her.

Tom swept his hand over the lid of the trunk as he approached the driver's side door.

"Do you think it's okay if I leave my car in the garage overnight?" Olivia asked as he slid behind the wheel. "Will anything happen to it?"

Tom smiled and patted her arm reassuringly. "It'll be fine. The police will have the place under surveillance. And when you need a ride to come get it, I'm happy to oblige."

Olivia nodded and turned to the window; her face reflected in the dark glass.

"Where do you live?" he asked, ignoring the fact that he'd heard her address when she'd given it to the police barely two hours ago.

"I'm about eight miles out of town, on Pontoc Road. Just before you get to the turnoff to Granger."

Tom swung the car slowly in a U-turn. "There's no traffic at this time of night. We'll be there in twenty minutes. How long have you lived out there?"

Olivia kept her head turned toward the window. "My whole life, really. My grandmother raised me and that's her house… actually, it's my house, now."

Tom remained silent and waited for Olivia to continue. Could this young woman have inherited money, too? He was a financial planner—she might need help with her investments. There were so many unscrupulous people out there who preyed on people who recently inherited money. He'd hate to see her fall into the wrong hands.

"I don't know if you heard this part of my conversation with the police, but my grandmother died recently and left the house to me. So now it's my house."

"I'm sorry for your loss," Tom said. "Do you have other family in the area?"

Olivia shook her head. "No. I was an only child. My mother died when I was little, which is why I was with my grandmother. My grandpa died long before I was born, and Grandma had no family. It was always just the two of us."

"As I said, my deepest condolences. Will you stay in your house?"

Olivia glanced in his direction and paused. *Why is he asking so many questions?*

Tom shifted his gaze from the road ahead and smiled at her.

He's just being nice. Don't be so prickly, she chastised herself. "Of course I will. It's my home. What else would I do?"

"I don't know. You could sell it and move closer to town. The upkeep must be a chore. And you're pretty isolated out there. Aren't you lonely?"

"I've got cats and they're great company. We used to have a miniature schnauzer but she died shortly before my grandmother did. I've been thinking about getting another dog. As for upkeep, that's no problem. I'm quite handy around the house."

"Ahhh…. Well…." He cleared his throat. "I'm a financial planner and I'm accustomed to helping people in your situation figure out what they should do. If you ever want to talk to me about anything, I'm happy to listen."

Olivia fidgeted with the strap on her purse. It would be nice to have someone to talk to. Sam had always been a good listener—at least until recently. Now that her grandmother was gone and Sam was so preoccupied, she had no one to confide in. Maybe Tom was as kind as his brother. They continued on in silence as she considered this. She soon pointed to an asphalt driveway that intersected the road at the far edge of the headlights' illumination. "There," she said. "On your left."

Tom slowed the car and swung into the driveway. The asphalt was in disrepair and he winced as his tires propelled loose chips into the undercarriage. He veered left onto a portion of the driveway that circled in front of the house, pulling to a stop by a short flight of steps that led to a deep porch spanning the width of the house. He was unbuckling his seat belt when she put out her hand to stop him.

"You don't need to walk me to my door," she said. "I'm fine from here."

"At least let me see you safely inside."

She gestured to the door. "I don't have a key for the front door. We lost it years ago and never replaced it. I always go around to the back and it's muddy there. You'll ruin your shoes." She opened her door and got out of the car quickly. She leaned down before she shut her door, bringing her hand to shield her mouth.

"Thank you for the ride home and for being so kind. Don't worry about me. You've done enough."

Tom shot her his most reassuring smile. "You're welcome," he mumbled as she shut the door. Tom shifted his car into gear, proceeded around the circle, and headed back to the main road.

Olivia made her way around the side of the house to the back steps. The sliver of a moon provided scant light and she was thankful for the illumination afforded by Tom's headlights. She rummaged through her oversized purse to find her house key. The headlights swung away at an angle and disappeared as Tom retreated down the driveway, plunging her into darkness.

Olivia cursed under her breath. She was sure she'd turned on the porch light before she left. Had the bulb burned out or had someone tampered with it? The wind was picking up, rustling through the trees in the wooded copse that ran along the far side of the house. A twig snapped and she turned in the direction of the sound, crouching low on her door stoop, straining to see if anyone was watching her from the shadows. She froze, allowing her eyes to adjust to the low light. A dark object, the size of a small dog, darted across the lawn. She followed the raccoon with her eyes to the trash can by the shed. She really should chase the bothersome creature away, but she couldn't force herself to move.

She turned her attention back to the shifting shadows at the edge of the woods. If someone was out there, they were concealing themselves. Olivia brought her hand to her chest and felt her heart hammering through the layers of clothing. She forced herself to breathe evenly. The woods were full of nocturnal creatures. It was probably another raccoon.

Olivia remained crouched and slowly churned the contents of her purse until she found her key. She withdrew her cell phone, intending to click on the flashlight function to help her insert her key in the lock. She was about to illuminate the door when she stopped abruptly and dropped the phone back into her purse. If someone was out there watching her, she didn't want to shine a spotlight on herself.

Olivia pulled open the screen door and leaned into it with her shoulder. She ran her hand over the keyhole. Her hand shook as she brought the key to the opening and the key slipped to the right of the hole. She quickly brought it back to the opening and slid the key over the metal but, try as she might, could not insert it.

She jumped as the raccoon pried the metal lid from the trash can and sent it clattering to the ground. She glanced quickly over her shoulder as another raccoon joined the offending creature. She'd have a mess to clean up in the morning, but right now she didn't care. She needed to get into her house. She turned back to the keyhole and traced the opening with her fingernail. This time, she successfully guided the key into the lock. She turned the key and the door swung open. She stepped quickly inside, slamming and locking the door behind her.

Olivia sagged against the closed door and paused, allowing her pulse to return to normal. Tinker, the most outgoing of her two cats, sidled over to her mistress and greeted her with a loud meow that expressed her dissatisfaction that dinner had been delayed. Olivia scooped up the calico who settled into her familiar place under Olivia's chin.

Olivia deposited her purse in its customary spot on the kitchen counter. She released Tinker onto the floor and called to Bell. The more timid cat appeared from the shadows and wove a figure eight around Olivia's feet.

"Sorry I'm late, guys," Olivia said in a soft voice. "You wouldn't believe the day I've had." She flipped on the overhead kitchen light and started toward the cupboard where she kept their food. She'd taken no more than two steps when she caught her reflection in the kitchen window, black against the dark night. Fear coursed through her veins and she quickly turned the light out. If he was out there, watching her, she was a sitting duck in here.

Olivia sank to the floor, her back to the cabinets. Her mouth tasted like metal and she realized she'd chewed a sore in her cheek. She raked her hand through her hair, releasing it from the tight bun she always wore when she went out. The long blond hair cascaded around her shoulders and down to her waist.

The images of that night—the terrible images from the parking garage—flooded her brain: the woman's neck at that terrible angle and the eyes of the man behind his mask as he lunged toward the elevator door. A wave of nausea washed over her and she choked on her saliva.

Bell climbed into her lap and Tinker settled at her feet. Olivia stroked her cats as her thoughts calmed down. She checked the digital clock on the microwave. It was almost ten. Too late to call one of her grandmother's friends to see if she could come stay with them. She didn't have any close friends of her own. She didn't have her car anyway.

Tinker stirred and released another pleading meow. Olivia needed to get control of herself. If anyone was out there, they would have tried to get into the house by now. It was ridiculous to think that the masked man would have been able to identify her and track her down. She needed to feed her cats and go to bed. She had to be at work in the morning.

Olivia started to stand up, then quickly dropped to a crouch. She wouldn't walk in front of the kitchen window. She crawled beneath the window and rose on the other side, keeping her body close to the cabinets as she retrieved two tins of cat food. She fed the cats and realized that her own stomach was growling.

She crawled to the refrigerator, raised her hand to the handle and then stopped, glancing at the dark kitchen window. She wouldn't risk illuminating herself in the light from the refrigerator.

Olivia crept back to the counter and found the glass jar where her grandmother kept snacks. She fished a stale granola bar out of the jar, retrieved her purse from the floor, and scrabbled into the short hallway that connected the kitchen with the two bedrooms in the house.

Olivia stood in the windowless hallway and was walking to her bedroom at the end of the hall when a loud thwack sounded behind her. She flattened herself against the wall and listened, but the only sound she heard was her pulse hammering in her ears. Maybe she'd imagined it? She resumed her progress to her bedroom.

The sound came again, this time softer. Someone was trying to get in. She dumped the contents of her purse on the floor at her feet and picked up her cell phone. For the second time that evening she was punching 9-1-1 into her phone when the telltale creak of the screen door's hinges sounded, followed by the crack of the door. She brought her phone to her side, allowing the call to go uncompleted. She hadn't secured the latch on the screen door to the kitchen. The door was banging open and shut in the wind.

She inhaled deeply and exhaled slowly. *You're being ridiculous.* She forced herself back into the kitchen. She fought the urge to drop to her knees as she passed by the kitchen window. Olivia didn't glance at the dark glass but kept her eyes focused on the door. Without pausing to allow herself to change her mind, she grasped the door knob and opened the door. She reached for the screen door as a gust of wind sent it out of her reach. Olivia hurriedly stepped across the threshold with one foot and leaned into the icy wind, grasping the screen door and pulling it back into place. She secured the latch with shaking hands.

She shut and locked the kitchen door in one fluid motion and retreated to her bedroom.

Her blackout drapes were firmly drawn. Olivia turned on the small lamp on her nightstand and fatigue enveloped her like a fog. She kicked her shoes into the corner and unzipped her jeans, leaving them in a puddle at her feet. She tossed her turtleneck over the doorknob and called softly to her feline companions. They came running and settled themselves in their customary spots on her bed.

Olivia closed her bedroom door and forced the lock into position, making a mental note to oil it in the morning. She'd never locked her door before—she hadn't needed to lock it. Until now. She positioned the small wooden chair from her dressing table beneath the door knob and withdrew her cell phone from her purse.

Clutching her phone tightly, she crawled beneath the covers, bringing them up to her chin. Her eyes darted to every corner of the room. No one's here, she told herself firmly. She forced herself to shut her eyes and was, once more, stepping out of the elevator to the terrifying scene etched into her mind. Olivia let out a cry of frustration and pulled Bell close to her. She stroked the cat and concentrated on Bell's rhythmic purring. A fitful sleep finally enveloped her.

CHAPTER 6

The man turned his car toward the crematorium in the industrial section of town. The funeral home was the only mortuary in this part of the state that offered cremation services to other undertakers within a two hundred-mile radius. When he planned his killings, he made sure that he'd be able to dispose of the bodies through cremation without being detected.

That's what he had done four years ago when he'd killed the first batch of widows—six of them in a little over eighteen months. No one had suspected a thing. It had been a relief when he'd gotten control of himself and stopped killing. But then he had relapsed and started again. He'd been a fool to tell himself he could control it. He had promised himself he'd be more careful than ever this time.

He hadn't kept that promise this afternoon. He hadn't stuck to his plan. He'd acted on impulse and out of anger. Now he was paying for his rash behavior.

State law required all cremations to be completed within daylight hours. At this time of the year, the sun went down early. He thought Steve Darrel—their cremation director for over thirty years—should have locked up and gone home hours ago.

The man checked the clock on his dashboard. He pushed the accelerator down hard and felt the impressive response from the fine German engine, then quickly backed off. The last thing he needed was to be stopped by the highway patrol.

He approached the nondescript cinder block building from the back side. At nine forty-five in the evening, the auto body shops and light manufacturing businesses surrounding the crematorium were dark and deserted. He pulled slowly around the corner and drove past the crematorium. The one window—into Steve's office—was dark and the gate was shut, the padlock in place. Steve was not working late, catching up on paperwork, as he sometimes did.

The man circled the block and pulled his car up to the gate. He cursed as he fumbled with the heavy iron latch. The gate creaked loudly when he pushed it open on its track. He cast a glance into the street. No lights came on in any of the adjacent buildings. He quickly pulled his car up to the overhead door leading into the oven room and closed the gate.

His victim was on the small side. He'd be able to finish up and be on his way in a couple of hours.

The man stumbled in the dark as he made his way to the office door along the far side of the building. He held his keyring up to his face but couldn't pick out the correct key in the thin light. Unwilling to risk using his cell phone's flashlight, he tried each of the keys in turn. The third key turned the deadbolt. He stepped into the office and put his hand on the wall, feeling his way to the desk in the corner and the small lamp that he knew sat on the desk. He switched it on.

He looked at the desk, now illuminated in a narrow cone of light. The crematory log book sat in its usual spot in the upper right corner of the desk. Steve's collection of pens was neatly lined up in a tray next to the book. He shook his head. Nothing was ever out of order in Steve Darrel's world.

He turned and entered the main workroom, hurrying past the large walk-in cooler where they stored bodies that couldn't be completed before sundown or that weren't released for cremation by the medical examiner. Even through the thick walls of the cooler he could hear the hum of the large fans that kept the air circulating and the putrid odors at bay. He'd worked at the crematorium all through high school; the ovens didn't bother him, but the coolers always made the hair stand up on the back of his neck.

He flipped on the overhead fluorescent lights and halted, allowing his eyes to adjust to the sudden brightness. The oven room was a large concrete block box with a cement floor. Heavy metal conduits for the high voltage electrical lines and massive gas lines traversed the ceiling and ran down the walls. While the small office was painted a crisp white, the oven room was an unbroken sea of gray.

Along the back wall was the industrial processor that was used to pulverize the bone and teeth that didn't burn into ash. In the center sat two large cremation ovens, only one of which was used on a regular basis. They'd kept the old, cold hearth oven as a backup. It was more expensive to dismantle and discard it than it was to leave it in place. He shook his head. And to think that he'd been the one to advocate selling it off when they'd purchased the new oven. Now he was the only one who ever used it.

The man debated employing the newer oven just this once; it would cut the required time almost in half. He decided against it. The compulsively orderly Darrel would almost certainly know that the oven had been used after he'd finished with it.

He flipped the electrical switch to activate the controls on the cold hearth oven and set the dials for the desired run time. He heard the hiss of gas in the lines and felt the familiar burst of warmth as the burners fired up.

The man found one of the low carts that were used to remove caskets from the delivery vans that brought bodies to the crematorium. The caskets—often only simple cardboard boxes—were slid onto the carts and rolled into the cooler or directly to the oven. When he had time to plan his killings, he'd had a large cardboard box handy for just this purpose. He had no box this time.

The man shivered. The prospect of lifting his victim out of the trunk of his car and placing her directly into the oven made his flesh crawl. He scanned the room and noted a stack of cardboard caskets along the far wall. The mortuary used these when the medical examiner sent them a John or Jane Doe for eventual cremation. The State didn't pay for fancy caskets. He counted the stack. There were only four cardboard caskets.

He hesitated. Steve would notice if one were missing. Damn it. He'd have to place her on the cart and shove her into the oven head first. He'd employ one of the long T-shaped poles used to stir the burning bodies mid-cycle to assure even results.

The man checked the temperature gauge on the oven. It was time. He switched off the fluorescent lights and waited a moment for his eyes to adjust, then opened the large overhead door. The glow from the oven provided enough light for him to make his way to his trunk without stumbling.

He picked up his jacket and ski mask from where he'd tossed them in the trunk. He forced his arms into the sleeves and stuffed the mask into the left pocket. They were already tainted with the dead woman's DNA. He'd use them now to protect his clothes and toss them into the oven to destroy the evidence. He returned to the trunk and contemplated his victim with disgust. Rigor mortis had begun to set in and her form was set in grotesque angles. He attempted to place his arms under his victim's shoulders, but his injured hand throbbed and he couldn't get a firm grip on her. He tugged the body out of the trunk by her head and one leg. The man hoisted the body onto his shoulder and brought his victim inside. He placed her on the cart and quickly closed the overhead door. The woman's lifeless form was silhouetted against the orange glow of the open oven.

The man found Steve's protective gloves in their usual place by the new oven. He pulled them on, grasped the twelve-foot pole, and began his grizzly task.

CHAPTER 7

Ashley Hilton turned to survey herself in the floor-to-ceiling mirror of the ladies' powder room at the Marquette Country Club. She had to admit, the Christian Dior couture gown was the perfect choice. The azure blue played off her eyes and complemented her skin, and it fit her well-toned figure like a glove. She was stunning. Tom would be furious with her over its cost, but the gown was worth every penny.

Deep creases settled into her thirty-six-year-old forehead as she thought about her husband of barely three years. She snatched her Judith Lieber evening bag from the stool at her feet and checked the time on the cell phone that she'd stuffed into the bag. Tom was supposed to be here half an hour ago. She scrolled through her text messages but there were none from him.

Ashely placed another call to Tom's cell phone and hung up quickly when it went directly to voice mail. She'd already left him half a dozen messages and he hadn't returned any of them.

She took a steadying breath and faced the mirror, blinking hard. She'd be damned if she'd ruin her makeup by crying over that thoughtless bastard.

The door to the powder room opened and her sister-in-law, Nancy Hilton, swept into the room. In her late forties, Nancy was short with graying dark hair, deep green eyes, and a once-trim figure that now sported an extra ten pounds that Nancy couldn't get rid of no matter how much she dieted and exercised. Nancy and Ashley were as different from each other as the twin brothers that were their husbands were similar.

"Hi, sweetie," Nancy said. The women exchanged air kisses. "Don't you look amazing. No one will be able to take their eyes off of you."

Ashley squeezed her sister-in-law's hand. "You always know what to say to make me feel better."

Nancy stepped back. "Why in the world are you feeling bad? This event has been sold out for weeks. It'll raise a record amount for the new children's wing at the hospital. It may even fund the whole thing."

"You think so?"

"I most certainly do. You've attended to every detail. The silent auction items are way nicer than last year's. People are bidding like crazy out there. I've got my eye on the three-week European vacation. I'm going to hang by the table, pen in hand, until they close the bidding. It would make a perfect graduation trip for Ben. I'm going to go home with that one or die trying."

"I just wish Tom were here. I want him to see what I've done with this. He needs to know what I'm capable of."

Nancy took Ashley's chin in her hand. "I'm sure he already knows that about you. We all know that. He couldn't not know."

"Why isn't he here? He promised me."

"I'm sure he's gotten hung up unavoidably and he's doing his best. He's probably feeling worse about this than you are right now." Even as she said this, Nancy doubted it.

Ashley rolled her eyes. "I wish Tom were more like Sam. He's always so reliable. I'll bet he's out there now, waiting for you. I wish Sam hadn't gotten all of the 'dependable' genes in the family."

"Don't be silly," Nancy said, making a show of checking her watch. "It's time for you to step to the podium, Mrs. Hospital Auxiliary Board Chairwoman. Let's get this party started."

Ashley's shoulders sagged.

"None of that," Nancy put her arm around her sister-in-law's shoulders. "You can do this without Tom. He'll probably rush in while you're making your speech. He'll be thinking what the rest of us will be thinking—that you are a brilliant, beautiful, and talented woman, and we're lucky to have you."

Ashley straightened and gave herself one last approving glance in the mirror.

"Go out there and take that room by storm," Nancy said.

Sam slid into the empty chair next to his wife at the round table in time to join Nancy and four other well-to-do couples for dessert. His brother's wife had done a marvelous job organizing this year's charity ball to raise money for the hospital, and he knew that he should be showing more enthusiasm for the cause. In truth, he was glad he'd missed her speech and the program presented by the hospital board. The only thing on his mind these days was the financial strain he was under.

The renovations and repairs to Hilton Mortuary were running two hundred percent over budget. Every time he turned around, someone was asking him for money. All he wanted to do now was get away from this fundraiser with his wallet intact. He lifted his fork to attack the twelve-layer red velvet cake that teetered on the plate in front of him, then quickly set it back on the table.

Nancy leaned toward her husband. "I thought you were going to stand me up—just like your brother is standing up Ashley." She gestured to the empty chair at the head table.

"Tom isn't here either?" He glanced at his sister-in-law. "I can't believe that." He took Nancy's hand. "I'm sorry, sweetheart. I got held up at the mortuary."

"All you do these days is work," Nancy said. "I don't think you've done anything fun in ages. I thought a night out tonight would be good for you."

"I'm too exhausted to enjoy myself. Can we skip the dancing and sneak out of here?"

Nancy patted his knee and peered into his face anxiously. "You're running yourself ragged, sweetheart. You're starting to act like your brother."

Sam shook his head. "I can't imagine why he didn't show up. If he's not careful, Ashley will soon become his third ex-wife." He stood and Nancy took his hand.

Sam winced and pulled it back.

"What's the matter with your hand?" Nancy asked, drawing it to her and examining the growing discoloration on the side of his right hand.

"I tripped on construction debris in the back parking lot and fell. Caught myself with my hands." He massaged his right wrist with his left hand.

"You'd better get that x-rayed," she said. "It might be broken. We can stop at the emergency room on our way home."

"That's the last thing I need—an ER visit. That'll cost a fortune." He held up his left hand to silence her protest. "It'll be fine in the morning—I'm sure of it. If not, I can call the doctor then."

Nancy raised an eyebrow and looked at her husband. "Alright, Sam Hilton. But you'd better promise me you'll do just that if it's not better."

"I promise. Now let's get out of here."

"We've got to stop at the cashier first. I was the successful bidder on the European vacation. I'll just give them our credit card on the way out."

Sam sucked in his breath.

"Is something else wrong?" Nancy asked. "Are you having trouble with indigestion again?"

"I'm fine," Sam said. They made their way to the cashier. "How much was our winning bid?"

"Twenty-five thousand," Nancy replied as she turned her back on her husband to join the queue waiting to pay the cashier.

The color drained from Sam's face. If he spread the charge on every credit card in his wallet, he wouldn't have enough. He'd run all of his cards up to the maximum months ago. He pulled Nancy out of line.

"What?" she asked, swiveling to him in surprise.

"You're right—I'm not feeling well. I need to get home."

"Of course, dear," Nancy said. "I'll text Ashley in the car and tell her that I'll come by in the morning with the payment."

The couple stepped into the cool night air.

"Wait here," Sam commanded. "I'll bring the car around."

"You don't need to... I can walk," Nancy said, but Sam had already stalked away.

He pulled his sleek black Mercedes sedan up to the curb a few minutes later.

Nancy waited for him to slide out from behind the steering wheel to open her car door, but he made no move to do so. She got into the car and Sam took off at a pace too fast for the country-club parking lot.

"Okay, Sam Hilton. What in the world is wrong with you? Who's got your goat?"

"Nothing's wrong with me," Sam blurted out. "I'm wondering what's wrong with you."

"What are you talking about?"

"Spending all that money on a summer vacation?"

"We've been planning to take the kids to Europe for Ben's graduation trip for years," Nancy said, astonished at his tone.

"I know," Sam replied. "And last I heard, we were budgeting fifteen thousand. Now we're spending twenty-five?!" He forced himself to take a deep breath—he hadn't meant to yell at her.

Nancy stared at her usually calm, easygoing husband. "But we always support the hospital—it's one of our charities. And this year— since Ashley is chair of the fundraiser—I thought you'd want to be especially generous. We were going to spend money on a European vacation, anyway, so I thought I'd tack on our usual gift." She sniffed. "I don't understand what's gotten into you."

"I'm upset because we're hemorrhaging money everywhere I turn. I can't seem to get ahead of it."

"This is the first I'm hearing of this."

"The funeral home renovations are way over budget."

"Why didn't you say so?"

They rode in silence for several minutes.

"I can't react to thoughts you don't express, you know," Nancy finally huffed. She peered at him across the dark seat. "You're acting like you did four years ago. I thought we were done with all of that."

"I was under a lot of stress when Dad died suddenly and I took over the business."

"You refused to go to a counselor back then. Maybe you should go to one now. To help you with the stress."

Sam shook his head vehemently. "I'll get over this like I did before. I don't need any help."

"At least take up a hobby or a sport or something. Yoga, maybe? Sylvia's husband has gotten into that hot yoga and she says he's like a new man. You need to do something to relieve your stress."

"I've got my own ways of relieving stress." He faced his wife. "Just stop spending so much."

Nancy bristled. "You know darned good and well that I'm careful with our money, Sam. You've always said so."

They rode on in stony silence.

"I can tell Ashley that I made a mistake with the vacation and she can offer it to the next highest bidder," Nancy finally said.

Sam reacted to this comment like he'd been slapped across the face. He swung on her. "Of course not. You'll do no such thing. I don't need our name being made a laughingstock around town."

"You're exaggerating. It wouldn't be—"

Sam cut her off. "I'll get the money together. Just don't go off half-cocked again and get me into this kind of trouble."

Ashley stood under the porte cochere of the Marquette Country Club waiting for the valet to bring her car around. She stood on the pavement in her aching bare feet, her Jimmy Choo beaded sandals dangling from one hand. The evening had been an unmitigated success, but she wasn't thinking about that. All the happiness she should be feeling was overshadowed by her anger and frustration that her own husband hadn't bothered to show up—or even let her know that he wouldn't be there. Once more, when it was her turn to shine, he was conveniently absent. Ashley rubbed her bare forearm with her free hand and rehearsed what she would say to Tom about this latest indignity.

She didn't have long to wait. As the valet brought her car to the curb, Tom pulled his BMW alongside. He got out of his car, motor running, and intercepted the valet. He gave the man a twenty and requested that he return Ashley's car to the lot. The valet looked toward Ashley, who nodded imperceptibly. The valet slid behind the wheel and left Ashley and Tom staring at each other.

"Would m'lady like a ride home?"

"Don't m'lady me," Ashley said as Tom opened the passenger door for her. "Where the hell have you been?" She tucked herself into her seat, allowing the deep slit in her gown to reveal a long, tanned leg.

Tom got back in the car and glanced at his wife. Ashley was staring straight ahead. He steered toward the exit. "You won't believe it…"

"You'd better have a damned good, watertight excuse, Tom. This was so important to me—you knew that—and I was humiliated to have to do this alone." Her voice cracked, and she choked on her tears. "Everyone asked where you were. And you know what I told them? 'He's been detained—you know how he is—but he'll be here any minute.' And then you never showed."

"I'm sorry, sweetheart. How was it?" He turned to face her. "You look ravishing, by the way."

"Don't try to get out of this by flattering me."

"I think it was more important to you to be able to truss yourself up head to toe in designer wear than it was to have me with you," he sniped. "You got what you really wanted."

"That is complete bullshit," she said. "You're not going to change the subject and make this about me," she said. "I'm not falling for it this time." She faced him. "Where were you? Is there another woman?"

"Good grief, no. Why would you think that?"

"I'm your third wife, remember? And you cheated on the other two. 'Tigers don't change their stripes' my mother always said."

"I was helping a woman report a murder to the police."

Ashley gasped. "Who was murdered?"

"We don't know. The body hasn't been found."

"Then why do you think there's been a murder?"

Tom launched into the story that he'd rehearsed repeatedly on the way to the country club.

Ashley flattened herself into her seat. "That's really creepy. I'm glad you don't park in that garage."

Tom nodded his agreement.

She regarded him carefully. "You're a mess. Your hair is sticking out all over and you've got something on your pants." She reached over to pick at a smudge on his knee.

He intercepted her hand and held it with his right hand. "It's been a long day. I'll jump in the shower when we get home."

Ashley yawned. "Will it be in the morning papers? Will your name be mentioned?"

"I would hope so. Should be front-page news."

Ashley was silent, allowing this to sink in. "Good. That'll make the perfect excuse for your not showing up at the hospital charity ball. No one will gossip about me when they read about this."

CHAPTER 8

Kathy Karlsson picked up her coffee mug and headed down the hall to the employee break room at Hilton Mortuary. It was past time for her second cup of the morning. She glanced into Sam Hilton's office and was relieved to see that he had his back to the door, hunched over what looked like an excel spreadsheet opened on his computer screen. Kathy quickened her pace. Her normally amiable boss had turned short-tempered and demanding in the last six months—ever since they'd started the renovations on the mortuary.

Kathy had worked for the mortuary since Sam's father had been in charge. Almost forty years, she thought proudly. This was the first major construction project. She supposed that Sam was entitled to be out of sorts, if what Olivia told her was true. Construction was behind schedule and seriously over budget. That would put anybody on edge.

Kathy proceeded to the break room, inserted the pod into the coffee maker to brew a fresh cup, and deposited the stack of old newspapers that had accumulated on the counter into the trash. When the coffee stopped dripping into her cup and the machine made the low-pitched whine to indicate the water reservoir was refilling itself, she picked up her coffee and headed to the office that housed the mortuary's bookkeeper. Kathy had a soft spot in her heart for the shy girl. Olivia was smart, hardworking, and kindhearted. Very few people were allowed to see the real Olivia, however, because she retreated into her shell at every opportunity and pushed people away. It was all due to that botched repair of her cleft palate when she was an infant. She was outrageously self-conscious about it. The speech defect that it caused didn't help matters, either.

Kathy paused in the hallway and took a deep breath. She was going to have it out with Olivia. She'd promised Pearl Osgoode, on her deathbed, that she'd watch out for her best friend's granddaughter. She and Pearl had had many conversations over the years about Olivia. They both wanted her to see a plastic surgeon and have the childhood surgery repaired. She'd even driven Pearl to the university hospital for a consultation with a surgeon. Pearl had brought photographs of Olivia and the doctor had assured Pearl that modern surgical techniques would produce a transformative result on the girl. Olivia needed this surgery and Pearl had left her more than enough money to pay for it. She would keep her promise to Pearl and convince Olivia to take action.

Kathy was surprised to find that Olivia's door was closed. She knocked softly. When Olivia didn't answer, she tried the handle. The door swung open into an empty office. Her computer hadn't been turned on and her purse wasn't slung under her desk.

Olivia was late to work. Kathy had never known Olivia to be late.

Kathy turned on her heel and marched back to Sam's office. He remained hunched over his spreadsheets. Kathy knocked on the door frame.

"What?" Sam said, not turning around. "I'm busy here."

"I'm sorry, Sam," Kathy said, "but Olivia isn't in yet."

"So? What time is it?"

"It's quarter to ten."

"Maybe she had car trouble; maybe she overslept."

"Olivia? In ten years, has she ever been late?"

Sam glanced over his shoulder at Kathy, placing his finger on his computer screen to mark his place. "Did you ask any of the others? Maybe she called in." He turned back to his computer.

Kathy sighed in exasperation and headed for the lobby. Maybe their receptionist, Flora, had heard from Olivia and hadn't had time to pass the news along to Kathy. Hilton Mortuary was a busy place this morning. Still, that would be out of character for the ultra-efficient Flora.

Kathy was leaning against the reception desk, waiting for Flora to finish a phone call, when Olivia rushed through the front door.

"Olivia!" Kathy and Flora said in unison.

"Sorry. I know I'm not supposed to come in through the front entrance."

"It's not that," Kathy said. "I was worried about you. You're never late and you didn't call."

"I know. I had to take the bus this morning and I didn't realize that I'd have to change twice to get here. Plus, I got on the wrong bus and had to double back."

"Did you have car trouble?" Flora asked.

"You should have called me. I would have picked you up," Kathy jumped in.

Olivia paused and her eyes filled with tears. She brushed her hand across her eyes. The image of the woman, head dangling at an unnatural angle, filled her brain. "I've got to get to work," she mumbled. "Will you let me know when the family arrives for the boy's service at eleven? I talked to his father yesterday afternoon and want to introduce myself in person. Make sure he's not worried about paying for any of this." She swept her arm in the direction of the chapel. "I want him to be able to focus on himself and his family today."

"I can talk to him, if you want," Kathy said. "You seem," she hesitated, "not quite yourself today."

"I'm fine… I'll be fine." She tried to force a smile. "Just buzz me when they get here."

"Will do," Flora said as Olivia swept past them. "Something isn't right with her." She looked at Kathy over the top of her reading glasses. You're the only one that she confides in. Maybe you should talk to her."

Olivia extended her hand to a man in black slacks and a white shirt. The creases in the shirt told her that it had just come out of its packaging. The man took her hand and shook it. His palm was callused and rough. The unmistakable smell of Fels-Naptha soap wafted upward. She dropped her other hand from its habitual position in front of her mouth and placed it over their clasped hands.

"I'm Olivia Osgoode," she said. "We talked late yesterday afternoon."

The grieving father cleared his throat. "I thought you said all the expenses were covered," he began.

"They are. Everything's fine. I wanted to express my condolences to you in person and to see if you had any additional questions. If you thought of something overnight? I don't want you worrying about any of that today."

He lowered his gaze to the floor. "Thank you. I didn't sleep last night and I can't focus on anything." His voice broke.

Olivia squeezed his hand. "Be with your family and friends today. Take comfort in them. I'm holding you in my prayers and I'm here if you ever have any questions." She gestured with her head to the vestibule behind them. "People are starting to arrive. Would you like to greet them?"

He nodded.

Olivia put her hand on his elbow and escorted him to the comforting arms of the arriving mourners.

Kathy checked her watch. It was one o'clock. Olivia would almost certainly be in the break room, eating her sandwich with her nose in one of those repair manuals she was always reading. Collecting and repairing vintage toasters was an odd hobby for a young woman, but Olivia was not your average girl.

If she was lucky, they'd be alone, and Olivia might open up about whatever was bothering her.

Kathy made her way down the hall. The break room was empty. She found Olivia in her office, typing furiously on her keyboard.

"Aren't you eating lunch today?" Kathy asked.

Olivia glanced in her direction, then turned her attention back to her computer screen.

"I forgot to pack it."

"I've never known you to forget your lunch," Kathy said. "Or be late to work, for that matter."

Kathy waited but Olivia didn't respond.

"I've got leftover lasagna from last night and I've brought way more than I need," Kathy said, patting her love handles. "I'll split it with you." It was a statement, not a question. She regarded Olivia carefully.

Olivia sat back in her chair, then nodded slowly. "That would be nice. I didn't eat breakfast this morning or dinner last night. I'm starved."

"Why not?" Kathy asked. She put up a hand. "I'll go put the lasagna in the microwave and you can tell me about your evening as we eat." Kathy stepped out of Olivia's office before she had a chance to protest.

Olivia entered the break room as the microwave dinged, signaling that the lasagna was ready. Kathy removed the glass container. "Get yourself a paper plate," she said to Olivia.

Olivia complied, and the two women sat opposite each other at the round lunch table as Kathy divided up the fragrant pasta. She scooped a large serving out of the dish and moved it toward Olivia's plate, sticky strings of melted cheese clinging to it like guy-lines. Olivia encircled the strings of cheese with her fingers and gave a swift tug, breaking them free.

"Teamwork," Kathy said, smiling at Olivia as she placed the lasagna in front of her.

Olivia picked at it with her fork.

Kathy reached across the table and patted Olivia's arm. "Something's wrong, sweetheart. I know it."

Olivia's eyes were rimmed in red and a tear slid down her cheek.

"Are you missing your grandmother? Maybe you should join one of the grief support groups that we run right here at the mortuary," Kathy said kindly.

Olivia sniffed and turned her head away. "I'm never going to one of those groups where you sit in a circle and talk."

"Lots of people find them very helpful." She could see Olivia's spine stiffen. "You don't have to talk if you don't want to. You could just go and listen. It'll be…"

"It's not Grandma," Olivia said, cutting her off.

Kathy put her fork down and concentrated on Olivia. "Then what?"

"I saw a murderer last night."

Kathy recoiled into her chair. "What?"

Olivia drew a shuddering breath. "In the parking garage after my appointment with Grandma's lawyer. A man was putting a body in the trunk of his car."

"Oh my God!"

Olivia launched into her tale of the events of the prior evening.

"There was nothing in this morning's paper about it. Or on the news."

Olivia shrugged. "They haven't found the body."

Kathy stared at her coworker. "What do you mean?"

Olivia turned aside. "I really don't know."

"What do you mean you don't know?"

"The police haven't told me anything other than they didn't find a sedan with a body in it at the scene. Or the killer."

"They're looking for it, aren't they? This guy is still out there! They've got to find him."

Olivia nodded solemnly.

Kathy leaned over the table, digesting Olivia's story. "So what did you do last night?"

"What do you mean? I went home—Tom Hilton drove me home."

"Tom Hilton? What has he got to do with this?"

"He was the man from the office building that helped me call the police. That's where he works."

Kathy shook her head. "I can't wrap my mind around all of this." She looked up at Olivia. "So you spent the night at your house—alone?"

"Of course I did. Where else would I have gone?"

"You could have come to me! Weren't you afraid to stay alone after seeing the murderer? After he saw you?"

Olivia shrugged. "Not really. I was fine," she lied.

Kathy leaned toward Olivia and regarded her critically. "That's plain ridiculous. You can sleep at my house tonight—and you can stay until they catch this killer."

"That won't be necessary," Olivia insisted. "I'm fine at home." She paused. "If you wouldn't mind, I could use a ride to the garage to pick up my car. I left it there last night."

"That's why you took the bus? Your car is still in that garage?"

Olivia nodded. "If it's inconvenient, Tom offered to take me back to the garage to pick up my car."

"You won't need to do that," Kathy said. "I'll take you by there any time you want to go." She took Olivia's hand and squeezed it. "Are you sure about staying at your place alone? You're pretty isolated out there. If I'd seen what you've seen, I'd be mighty shook up. Why don't you stay with me until they catch this creep?"

Olivia shook her head emphatically. "I'm fine. I was pretty jumpy last night, but I got through it. It's ridiculous to think that the killer would try to track me down. He knows I can't identify him."

"Even so—" Kathy began and Olivia interrupted her.

"I've got the cats to take care of and I don't sleep well unless I'm in my own bed." She forced herself to look at the older woman and smile. "I'll be alright. If you can take me to my car after work, I'd appreciate it."

CHAPTER 9

Olivia finished filing the stack of invoices that she'd just paid and checked that her email inbox was current. She leaned out of her office and saw that Sam's door was firmly shut.

Now's as good a time as any.

She shut her office door quietly and returned to her desk. She dialed the general number for the Marquette Police Department.

"Detective Novak, please," she told the brusque male voice that answered the phone.

"Olivia Osgoode," she said. "Olivia Osgoode," she repeated as slowly and distinctly as she could. "I… witnessed… the man… carrying… the dead body… in the parking garage."

Olivia waited as her call was put through.

"Ms. Osgoode," Detective Novak said. "How can I help you? Have you remembered something else?"

"No," Olivia said. "I'm sorry, no." She sighed heavily. "I'm calling because I didn't see anything about this in the newspaper and I'm wondering what's happening."

"Were you looking for your name in the paper?" the detective asked.

"Of course not," Olivia said. "I wouldn't want my name mentioned, with a killer on the loose. I'm wondering where you are in the investigation. What have you turned up?"

"Those are all confidential police matters, Ms. Osgoode. We've got an ongoing investigation."

"Did you learn the identity of the victim?"

"We haven't found a body, and no one's been reported missing, so we don't have a victim yet."

"Maybe if you reported it to the press, someone would come forward with information."

"I think we know how to do our job, Ms. Osgoode. I wouldn't worry about this anymore if I were you."

"Not worry about this?" Olivia's voice rose an octave. "I've seen a murderer with his victim in his arms and he's seen me. I'd say I have a lot to worry about."

Detective Novak paused. "If at any time you feel unsafe, call 9-1-1 immediately."

"That's it? Call 9-1-1 if he comes after me?" Olivia felt the blood rise to her cheeks. "I might not have time to call if he's got his hands on me."

"I think your imagination is running away with you, Ms. Osgoode." The detective cleared his throat. "As I said, we're continuing with our investigation."

"That's very comforting, Detective," Olivia said, the words dripping with uncharacteristic sarcasm.

"We have very little to go on. If you think of anything else that might help us, please call me." The detective ended the call.

Olivia slammed the receiver down and cradled her head in her hands. The detective didn't believe her. He thought that she was making it all up to gain attention—like some pathetic publicity hound.

There was an elderly woman out there whose body wasn't buried in a proper grave—who might be at the bottom of some fetid pond or decomposing in a ditch. Some lovely older woman like her grandmother. *I can't let this woman rest in an unmarked grave.*

Olivia straightened and put both palms on her desk. If the Marquette Police Department didn't find the victim, they weren't going to look for the killer, either. How could she ever feel safe, knowing he was out there? What in the world was she supposed to do now? Find the victim for them? *How in the world am I going to do that?*

She sighed heavily and retrieved her purse from under her desk. She needed to clear her head and think, and she knew where to go to do that.

Olivia set her satchel next to the gravestone and removed the small brush from its holder. Although the stone bore no visible dirt or debris,

Olivia carefully traced the name—Pearl Osgoode—and the corresponding dates with her brush. Her hand lingered over the inscription: "Loving Grandmother and Friend to All." She sat back on her haunches and let the peace and calm that the cemetery always brought settle upon her.

Somewhere in the distance, thunder rumbled. She pulled her collar up around her ears and looked over the top of the headstone, into the woods beyond the cemetery.

"Sorry I haven't been here for a couple of days, Grams. I promise I'm thinking about the surgery. Kathy brought it up and I know you made her promise that she'd encourage me. I'm going to do it. Just give me some time."

Olivia tilted her face to the sky. "Something awful happened, which I think you already know about since you're on the other side. That murder. And now the police don't believe me. I'm going to have to prove that there really was a dead body. I'm not sure how I'm going to do it, but you always told me I could figure anything out. I'm hoping you're right, Grams."

Olivia rose to her feet and put one hand on the headstone. "I love you. I'm gonna make you proud of me." She bent to pick up her satchel and saw a familiar figure entering the plot from the far side.

The woman noticed Olivia at the same time and brought her arm over her head and waved. Olivia waved back and started across the grass to her.

"Hello, Olivia. It's been a couple of days since I've seen you. I guess we got off schedule."

"I haven't been here. Something came up."

"Good. I'm glad to hear it. A young woman like you shouldn't spend all her free time at the cemetery, like us old crones."

"I like visiting my grandmother, Mrs. Marshall," Olivia said in a quiet voice.

"And that's wonderful, dear. I didn't mean to be critical. I'm glad that you've had other things to do and I'm sure your grandmother would be glad, too."

"It's peaceful here—easy to think about things."

"That it is," Mrs. Marshall agreed.

"Last time I saw you, you said you have a mixer that needs fixing."

"I do. I know I could buy a new one, but it was a wedding present and I hate to part with it. It's been part of my kitchen for over fifty years. I've baked hundreds of cakes using that old thing. Are you sure you have time to work on it?"

"I'm sure. I love refurbishing old appliances. It's sort of like working a jigsaw puzzle."

"You're a very clever girl. I'd be grateful."

"Do you have it with you?"

The older woman nodded.

"When you're done visiting your husband we'll go to your car to get it."

"I also feed that stray dog that finds his way under the fence by the large maple." She pointed to the tree. "Have you seen him?"

"Small, short-haired? Some sort of terrier mix?"

"That's the one. I don't have the heart to call the dog pound. I know I shouldn't, but I've been bringing him table scraps every day. I'm hoping to catch him—although what I need with a dog, I don't know."

Mrs. Marshall reached into her oversize purse and withdrew a small tinfoil package. "Here's today's offering. Would you mind taking it to him while I visit my husband?" She gestured to the grave at their feet.

Olivia held out her hand to accept the package. "Will he come to me?"

"Just unwrap it and step back about ten feet and don't move. He may not come out right away, but if you remain still he'll make his presence known. Give it a few minutes. If he doesn't appear, just leave it. He might find it later."

"Or some other animal will get it."

"True. We can only do what we can do."

Olivia nodded and made her way to the break in the fence by the tree. She couldn't be sure, but she thought she saw movement in the brush as she approached.

She opened the foil package and set it on the ground. The scraps of cold pot roast looked enticing. Olivia stepped back. She didn't have long to wait. The creature, with ribs protruding and matted fur, slunk out of the trees and made a beeline for the food.

Poor thing, Olivia thought. He looks like he's starving. She regarded him carefully while he ate. She couldn't be sure, but it looked like there was a patch of dried blood above his right eye. She took a cautious step forward to get a better look and leaned toward him.

The animal stopped eating and stood stock still, head down over the remainder of his food. Olivia held her breath. After a long pause, the dog resumed eating. As soon as he finished he turned and dashed to the break in the fence. Before he squeezed under it, he turned back to Olivia and wagged his tail in thanks. Olivia was caught off guard by the warmth that surged through her. She smiled at him. He was under the fence in an instant and was gone.

Olivia watched as he disappeared into the woods. She hoped that the creature had somewhere to shelter from the storm coming their way. She turned back to Mrs. Marshall who was arranging flowers in a vase by her husband's headstone. Mrs. Marshall's jacket had fallen open and the wind caught the end of her scarf, sending it up into the air. Mrs. Marshall grabbed for it but was too late and the wind sent the scarf racing across the grass.

"I'll get it," Olivia called as she ran by the older woman. The wind died down momentarily and Olivia caught up with the scarf and secured it with her foot before the next gust of wind sought to send it sailing.

"Well done," Mrs. Marshall called.

Olivia picked up the scarf and a remembered image flooded her vision—a bright scarf, dangling from the neck of the dead woman in the garage. Olivia bent over suddenly, grabbing her knees to steady herself. She'd seen the dead woman's scarf before, right here in this cemetery. One of the widows who visited her husband's grave wore that scarf. She was sure of it.

"Are you alright?" Mrs. Marshall called out in alarm.

Olivia struggled to get her breath. Did she know the woman who had been murdered? Would she be able to identify the victim?

Mrs. Marshall came up to her and put her hand on Olivia's back. "What's happened, dear? Are you in any pain?"

Olivia straightened up slowly, shaking her head. "I'm fine," she lied.

Mrs. Marshall ran her eyes over Olivia's face. "You look like you've seen a ghost."

Olivia's mind raced. Should she share her newfound revelation with Mrs. Marshall? She might know the identity of the woman. On the other hand, she might think Olivia was crazy. The newspaper still hadn't reported the murder and Olivia remembered Kathy's reaction to her story. *No. I'll keep my own counsel on this for the time being.*

"I just got a stitch in my side. It happens to me from time to time. I'm fine now."

"If you're sure." Mrs. Marshall looked doubtful.

"Let's go get your mixer," Olivia said. "It's almost dusk and they'll be closing the gates soon. We need to get out of here."

Olivia clutched the broken mixer to her chest and watched as Mrs. Marshall started her car. The older woman rolled down her window and called to Olivia. "Are you sure you won't let me pay you?"

Olivia smiled and shook her head. "I'm sure. It'll only take me a few minutes to rewire it." She waved to Mrs. Marshall and stepped back.

Olivia checked the time on her cell phone. It would be dark soon. She hurried to her car, deposited the mixer on the back seat, and turned back to the cemetery. Olivia wanted to find the grave that the woman with the scarf usually visited.

She picked her way carefully in the growing dusk and concentrated on the image of the woman. Short and slender, with a thick head of white hair. Probably in her eighties, Olivia guessed. She didn't see the woman as often as she saw Mrs. Marshall and some of the others.

Maybe this woman didn't visit her loved one as regularly as the others did, or maybe she came at different times.

Olivia paused when she reached the section of the cemetery where her grandmother was buried—where she'd seen the woman with the scarf. Her mind was racing as she contemplated the scene in front of her. From this vantage point, she couldn't remember where she'd seen her.

She made her way to her grandmother's grave and stood in her customary spot, surveying the cemetery. *There,* she thought. *I've seen her over there.*

Olivia set off at a fast clip to the row of graves where she'd seen the woman with the scarf. She walked an area thirty-feet by thirty, perusing all the headstones in the fading light. She could eliminate any headstones with the name of a woman or a couple. That left her with three headstones bearing male names only.

Olivia took photographs on her cell phone of each headstone. If her hunch was right, the dead woman was either Mrs. Jonathon A. Mazur, Mrs. Robert Howard Robinson, or Mrs. Scott Williams.

How am I going to figure out whose widow she had been?

CHAPTER 10

"Good morning, Tom," Flora said as Tom strode through the front door. She sat up straighter in her chair and smoothed a stray wisp of the hair that had been Nice'n Easy 6R Light Auburn Red for the past forty years. Tom Hilton always made her want to look her best. His features were the same as Sam's, but the way he looked at her made her feel like she was the only person in the room. She respected Sam for his commitment to his wife and family and knew that Tom was a philandering ladies' man, but he still made her heart flutter when he looked at her.

"How are you, Flora? How's that grandson of yours? Still breaking state records in the freestyle?"

Flora beamed. "He sure is. You should see him. His coach says he's the best athlete he's ever worked with."

Tom sensed Flora was warming to her topic and was relieved when the phone rang. "Sam in his office?" he asked as she answered the call. She nodded and inclined her head toward Sam's office.

Tom started down the hall and stopped abruptly when Olivia stepped out of her office. "Olivia," he said, extending his hand. "How are you doing?"

She took his hand and he brought his other hand to rest on top of the clasped hands.

"Are you alright?" she asked, peering at him closely.

"I'm fine. Why do you ask?" He pulled his hand from her grasp.

"You grimaced."

"It's just a headache." He cleared his throat and looked over her shoulder. "I'm here to see Sam."

"He's in his office," Olivia said, stepping around him.

"Wait. How are you doing?" Tom asked again, touching her elbow. Olivia shrugged. "Alright."

"Did the police ever get back to you? Did they find the body?"

"I called them. Nothing." Olivia raised both palms upward and shrugged. "It's like it never happened."

"I'm sure they're working on it. Without a body, they don't have much to go on." Tom rubbed his arm. "Some crimes never get solved."

Olivia dropped her gaze to the floor. "I suppose."

"In the meantime, I think all you can do is put it out of your mind and go about your daily life."

"Maybe. I saw…" she began, when Sam emerged from his office, his car keys in hand.

"Tom," Sam said. "What brings you here? I was just on my way to the bank."

"Can I have a word?" Tom asked.

"Sure. Walk me to my car."

"What were you saying?" Tom turned back to Olivia. "I couldn't hear you over my brother, here."

"It's nothing," Olivia said. She smiled and made a dismissive gesture.

The two men proceeded out the employee entrance to the parking lot.

"Another successful fundraiser for the hospital. Your wife did a bang-up job. Too bad you missed it," Sam said, making no attempt to keep the sarcasm out of his voice.

"That's the reason I'm here, actually. Ashley sent me by to thank you and Nancy for your generous bid on the European vacation and to pick up a check for twenty-five thousand dollars."

"About that," Sam replied. "I don't have it right now."

"What?" Tom's voice rose several decibels.

"Keep it down, okay?" Sam glanced at the window to the left of the rear door. "That's Kathy's office. We don't want her to overhear." He motioned for Tom to follow him to his car.

Sam continued, "You're a minority owner in the mortuary. You've seen the reports. This renovation is killing us. We're over budget and have run into one snag after another. First the crack in the foundation and now these wiring issues. I've funded all of the overages out of my own account, but I'm tapped out."

"Then why did you bid twenty-five grand on a vacation? Do you know how embarrassing it will be if you renege on your bid and it goes to the next highest bidder?"

"Nancy bid on it, I didn't."

"Why didn't you stop her?"

"I wasn't there—I got held up at the office. And you've got no room to criticize on that score." He fixed his brother with his stare. "Why didn't you show?"

"Didn't Olivia tell you?"

"Tell me what?"

"About the man she says she saw carrying a dead body in the parking garage across from my office building."

"What?"

Tom recounted Olivia's story. "She was in front of my building, trying to call 9-1-1. Totally freaking out. I was on my way to the charity ball when I came across her. I couldn't leave her."

Sam nodded. "No. Of course not."

"By the time we were done with the police and I'd dropped her at her house, the charity ball was over. I got to the club as Ashley was leaving."

"Why hasn't any of this been on the news or in the paper? I haven't seen or heard a thing about it."

"I guess they didn't find the body."

"And no one's been reported missing?"

"Nope."

Sam leaned his forearms on the roof of his car. "Do you think they believe Olivia?" he asked, swiveling to face Tom.

"Why wouldn't they?"

"She's different. You know that. And she's deeply grief stricken over the loss of her grandmother. She's a loner and has very few friends, so her grandmother was her only outlet. Maybe she's gone a bit 'round the bend; maybe she's imagining things. Wouldn't be the first time that's happened to someone dealing with extreme grief."

"Seems unlikely to me. She'd really have to be unbalanced to make this all up."

"I know." Sam sucked in air through his teeth. "That's the last thing I need right now—my bookkeeper going crazy."

"She didn't tell you about the body? Or anyone else here?"

"No. Not that I'm aware of."

"Let me know how she's doing, okay? Since I got involved to help her, I feel obligated to see it through."

Sam raised an eyebrow at his brother. "It's not like you to be so concerned. Do you think Olivia will make an easy conquest? The last thing she needs is to get swept off of her feet by you. You're a married man, remember."

Tom opened his mouth to protest.

Sam cut him off. "Don't worry about Olivia. She'll be fine. I'll look out for her."

"It's not like that," Tom said. "She's not my type and you know it. I feel sorry for her." He fixed his brother with a stare. "I'm here for the twenty-five, anyway."

"I was headed to the bank to liquidate the last of my remaining certificates of deposit. I'll have to pay a penalty for selling them early. Do you think you could float me the money until they mature?" Sam swallowed hard. He hated asking Tom for anything. As brothers, they were fiercely competitive. Tom was the suave, flashy one while Sam was dependable and consistent. Fine Italian loafers versus sturdy English brogues. Just once, Sam wanted to come out on top.

Tom looked away from his brother. "I'm tapped out at the moment, too. I'm sorry, but I don't have it."

Sam took a step back. "Seriously? You always act like you have money to burn. He touched the watch on his wrist and pointed to Tom's new BMW sedan parked at the edge of the lot. "If you were having cash flow problems, why the Rolex for my fiftieth birthday?

Why the brand-new Beemer when your old car only had forty thousand miles?"

"Things can change on a dime, you know. I had the money when I bought the watches and the car."

"That's only weeks ago. What's changed so quickly?" Sam leaned in to stare into Tom's eyes. "Are you using again? Is that where your money's going?

"No, I'm not," he hissed. "Don't be so high and mighty with me."

Sam wiped the bead of sweat from his upper lip. "You'll have your money—day after tomorrow at the latest."

Sam yanked his car door open and flung himself into his seat. Tom started toward the BMW as Sam leaned out and yelled, "Get ready for a capital call next week."

Tom spun on his heel. "What?"

"We're out of money and can't pay the contractors. The bank won't advance us any further loan proceeds until we get caught up with our bills." He took a measure of satisfaction from the look of shock on Tom's face. "For once, you're going to have to put money into this place rather than always cashing your distribution checks."

"How much?"

"Olivia's running reports for me now. Maybe thirty thousand—to get all caught up. I'll let you know."

Sam and Tom stared at each other in silence. Sam slammed his door, started the ignition, and set off for the bank.

Tom walked slowly to his car, his back to the window of Kathy's office. He really should step up his efforts to manage the money that Olivia inherited. A new client would be most helpful right now.

Kathy stepped away from the glass, rubbing her temples. Hilton Mortuary was in financial trouble? She could hardly believe it. Old Mr. Hilton must be spinning in his grave. She needed to find Olivia to see what she knew about this new development.

CHAPTER 11

Olivia turned to look over her shoulder at Kathy. The older woman stood in the doorway, fidgeting with the buttons on the cardigan sweater that lived in Kathy's office in case she got cold. Kathy was always cold. Olivia couldn't remember a day when Kathy hadn't donned her cardigan. Olivia and Flora privately joked that the garment was Kathy's office bathrobe.

"I was wondering… how are you doing today?" Kathy asked.

"Fine." Olivia pointed to the stacks of paper spread across her desk. "Sam suddenly wants all of these invoices analyzed for parts, labor, and tax charges, matched up to the materials budget, and uploaded into spreadsheets. I suggested we do this when the renovation started but he said no. 'Waste of time' he said. And now he wants me to recreate all of it and have it to him by the end of the day."

Kathy stepped into the room and closed the door behind her. "Are we in financial trouble?"

"We're having some cash flow problems, but I think Sam's got money put away for a rainy day. This has happened before, and he's always been able to cover what we need." Olivia put her pencil on the table and leaned back in her chair, stretching her arms overhead. "We should have been keeping track of this all along. Don't let this worry you," she said, sweeping her hand across the papers in front of her.

"I just heard Sam and Tom arguing in the parking lot. Over money," Kathy replied. She stared down her nose at Olivia.

"Were you eavesdropping?" Olivia raised her eyebrows.

"I was. I didn't mean to, but I heard raised voices outside and went to see what all the fuss was about. As soon as I saw who it was, I couldn't help myself." Kathy twisted her hands. "I've been here for over forty years and I'll be able to retire in a couple more. I need this job until then."

"It's not as bad as all that, I'm sure."

"Sam hasn't been himself for months. Grouchy as a bear. Short-tempered. You have to admit—that's not like him. At least not since right after his father died and he took over running this place."

Olivia shrugged. "Maybe he's got stuff going on at home, too. He has a house with three teenagers, you know."

"Those kids are great—they're not causing trouble."

"Whatever it is, Sam is going to be much grouchier if I don't finish these spreadsheets."

Kathy reached for the door. "You're right. I've got to follow up on the Henderson funeral tomorrow."

Olivia picked up her pencil, fished her calculator out of her drawer, and resumed her work. She skipped lunch and plugged along diligently until she printed off the last spreadsheet at four twenty-five.

Olivia gave her work a final review and slipped the papers into a manila folder that she slid under Sam's locked office door.

She returned to her desk and opened her browser. With Sam out of the office, it was an ideal time to see if she could find information about the three men buried in the cemetery. *I've got to figure out who that dead woman was.* Olivia cradled her head in her hands as the terrible images flooded her consciousness.

She opened the photo library on her phone and scrolled to the picture of the first grave. Jonathon A. Mazur was not a common name and she hit pay dirt at the top of the second page of Google results.

Jonathon Mazur's obituary had been published in the local paper eight months ago. The short write-up stated that he was survived by three sisters and two children. A wife was not mentioned so he was probably divorced. He'd been in his mid-sixties when he'd died.

Olivia closed her eyes and conjured up the image of the dead woman, head at an awkward angle, held in the masked man's arms. The image appeared, fully fleshed out and in technicolor, every night in her dreams. Her face had been angled to the floor and she didn't see any facial features.

The dead woman had a shock of white hair and must have been in her seventies or eighties. She felt sure of it. She could not have been one of Jonathon Mazur's grieving daughters.

She was typing Robert Howard Robinson into her search box when she heard Sam's heavy tread in the hallway, approaching her office. He must have come in through the front door. She punched the 'delete' key and held her breath. The evidence of forbidden personal use of her computer faded from the screen as Sam entered her office.

"Great job, Olivia," he said, waving the folder with the spreadsheets in front of him. "This is all of it, right?"

"Yes. I even added a couple of invoices that the contractor brought by today."

Sam's head snapped up. "Today? How much were they for?"

"One was for electrical—for $1,123," she said, pulling the spreadsheet up on her computer. "The other was $240 for painting. Not bad at all."

Sam sighed heavily. "Okay, then. Thank you." He stepped through her doorway and turned back to her. "Tom tells me you had quite the scare the other night."

Olivia opened her mouth to speak but Sam raised his hand to silence her. "You don't need to tell me a thing if you don't want to. But maybe you should take a few days off to recover. You've been here every day since your grandmother died."

Olivia blinked hard and turned away.

"Sometimes we have to be gentle with ourselves," Sam said quietly. "Take some of the advice we give to others here—allow yourself time to grieve. You're welcome to join one of our support groups, you know."

Olivia nodded.

"Get your things," Sam said. "It may only be a few minutes, but I'm letting you go early today."

"You don't need to do that," Olivia protested. She wanted nothing more than to continue her research of the men in the cemetery. Not for the first time did she bemoan the fact that she didn't own a computer at home.

"I insist. The work will wait until tomorrow." Sam smiled at her and she realized it was the first time she'd seen him smile in weeks.

Olivia slowly shuffled her papers into a neat pile, logged off her computer, and followed Sam out the door.

Olivia stopped at the mailbox that sat at the entrance to her driveway. The rain that started in the late afternoon had turned to sleet. She considered continuing to her house without collecting the mail, but she was religious about picking up the post on a daily basis. Her grandmother always insisted that you never knew when you'd find a check instead of a bill; a handwritten letter instead of junk mail.

She maneuvered her car as close to the box as possible, pulled the hood of her jacket over her head, and dashed the few feet to the mailbox and back. She tossed the stack of mail on the seat next to her and rummaged through it quickly. As usual, it was all advertising flyers and junk mail.

She opened the garage door and pulled into her spot. She snatched her purse and the mail and was about to deposit the mail into the trash can that lived on the side of the garage when the heavy manila envelope, bearing the return address of Howard Asher, Esq. slid out from the folds of the weekly grocery store flyer and fell to the ground.

Olivia consigned the rest of the mail to the bin and lowered her face to avoid the pelting sleet as she hurried to the kitchen. She placed the envelope on the trestle table in the breakfast room at her grandmother's customary spot and stared at it. This was bound to be the letter that the attorney had spoken of during her appointment with him on that fateful day recently. The letter with the recorded copy of her deed to this house—now her house—and a check for the money that her frugal grandmother had scraped and scrimped to save all her life. And had now left to Olivia.

Olivia deposited her purse on the table next to the letter. Tinker bounded over to her as Bell stretched herself in the leisurely fashion that cats have perfected. Knowing she'd have no peace until she filled their bowls with kibble, she quickly attended to the task.

With the cats happily occupied, she went to the hutch in the breakfast room and selected her grandmother's favorite china coffee mug with the yellow daisies and the stenciled scripture: "This is the day the Lord hath made; we will rejoice and be glad in it."

She turned on the burner under the old copper tea kettle that waited faithfully on the white O'Keefe & Merritt stove. The stove held pride of place in the kitchen and occupied a special place in Olivia's heart. When the repairman had advised her grandmother that the stove couldn't be fixed and that it was time she got a new one, her grandmother had been heartbroken. Grams didn't want a new stove—she wanted her beloved O'Keefe & Merritt.

Olivia had dismantled the stove and painstakingly repaired it, bit by bit. She'd just turned twelve. Her grandmother had never fussed or tried to hurry her—saying that she knew Olivia would figure it out and they'd get along fine with a Crock-Pot and a hot plate. After six months of concentrated effort, Olivia had restored the stove to its original glory. Olivia then moved on to repairing every small appliance that her grandmother owned, and the hobby she still enjoyed had been born.

She made herself a cup of strong tea with the Lady Londonderry tea bags that her grandmother had ordered for Olivia all the way from England.

Olivia pulled out her grandmother's chair, relaxing into the wooden frame that had supported her grandmother during a lifetime of meals, countless cups of coffee, and endless hours of listening to Olivia's hopes, fears, and dreams. She took a sip of her tea and opened the envelope.

The contents were partly as expected. The deed to the house was now in Olivia's name and the attorney had kindly included a long letter detailing her legal and financial responsibilities as a homeowner. Olivia gasped when she saw the amount of the check. She blinked hard and shook her head before looking at the amount again.

Her grandmother had left Olivia four hundred and eighty-five thousand dollars. Olivia stared at the check. The numbers became a blur as her eyes filled with tears. She'd had no idea. Why on earth hadn't her sweet grandmother spent this money on herself—on making her own life easier?

Olivia swallowed hard. The envelope also contained a letter, addressed to her in her grandmother's unmistakable—if shaky—hand. The date at the top of the letter was six weeks to the day before she died.

My Dearest Olivia,

You have been the joy of my life. Don't ever think, for one moment, that you've been a burden. You are a kind, compassionate person with a heart as big as all outdoors and an intellect to match. I'm so proud of the woman you've become.

For some reason, you were born with a cleft palate. The surgery when you were an infant should have repaired it, but, if anything, it made it worse. I know that you were teased and bullied as a child. Maybe those experiences contributed to your empathy as an adult. But you've become increasingly withdrawn and fearful as the years have gone by.

You are a wonderful person and will make a terrific wife and mother. I know you want those things and you deserve them.

You need to go to the best surgeon you can find and have this botched surgery repaired. I want you to see yourself as the beautiful person that I know you to be. I've been saving for this since you first came to live with me. As you now know, I saved quite a bit. Your old Grandma was a savvy investor.

You have more than enough money to pay for the surgery. I'm directing you to do that now. I've seen the stack of papers you keep tucked away in your room about the surgery. You know it isn't a big deal. Don't allow your fear of doctors dissuade you.

When you've recovered, take some of this money and buy yourself a nice new wardrobe. Burn those black turtlenecks and gray cardigans. I think you'll be lovely in violet, so buy yourself something to match those remarkable eyes of yours. Wear your hair down and let the world see how pretty you are.

Finally, take the rest of the money and get your degree. You're too smart to spend the rest of your life working for the mortuary. With your ability to fix anything electrical or mechanical, I think you would be a wonderful engineer.

You always did what I asked of you when you were growing up, so I'm asking these three things of you now. And don't feel badly that I didn't fritter the money away on clothes or travel for myself. I had everything in life that matters in the love of a remarkable child: you.

I'll be cheering you from up here as you move into your happy future. And remember my favorite Bible verse: Fear not, for I am with you.

With unending love and faith in you,

Grams

CHAPTER 12

Olivia clutched the letter with trembling hands. *How in the world am I going to get along without her?* She flipped away a tear that landed on the letter, smearing the ink.

She took a sip of her tea which had long since grown cold. There was so much to think about. Her grandmother was right about everything in that letter.

Olivia rose from the table. It was too late to go to the cemetery. She'd have to settle for the second-best place where she could really think. She crossed to the corkboard by the back door and retrieved the key to the henhouse. Pearl hadn't kept chickens for more than forty years and had allowed Olivia to fix up the structure—first as a play house when she was a child and later as a workshop when she became an adolescent.

Olivia gathered her jacket around her and peered into the darkness. The roof of the workshop was outlined against the clouds skittering across the night sky. She shifted her gaze and her reflection stared back at her. *Am I going to hold myself hostage in my own home each night?* She paused, searching for answers from the anxious woman looking back at her. *I'm being ridiculous. I've got Mrs. Marshall's mixer to repair. I need to get out there and do it.*

Olivia forced her hand to grasp the door handle and open the door. She propelled herself into the yard and ran to the workshop. She unlocked the deadbolt. The wide door swung open to reveal a long, high workbench along one wall. A pegboard over the bench held a tapestry of tools, wires, and fittings. Lining the walls from floor to ceiling on two sides were shelves of toasters. Some were clothed in shiny chrome and colorful Bakelite while others were coated in grime and rust, waiting for her ministrations.

She closed and latched the door behind her and ran her hand along a shelf of the restored appliances. She'd acquired them all from yard sales or junk yards. She had a keen eye for what was valuable and marketable, and she knew how to restore them to their former luster. She rarely sold any of her restorations, however. They all ended up, tidy and secure, on the shelves in her workshop.

Olivia knew what she must do—she must have the surgery. Her grandmother was right. In the morning, she should call the surgeon whose website she'd visited at least a dozen times. In the meantime, she needed to keep her mind busy so she wouldn't chicken out. She'd make the repair she'd promised Mrs. Marshall and then she'd tackle one of her more challenging finds. Restoring old toasters was completely absorbing for her, like playing the piano or working a jigsaw puzzle had been for her grandmother.

Olivia brought the mixer to her workbench and then scanned the rows of garage sale finds waiting for her attention. As soon as she finished the mixer, she'd start in on a particularly rusty General Electric D-12. Decades of grime hid the flowers on its base. Perfect, she thought. She turned back to her workbench and set to work.

Olivia surveyed the parts neatly arranged on the towel spread across her workbench. The General Electric D-12 had been harder to disassemble than she'd anticipated, but she'd stuck with it and was satisfied with the results of her efforts. She checked the time on her phone and was shocked to see that it was almost ten. She was more relaxed than she'd been in weeks.

She stretched her arms over her head. She had to work the next day and she hadn't eaten dinner. It was time to close up her workshop and go back to the house.

Olivia placed the mixer, now as good as new, in a sturdy carrier bag. She'd put it into her car tomorrow. She cast one last glance around her workshop to make sure her tools had all been returned to their allotted homes, then moved to the large door. She flipped the switch to turn out the overhead light and began rolling the door open on its creaky track. She paused in the opening, allowing her eyes to adjust to the dim light outside her workshop. The freezing rain had stopped, but the temperature had dropped and the gravel path from the workshop to her back door was coated in ice. The moon was shrouded in clouds.

Olivia closed the door behind her and secured the deadbolt. She positioned her house key in her right hand. The woods that skirted her property were an inky sea of shadows that surged in the wind. Did something metallic glint from the perimeter of the woods? A belt buckle, perhaps? *Is someone lurking in those shadows?* She wanted to sprint the fifty feet to her back door, but knew that the ground was too treacherous. She stepped carefully onto the gravel path and gingerly made her way to her door.

Olivia had almost reached the bottom step when the neighbor's dogs erupted in urgent barking in the distance. She quickened her pace and slipped to her knees as she lunged for the handrail, her keys skittering into the darkness.

Olivia cursed under her breath and crouched, feeling the ground where she thought her keys had landed. With the icy coating on the concrete, they could have skittered anywhere.

She reached in her jacket pocket for her cell phone. Her flashlight function would help her find her keys. Olivia searched one pocket and then the other. She patted the pockets of her slacks. "Damn it," she whispered. She must have left her phone in the workshop.

The plaintive wailing from the dogs continued. Had someone hiding in the woods drawn their attention? She dropped to her hands and knees and crawled in an ever-widening circle around her back steps, feeling her way in front of her for her keys. On her second sweep through, her left hand touched something metallic and serrated. She gathered the keys to her and sat against the bottom step. She wanted nothing more than to get into her house and lock the door behind her, but she needed her phone. Sleep was a fitful companion since she'd seen the man in the garage and she wouldn't sleep at all without her phone at her side.

Olivia took a deep breath. She was allowing her imagination to play tricks on her again. *The dogs are barking at a stray cat or a raccoon.* She forced herself to stand and walk slowly back to her workshop. She unlocked the deadbolt, turned on the light, and spotted her phone on the far end of her workbench. She retrieved the phone and was about to turn off the light when a resounding crack sounded from the edge of the woods. She spun in the direction of the sound and clutched the door frame as her knees buckled. A man in an overcoat, his face shrouded in the shadows, stood at the edge of the woods.

Olivia's scream was borne away by the wind as she slammed the door shut and secured the latch from inside. She fumbled with her cell phone and, for the second time in a week, placed a call to 9-1-1.

CHAPTER 13

The man stepped back into the shadows. *Shit! She's seen me!* He had to get out of there before the place was crawling with cops.

He'd been driving by on his way home when he'd decided to do some clandestine snooping on Olivia. He had no reason to believe that she could identify him from the garage, but there might come a time when knowledge of her daily habits would prove useful to him.

He'd parked his car in the heavy overhang of trees at the entrance to her driveway. He'd walked around her house and assumed she'd gone to bed when he'd rounded the corner and seen the light in an outbuilding. He'd stepped into the shadows at the edge of the woods as she'd exited the building and made her way to her back door. The cold was seeping through the smooth soles of his leather shoes and he was anxious to return to the warmth of his car.

Olivia wasn't the only one who had cursed silently when she lost her footing and dropped her keys. He remained rooted to his spot until she eventually made her way back to the outbuilding.

The man had waited until she was safely inside before he turned to retrace his steps to his car. He hadn't meant to step on the rotten branch that broke under his weight with a resounding crack.

He'd heard Olivia's scream and knew he had to get away. He watched her close the door behind her, then turned and ran for his car.

"Tucker," the familiar voice said into the phone. "Novak here. I just got a call from dispatch. They've heard from that Olivia Osgoode. Remember her? That nut job from the parking garage?"

Byron bit his tongue. Now was no time to take his superior to task for his assessment of the woman. "I remember Ms. Osgoode," he replied. "Did she recall something?"

"No. She called 9-1-1 because she thinks she saw a man in the woods next to her house. Thinks it might be the man from the parking garage."

Byron was quiet, taking this in.

"On a night like this," Novak said. "Dispatch sent out a squad car. They called me. I'd like you to go out there. She's so damned hard to understand, but she seemed to calm down around you. Can you take her statement?"

"I'll take Missie over to my sister's. I can be there in half an hour."

"Hate to drag you out for this. It's probably just her overactive imagination."

"I'm not so sure," Byron said. "I'm happy to go."

"You can fill me in on everything in the morning." Detective Novak hung up.

Byron parked next to the squad car angled toward the back of the property, its headlights illuminating a wide swath in front of it. The freezing rain from earlier in the evening had returned and he pulled his cap low over his ears. He removed the sunglasses that were always perched on the rim of his cap and tossed them on his dashboard.

One of the two uniformed officers on-site approached him. Byron listened carefully as the man repeated what Olivia told him. "Did you find evidence of an intruder?" he asked the man.

"Conditions aren't ideal for a search," the officer said, pointing to the sky. "She took us to the spot where she thinks she saw him."

"And?"

The officer shrugged. "Hard to say. There's a large branch on the ground that's snapped in two. Impossible to tell how recently."

"But it could have happened tonight?"

The officer nodded. "I think so."

"Show me," Byron said. The officer switched on his flashlight and the pair set off for the woods.

Byron took the flashlight from the officer when they reached their destination. He examined the broken branch. "It's a recent break—no rot or insect damage." He swung the flashlight over the area. "The ground's a blanket of wet leaves. I can't see any footprints but we'll need to look in the daylight. Did you check with the neighbor whose dogs were barking?"

The officer nodded. "Said their dogs bark all the time. They didn't see anything, but they didn't get up to investigate."

"Where's Ms. Osgoode?"

"She's in the kitchen with Smith. We told her we didn't find anything, but she's really shaken up."

"She identified him as the man she saw in the parking garage?"

"Says he might have been. She thinks he's the same size as the man in the garage."

"Did she see his face?"

"No. Too dark."

They turned and began to walk to the house.

"She could be making this all up to get attention. Just like the story about the body in the parking garage," the officer said. "That's what Detective Novak thinks."

Byron spun on the officer. "We've got no reason to think that she's making anything up. Until we do, we treat this like any other open investigation."

The man stepped back and nodded. "Yes, sir."

Byron knocked softly at the back door and entered the kitchen.

"Ms. Osgoode," he said, as he crossed the kitchen to the breakfast room. Even in the bright light of the overhead fixtures, the rooms felt warm and cozy with their wide-planked maple floors and soft white cabinets. "We met the other night."

Olivia began to rise.

"Don't get up," Byron said quickly. "You've had quite a scare here tonight."

Olivia wrapped her arms around herself and nodded. "Do you think he was here?"

Byron said, "I don't know."

"Do you think someone was out there, spying on me?"

"It's possible." He looked into her eyes. "The branch at the edge of the woods that you pointed out looks like it was broken recently." He pulled out a chair at the trestle table and sat down opposite her.

"Is there somewhere that you'd like to go tonight? Someone you can stay with? You won't want to spend the night here."

Olivia shook her head firmly. "I've got my cats to take care of. I need to stay here."

"Surely they'll be fine for one night."

"I'm sure they would be, but then what about tomorrow night and the night after that? This is my home and I need to be here." She swallowed hard. "I'm scared, though."

Byron leaned toward her. "That's understandable. We'll keep your house under surveillance the rest of the night. That's all we can do."

"Thank you. That'll let me sleep." She raised her eyes to his. "I'm not stupid."

"No one said you were."

"That Detective Novak thinks I am. People always think that because my speech is a bit," she hesitated, searching for the right word, "labored. They think that I'm dumb. But I'm not—I have a speech defect. And I'm not an unbalanced attention seeker, either."

Byron shifted uncomfortably in his chair.

"I'm neither of those things. I'm telling the truth. I saw a man carrying a dead woman's body in the parking garage and I saw someone out there," she gestured toward the woods, "tonight. I'm not sure if it's the same man but it could be."

"I believe you," Byron said. "Could it be someone else? Someone you know? An ex-husband or old boyfriend? A disgruntled employee or coworker?"

Olivia shook her head vehemently. She didn't have an ex-husband; she'd never had a boyfriend. No one at the funeral home had anything against her. "No. Nothing like that."

"We can only keep you under surveillance tonight. I suggest that you find somewhere else to stay for a while."

Olivia set her shoulders. "I'm staying here."

"Consider installing a security system."

Olivia nodded. "I can do that."

"Have it monitored. But keep in mind that our response time out here will be at least ten minutes. Your best bet is to vacate while we search for the killer."

He looked at the resolute woman who sat across from him. She reminded him of his late wife—smart and unflappable. He'd find time to drive by here while he was on duty.

CHAPTER 14

Olivia cradled her office phone on her shoulder as she logged into the bank's website and checked the balance in the mortuary's operating account. "There's no problem," she said into the receiver. She paused and listened to the irate banker on the other end of the line.

"I know today is the day that our payment is due and I see that we don't have enough in our account to cover it." She took a deep breath, her mind frantically searching for something comforting to say to the banker they'd done business with for over twenty years.

"I'm not sure why we didn't make a bigger deposit today. We certainly have the revenue," she lied.

She paused to listen and a flush spread from the top of her turtleneck to the tip of her head. She repeated herself, more slowly and distinctly. "I assure you that I'm very careful with our accounts," she continued. "We'll deposit the additional money tomorrow." She hung up the phone without waiting for his reply.

Olivia cradled her head in her hands as her annoyance grew. Why was she taking criticism from the banker when none of this was her fault?

She pushed herself to her feet and headed to the reception desk. "Any word from Sam yet?"

Flora hastily put aside the *People* magazine that she'd been reading surreptitiously while the phones were silent and shook her head. "He used to tell me when he wasn't coming in, but not anymore."

"Have you tried calling him?"

Flora shook her head emphatically no. "And get my head bit off? No thank you."

Olivia nodded and started back to her office as Sam burst through the door.

"Thank goodness," Olivia said. "I need to talk to you, Sam."

Sam brushed past her without looking up. "I just came in to get something. I'm late to an appointment. It'll have to wait until tomorrow."

"It can't, Sam." Olivia stepped in front of him.

Sam brought his head up. "What can't wait?"

"The bank called. We don't have enough to make the payment on the construction loan."

"How's that possible? I saw the deposit."

"Payroll has to come out of that, too."

Sam threw up his hands. "Then the bank will have to take its payment tomorrow."

"It's not just the bank, Sam," Olivia continued. "We're supposed to pay for cost overruns and we're behind. The contractor called me this morning and two of the subcontractors are going to file mechanic's liens." She paused to let this news sink in. "If they file liens, the bank may call our loan. It's an event of default under our loan agreement and they'll be entitled to default interest, too."

Sam stared at her. "You've got access to all of our accounts. Move some money around." He waved his hand dismissively. "Fix it."

He walked into his office, took a small wrapped gift from his desk drawer, and strode to the exit without glancing at Olivia.

The rear door slammed shut.

Kathy rose from her chair and joined Olivia in the hallway.

"Did you hear all that?" Olivia asked.

"I most certainly did. I can't understand what's come over him." Kathy faced Olivia. "It's not fair to ask you to make excuses to the bankers. That's his job. I've got half a mind to sit him down and tell him so."

Olivia touched her arm. "Don't do that. I'm afraid it'll only make matters worse."

"So what are you going to do?"

"I'll see if I can move money from another account. Maybe the bank will accept part of it tomorrow and the rest by the end of the week."

Kathy cocked her head to one side. "You're a smart cookie, you know that."

Olivia flushed.

"Speaking of being smart—are you going to coach a team in this year's sixth-grade science fair? If I remember correctly, your team placed fifth at the state competition last year. Very impressive. And you had a lot of fun." Kathy cocked an eyebrow at Olivia.

"I don't know. Grams was the one who signed me up for all of that."

"And your grandmother would want you to continue—in her memory. I'm in a Bible study with the sixth-grade science teacher and she mentioned to me that they were hoping you'd volunteer again this year. She said you have a way with the kids."

A smile played at the corner of Olivia's lips.

Kathy brought her hands together. "Perfect. I'll tell her that you're in. I'll give her your cell phone number."

"I guess that'll be fine. I have the time and it is fun. More fun than talking to cranky bankers.

CHAPTER 15

Sam pulled his car into his garage and sat quietly behind the wheel. He needed a moment to compose himself before he went in to his family. He'd been irritable around them far too frequently lately.

Tonight's dinner was a celebration of his son's acceptance into Sam's alma mater. Even without a scholarship, he could swing that tuition.

Sam turned over the package that he'd stopped by his office to retrieve. A T-shirt to Ben's new university might not be much of a celebratory gift, but it would have to do for now.

"Hey everybody—head for the hills. The old man's home." Sam called his customary greeting as he came through the kitchen door.

Nancy was working in high gear. Her favorite apron bearing the message "The Soup's Good when the Cook's in Love" was tied around her waist.

"Something smells great," Sam said, bending to kiss Nancy's cheek as she whisked a creamy sauce, bubbling on the stove.

"Thanks. I'm making all of Ben's favorites."

"You're a wonderful mother."

She glanced in his direction. "Can you go light the grill? We're having filets."

Sam laid his package on the corner of the kitchen island.

"What've you got there?"

"A T-shirt to the university. It's not much, but I thought he'd like to have it to wear this summer."

Nancy stopped stirring and brought her head up sharply. "Didn't you get his text?"

Sam frowned. "I haven't been paying much attention to my phone today. Why?"

She gestured to the phone that he'd pulled out of his pocket and grinned. "Read it for yourself."

Sam located the message from Ben and read aloud. "Accepted to Cornell!!! Food science program."

Sam brought his head up to look at Nancy. She wiped her hand over her eyes. "Makes me teary every time I think about it. It's his dream. I'm so proud of that kid of ours."

Sam cleared his throat. "Did he get a scholarship?" he finally asked.

"A small one," Nancy replied. "It's still going to cost an arm and a leg. I'm glad we can afford it."

"About that." Sam slumped onto a stool at the kitchen island. "I'm not sure that we can."

"Oh—go on. Sure we can. You've said yourself the funeral home was doing great. That's why you're renovating it." Nancy peered at him anxiously.

Sam glared at her. "We just talked about this when you bid on that European vacation. We're overspending on everything. There've been thousands of dollars of unexpected, necessary repairs at the mortuary. I'm completely tapped out."

She moved to him and put her arm around his shoulder.

Sam continued. "We've had lean times before, but I can't believe how quickly everything's spiraled out of control." He shook his head. "Ben's going to have to turn down Cornell and go to State as we originally thought."

Nancy stiffened. "He'll do no such thing." She took Sam's chin in her hand and turned his face to hers. "That's exactly what your parents did to you—made you turn down your scholarship to Vanderbilt to go to the local university so you could work at the mortuary while you went to school. You had to abandon your dreams of becoming a doctor."

"And look how that worked out for me," Sam replied. "I married you, have three terrific children, and am happy as a clam."

"We've built a wonderful life, I'll grant you that, but I think you've always resented that you didn't get to pursue your own dream." She lifted her chin. "We're not going to make the same mistake with Ben. It's almost impossible to get into this program. It's one of the most prestigious in the country. When he graduates, he'll have employers chasing after him." She inhaled slowly. "He's going to Cornell. We'll find a way."

Sam nodded slowly and drew his wife to him. "You're right. Ben deserves this chance." He sighed heavily. "Tom's always said that he'll help with college tuition for our kids since he doesn't have any of his own. I'll ask him.

CHAPTER 16

"That's it, Grams. That's all I know. For now. I'm going to figure out who she is." Olivia picked up her satchel. She took a step away from the grave and headed toward her car. A lone woman appeared in the distance and began walking into the cemetery. Olivia slowed her pace and froze when the woman stopped in the section of the graves that Olivia was interested in. Could she be one of the widows on her list of possible candidates that might be the dead woman from the garage?

Olivia busied herself tending to the grave in front of her but she kept her gaze on the woman. Olivia had seen her in the cemetery before.

The woman took a small bouquet of flowers, wrapped in newspaper, out of her large purse and laid them in front of the headstone.

Olivia checked the time on her phone. Her lunch hour was almost over and she needed to get back to work. She shoved the phone into her purse. She would stay until the woman left and she could see whose grave she had visited. She pulled weeds around the headstone and kept her eyes trained on the woman.

Olivia didn't have long to wait. In another five minutes, the woman put her fingers to her lips and pressed them to the headstone before walking away.

As soon as the woman was out of sight, Olivia made a beeline for the grave the woman had been visiting. Her heart lurched in her throat when she read the name on the headstone: Scott Williams.

What a lucky break. She'd tried to research the remaining two names on her list, but Robert Howard Robinson and Scott Williams were common names and Google turned up page after page of entries. It would have taken a month of Sundays to work through them all. But now, as chance would have it, Scott Williams had had a visitor who was most likely his widow. That left only one name on her list. The woman who she hadn't seen at the cemetery since the fateful night in the parking garage—the one that wore a scarf that matched the one she'd seen around the dead woman's neck—must be the widow of Robert Howard Robinson.

Olivia had to stop herself from running to her car. With any luck, she wouldn't have anything pressing this afternoon and could do some internet research to find out more about Robert Howard Robinson—and, most importantly, if he had a widow.

Sam knocked on Olivia's door late that afternoon. "I know you don't like to work in the front, but I was wondering if you could stay late?"

"Sure."

"Thanks. We've got two viewings tonight and we're a bit short-staffed."

"I'm not dressed to be out front," Olivia said, pointing to her jeans and turtleneck.

Sam nodded as he took in her attire. "If you could just be here in case anyone needs anything? Keep pens by the guest book and make sure the remembrance cards are fully stocked. That would be a big help."

"I can do that," Olivia replied.

"Good. I'll tell the others. Just stay right here in your office. They'll come find you if they need anything."

Olivia smiled. This was working out perfectly. "Do you mind if I surf the net on my computer? You won't even have to pay me for tonight."

"That's fine," Sam said as he exited her office. "But we'll pay you."

Olivia clicked the icon at the bottom of her computer screen and the page she had been reading on Robert Howard Robinson jumped back into full view.

His obituary recited that he'd died almost three years ago in Marquette at the age of ninety-two. He was survived by his second wife, Cheryl Robinson, and his two children by his first marriage. Services were provided by Hilton Mortuary.

"Yes!" Olivia whispered. She opened the mortuary's internal records and retrieved the file on Robert Howard Robinson.

She scrolled down the page until she found the entry she was looking for. She picked up a pen and piece of paper and made note of the Robinson's address. He was married to his second wife, Cheryl, when he died. The last entry told Olivia that the visitation book from his funeral service at the mortuary had not been collected by the family and would be stored by the mortuary for five years, after which time it would be destroyed.

Olivia sighed heavily. She knew just where that visitation book would be stored now that the mortuary was undergoing renovation. The records that were usually kept in carefully labeled cabinets were currently loaded into cardboard banker's boxes stacked precariously in the old shed at the back of the property.

She stood and shrugged into her jacket. She retrieved the pocket flashlight from the bottom drawer of her desk and sidled toward the entrance to the public viewing areas. Olivia noted that the stack of remembrance brochures perched next to the guest book looked sufficient. She caught Flora's eye and inclined her head toward the back door, raising her hand holding the flashlight. Flora nodded in understanding and waved a hand toward the back door.

Olivia grabbed the key to the shed from the hook by the back door and made her way quickly across the parking lot and back lawn. The waning moon was obscured by clouds and provided only a sliver of light. She switched on her flashlight.

The disorder in the shed was worse than she remembered. The boxes weren't labeled and she had to open each one and rummage through the contents. Records from services that had been held three years earlier were contained in four separate boxes. Holding the flashlight in her teeth, she found what she was looking for in the fourth box. Olivia's hands were stiff with cold as she lifted the records onto a makeshift table that she'd fashioned out of other boxes.

The thin guest book creaked as she opened it and ran her left hand along the spine. There had been only a handful of people at either the visitation or the funeral. His eighty-one-year-old second wife, Cheryl, had been there but no one with the names of his children attended. The signers of the guest book were all from the local community. If Cheryl had children from a prior marriage, none of them bothered to attend their stepfather's funeral.

Olivia hurriedly replaced the guest book in the box and hoisted it to the top of the stack of boxes where she'd found it. Her teeth were chattering and she was anxious to get back to the warmth of her office. She locked the shed and was striding toward the rear parking lot when the moon came out from behind the clouds and a man stepped from between two parked cars and into view. He was tall, with an athletic build, and wore a dark ski jacket. Olivia froze. Could it be? From this vantage point, he looked like he could be the murderer.

The man swiveled his head in Olivia's direction. She crouched low and kept her gaze fixed on him. Had he seen her? Her heart hammered in her chest.

The back door opened and Flora stood, outlined in the yellow light of the hallway behind her. "Olivia? Are you out here?" she called.

The man turned to Flora.

"Hal," Flora said as the man approached her. "When did you get back into town?"

"Just a few minutes ago. I flew in to pay my respects to Larry Thompson and his family."

"Will you be here long enough to have dinner with your favorite aunt?" She straightened the collar on her shirt and smoothed down the front of her skirt.

"I wish I were, but I'm on the first flight out in the morning."

"You work too hard. One of these days, you need to take a break and come for a proper visit."

"I agree." He approached Flora and leaned over to give her a hug.

"Have you seen Olivia?"

"Who's Olivia?"

"She's our bookkeeper. Maybe you've never met her. She doesn't work out front."

"I haven't seen anyone."

"She came out here quite a while ago. I'm looking for her to ask her to make more coffee for the viewing."

"Do you want me to search?" he offered.

Olivia held her breath. He'd been a normal visitor to the funeral home, and Flora's nephew, to boot. They'd think she was a paranoid fool if they found her out here, crouching in the shadows.

"No. You go see the Thompsons; they'll be glad you're here. I must've missed her in the ladies' room or something." Flora and Hal stepped through the door.

Olivia stood and made her way to the back door. She opened it slowly and was relieved that Flora and Hal were nowhere to be seen. She was in the kitchen, making coffee, when Flora stepped into the room.

"Where in the world did you come from?" Flora asked. "I've been looking all over for you."

Olivia gave her a quizzical look. "I put a box of old invoices in the shed and then I checked on things out front," Olivia lied. "Looks like we need more coffee."

Flora nodded. "That's why I was trying to find you." She arched her back and rubbed her hands along her sides. "Everyone thinks being a receptionist is an easy job, but it's tiring to sit in one spot all day."

"I'm sure it is," Olivia said sympathetically.

"I'd better get back out there."

Olivia waited impatiently while the coffee finished brewing and then unobtrusively replenished the dispenser by the viewing room. She scanned the room and, finding everything in order, retreated to her office. She was anxious to continue her computer sleuthing.

Olivia entered the name Cheryl Robinson into the search engine of the mortuary's software program. She wanted to see if Cheryl had died and they'd handled her services. Just because her name didn't appear on the headstone didn't mean anything. Sometimes people took years to attend to those details; sometimes they never got done at all.

Her cursor continued to blink and the words "No Matches for Search – Try Again" flashed on her screen. Olivia next looked for Cheryl's obituary on the newspaper's website and came up empty-handed.

Olivia was about to log off of her computer when another thought hit her—maybe Cheryl Robinson had sold the marital home and moved out of town.

Olivia went to the county assessor's website and searched the address that she'd just recovered from Robert Howard Robinson's file. The tax records showed that the property was owned by one Cheryl Robinson and indicated that all taxes were paid current.

Olivia sat back in her chair and a chill ran down her spine. The dead woman she had seen in the garage had to be Cheryl Robinson. Her body had never been found and it appeared she had no one in her life that was looking for her.

She leaned over her desk, head in hand. She needed to go to the police with this. Now they'd have something concrete to investigate. *They won't think I'm crazy now.*

Olivia dug Detective Novak's card out of her wallet and placed her call. The woman who answered took her number and told her the Detective was gone for the day and she'd give him Olivia's message in the morning.

He has to believe me. Olivia exhaled slowly and logged off her computer.

CHAPTER 17

Olivia checked the time on her phone for the hundredth time. It was now 1:41. She'd been sitting on the grimy straight-backed chair in the Marquette Police Department lobby for almost an hour, waiting to be ushered back into Detective Novak's office. Her lunch hour was long over and she needed to get back to work. She was approaching the woman who sat behind the window of bulletproof glass when the woman looked up and spoke to her through the small round opening.

"Detective Novak will see you now." She pushed a button, a buzzer sounded, and the lock on the door at the end of the room clicked. "You can go through to the elevator. He's on the third floor, second office on your right." The woman turned her back on Olivia.

Olivia followed the woman's directions and soon stood in front of an office with a name plate that read "Detective Novak." The office was empty and Detective Novak was nowhere to be seen. His desktop was littered with paper and three Styrofoam cups of partially consumed coffee perched at precarious angles in the mess.

She hesitated, then stepped into the office and sat in one of the stiff chairs across from his desk. I'm going to sit here all afternoon, if I have to. *Surely this will be enough evidence for him.*

Olivia waited, rehearsing her story over and over in her mind. She was on her fourth rehash when the detective burst through the door.

"Sorry to keep you waiting, Ms. Osgoode. Lots going on." He settled into his chair and glanced at the stack of papers in his inbox. "You said you needed to see me? Have you remembered something else from the other night?"

Olivia nodded. "I have."

Detective Novak's eyebrows shot up.

"I've remembered that the victim wore a colorful scarf around her neck. It was actually draped across her body, like this." She drew her hand across her torso. "It dangled away at the end."

"Can you describe this scarf?"

"It was shades of red and purple."

"Was it flowers? Or a geometric pattern?"

"I'm not sure. They were too far away."

"Was it a winter scarf or one of those silky kinds?"

Olivia shrugged and shook her head.

The Detective put down his pen abruptly and began to rise. "Thank you for taking the time to come in to tell me this."

"There's more," Olivia said, and the Detective sat back down.

Olivia continued. "I've seen that scarf before. There's a woman who used to visit the cemetery on a regular basis who wore that scarf."

"How do you know that?"

"My grandmother is buried there and I visit her almost every day." Olivia looked at her hands in her lap. "There are a number of us 'regulars' and the woman with the scarf was one of them."

"I thought you said you didn't know the victim."

"I don't. I'm friendly with some of the other women—they're all older widows—but I've never spoken to Cheryl."

Detective Novak shook his head. "How do you know her name?"

Olivia took a deep breath and recounted her story of how she'd identified the woman with the scarf.

Detective Novak leaned back in his chair. "That's some pretty fancy detective work you've done, Ms. Osgoode. The trouble is that it's all unsubstantiated conjecture." He gave her a sallow smile. "We'll look into this. There are a multitude of explanations as to why you haven't seen her: maybe she's out of town; maybe she's ill. Thank you for coming in, but from here on out, leave the police work to us."

He rose to his feet and gestured to Olivia to follow him. "You've taken enough of my time."

Olivia stared at him, rooted to the spot. *How dare you patronize me? She'd taken enough of his time?' After you kept me waiting for over an hour?* She curled her hands into fists and her nails bit into her palms. "Tell me how much progress you've made, Detective? Found the body? Even the tiniest clue as to who the killer in our midst might be?"

The detective stiffened and narrowed his eyes.

"What about the man lurking in the woods outside my house, spying on me. It's got to be the same man. Are you 'working on' that?"

Detective Novak took her arm and escorted her to the elevator. "As I've told you before, if you feel unsafe at any time you can call 9-1-1." He pushed the button and held the door for her when the elevator arrived. "As I said, we'll continue our investigation."

Olivia yanked herself free from his grasp and stomped onto the elevator. She was still seething when she exited the elevator on the ground floor and almost collided with Byron.

"Ms. Osgoode." He smiled at her and she didn't look away like she usually did.

Olivia nodded.

"What brings you here?"

"I remembered something about the dead woman that I thought might help you find her and the killer."

"Excellent. I'm sure Detective Novak was very pleased."

"Not really," Olivia snapped. "I'd be surprised if he does anything with the information."

"I'm sure you're wrong."

"He basically told me to mind my own business."

Byron couldn't hide his surprise. "Why don't you tell me what you remembered?"

Olivia shook her head. "I'm over an hour late getting back from lunch as it is. Ask your detective. I'd be interested to know if he actually took down my statement or not."

"Alright, I will."

"Thank you." Olivia stepped to the entrance. She turned back to him. "Any luck finding the man that was hiding in the woods outside my house?"

Byron shook his head. "We drive by at least twice each night but haven't seen anything suspicious." He didn't mention that he drove by every chance he got and on his days off, too. "I'm sorry that we don't have the resources to do more. As I recommended, if you're still uneasy, you might want to stay with a friend for a while."

"I'm having an alarm system installed on Saturday. I'll be fine." Olivia turned away from him. "It'd be nice if somebody took me seriously."

"I'm taking you seriously," he said as she pushed through the door.

Byron watched her as she walked away, then punched the elevator for the third floor and Detective Novak's office.

The detective looked up as Byron walked into the room. "What's up?"

"I just ran into Olivia Osgoode coming out of the elevator. I was curious to hear what she had to report."

"Wait until you hear the ridiculous story she's dreamed up now," Detective Novak snorted, and launched into his tale.

Byron's shoulders tensed. "I don't think that's ridiculous. We've got a name—it's something we can investigate."

Novak bristled. "I've got it all right here." He tapped a legal pad with his pencil. "We'll look into it."

"I know that you've had precious little to go on," Byron said, trying to placate the senior officer. He'd been angling for a promotion into the detective unit for months. The last thing he wanted to do was offend the man that headed it up. "It's not your fault that the garage was free so that you couldn't get any data from a ticket machine. Or that it isn't equipped with cameras."

"I recommended to the city council that they install a camera system in there two years ago." He slumped back into his chair. "You know how that goes—it wasn't in the current budget but they'd keep it in mind."

Byron nodded in sympathy. "Did any of the neighboring businesses have cameras that might have captured one of the entrances to the garage?"

"The building across the street has a system that films part of the street in front of the garage."

"So you could get license plates of any sedans driving on the street during the time of the crime."

Novak nodded. "Only trouble is—the camera was on the fritz the week this happened."

Byron sucked in air through his teeth. "We just can't get a break, can we?"

Novak's phone rang and he picked up the receiver, placing his hand over the mouthpiece. "We'll look into this," he said, tearing the sheet of paper with Cheryl Robinson's name off of his pad and stuffing it into his top desk drawer. He picked up his pen and began making notes as he turned his attention to his caller.

CHAPTER 18

Tom approached the first tee at the Marquette Country Club. The dew sparkled on the grass in the early morning light. He raised his hand in greeting to the three men in his foursome. He'd been trying to get close to two of them for years. Successful retired businessmen, they were rumored to be loaded. Tom would love to handle their investments. Unless he missed his bet, they'd be more focused on their handicaps than their brokerage accounts and he'd be able to rack up hefty trading fees.

"Good morning, Stan," he said, extending his hand. "I'm glad we're finally playing together. I understand that I'll get some good pointers from you."

"I don't know about that," Stan replied. "I hear you're a scratch golfer. We were hoping," he pointed to the other two men in their group, "that you'd give us some advice."

"We're up next," one of the other men said. "Where are your clubs?"

Tom looked over at the two golf carts waiting on the cart path. Three bags of clubs were neatly stowed on the backs of the carts. He frowned. "I don't know—they always have them ready for the members. Let me find out. I won't be a minute."

Tom strode toward the clubhouse and was intercepted by the golf course's general manager. "Mr. Hilton," the man said. "A word?"

"Where the hell are my clubs?" Tom hissed. "My foursome is about to tee off. We're going to miss our tee time. These are very important prospective clients of mine."

"Your membership has been frozen, Tom."

"What the hell are you talking about?"

"You're six months in arrears on your dues and that's the rule. You know that—you've been on the board here." The man inhaled deeply. "I'm sorry to tell you, but we can't let you play."

"There's been some sort of misunderstanding. Why didn't you notify me?"

"We've sent notices to your home. Repeatedly."

Tom clenched his jaw. He could visualize the letters from the Club, stacked on the corner of his desk. Unopened.

"I'll get this straightened out, I promise." He glanced over his shoulder at the three men who were now staring at him. "Just let me play today and I'll get back to you."

"I'm sorry, but I don't have the authority to do that. I've only kept your clubs here out of respect. We should have sold them to apply to your arrearages. The club's attorney has been directed to file suit against you."

Tom felt the blood pounding in his temples and knew his face must be beet red. He put his back to his foursome. "This is ridiculous. When I get to the bottom of this, there's going to be hell to pay. I know I've made my payments and your accounting department has screwed this up. Misapplied them or something."

The general manager remained silent.

Tom took a step closer to the man. "What do I need to do to be able to play today?"

"Bring your account current."

"How much is that?" Tom asked through gritted teeth.

Tom rocked back on his heels at the number the general manager supplied.

"That doesn't include late fees or interest," the man said. "If you pay me right now, I can deduct those."

Tom turned and waved to his compatriots who were now anxiously milling around their carts. He cupped his hand around his mouth. "Be right there," he called.

"I've got the cash on me, as a matter of fact. You do take cash, don't you?"

The man nodded.

"Let's step inside—I don't want to flash my bank roll in public."

The general manager signaled to one of the attendants. "Go get Mr. Hilton's clubs and put them on that cart over there." He gestured toward the first tee. "And hurry. Hold up the next foursome until they tee off."

The attendant took off at a run as Tom followed the general manager into his office. He took his money clip out of his pocket and peeled off a stack of one hundred dollar bills. He folded the remaining bills—a thin stack of ones and fives—and replaced it in his pocket.

"There," Tom spat. "Are we good?"

"We are."

"Make sure my food tab is open, too. I'll need to treat these guys to breakfast when we're done and I don't want any hiccups. Your incompetence has already embarrassed me enough." He spun on his heel and headed for the tee.

Tom was relieved to see his clubs in place on the cart.

"Seems they lost my clubs," Tom said as he approached his fellow players. "Can't imagine how that happened. These are custom made and cost a pretty penny. Had to raise a little hell with them back there."

"That's terrible," one of the men said. "You can't trust anybody these days. At least you've got them now."

"That's right," Stan said. "Just concentrate on your game."

Tom placed his ball on a tee and stood, surveying the lush green fairway in front of him. His mind wasn't on his game, however. He needed that stack of cash to buy the opiates that had become an essential part of his daily life. He was out and overdue on his payment to his supplier. This guy would do far worse than sue him for the arrearage.

He took a deep breath. He'd have to think of something. He swung his club and sent his ball far to the left, into the deep rough.

Tom pulled his car into his garage, switched off the ignition, and pressed the button to close the door. He reached for the door handle, then slumped back into the seat, allowing his hand to fall to the armrest. By the time they'd finished their round, he had been coming off his high. He'd managed to play the jovial host to the group at the 19th hole and had even secured a couple of promising referrals, but he'd been exhausted by the time he'd gotten to his car. He'd almost fallen asleep in the country-club parking lot but had pulled himself together enough to move his car to a shady spot behind an adjacent strip mall where he'd spent the remainder of the day passed out in his car.

He'd finally come to when Ashley called him shortly before midnight. He'd let the call go to voice mail and then listened to her tell him that she had a migraine and was going to bed and would he mind sleeping in the guest room when he came home so he didn't disturb her. That was fine by him. If she only knew how much he wanted to avoid scrutiny right now.

The cash he'd used to bring his country-club dues current had been meant to pay his debt to his dealer, with enough to buy pills to get him through the weekend. Now he was out of everything and would have to detox on his own. It was better that she didn't see him this way.

The overhead light in the garage went out. He leaned over the steering wheel and was reaching for the door handle when the door was jerked open. A pair of powerful hands grabbed him by his shoulders and dragged him out of his car.

"What the…" Tom sputtered.

"We were expecting to see you today, Tom," a man leaning against the wall in the shadows said quietly. "What happened?"

"I got very busy at the office."

The man who had hauled him out of the car slapped him hard along the side of his face with an open palm. Pain exploded inside Tom's head as his eardrum broke. Tom cupped his throbbing ear with his hand and moaned softly.

"I don't think you made it to your office today, Tom. I think you played golf at your fancy country club and then you slept it off in your car. Isn't that what happened today?"

Tom nodded imperceptibly.

"That's better. We like it when you tell the truth," the man said. "In fact, we think you usually tell us the truth and we generally like you, Tom. You've been a good customer and all. When you didn't show up with the money, we were going to visit with your wife about your payment," he continued.

Tom stood stock still, his moan freezing in his throat. "Leave her out of it."

"Doesn't she enjoy our product from time to time?"

"She's clean. Always has been."

The man chuckled mirthlessly. "I'll bet she doesn't even know you're using, does she?"

Tom stared at the man.

"Because we like you—you're such a fine, upstanding member of our community—we decided to pay you this courtesy call instead of delivering this same message to your wife. Quite a looker—it'd be a shame for something to happen to her that would mess her up."

"I'll get you your money."

"Except now it's more, Tom. We don't like it when people break their promises to us. Now you owe late fees and default interest. Just like at the bank." He snickered at his allusion. "We're like an institutional lender. The amount is now double. And unlike the banks, we have more ways to get your attention." He nodded to the man who still held Tom's right arm in a vicelike grip. The man brought his free hand to Tom's forehead and slammed his head back against the roof of his car.

Tom staggered and fell to his knees, cradling his head in his hands.

"You've got until the end of the week," the man said. "Don't disappoint us again. We won't go easy on you next time."

The man reached up and hit the garage door button on the wall behind him. Tom remained on his knees as the two men walked slowly past him and into the night.

CHAPTER 19

Olivia opened her eyes to sun streaming through the crack in her blackout curtains. She couldn't remember the last time she'd slept past dawn. She reached her arms over her head and pushed her toes into the footboard of her antique bed and stretched. For the first time in months, the gray cloud of grief had lifted.

She sprang out of bed and checked her bedside clock. If she hurried, she could still make the Saturday flea market in Lewisville when it opened at nine. She hadn't gone since her grandmother had died. She felt the customary frisson of excitement when she was about to embark on the hunt for a forgotten and discarded toaster for her collection.

Olivia stepped to the large pedestal sink in the hall bathroom and splashed water on her face. She checked her reflection in the beveled glass mirror and was relieved that her hair was not a tangled mess. She ran a brush through her hair, pulled on her jeans and turtleneck from the edge of the claw-foot tub where she'd tossed them the night before, and was on her way.

The twenty-minute drive to the nearby town was beautiful in the soft morning sunshine. Olivia found a parking spot at the end of a row by the west entrance to the market. She stopped by her favorite coffee vendor inside the gate and splurged on a large mocha latte and a lemon blueberry muffin. She peeled away a portion of the wrapper and ate the muffin as she perused the vendor's stalls, trailing crumbs in her wake.

Olivia scoured the stalls of the two antiques vendors where she often found items of interest, but came away empty-handed. Her disappointment in her lack of success didn't spoil her ebullient mood. Instead of scurrying to the exit like she usually did when she had exhausted her hunt in her usual stalls, she sauntered through the remainder of the market.

How had she never noticed all the interesting things offered by local farmers and artisans? She bought a sack of heirloom tomatoes that were almost too beautiful to eat and a jar of local honey.

Olivia rounded the corner to the outside row of stalls and was drawn to a vendor, halfway down the row, that displayed row upon row of hand knit sweaters, scarves, and blankets. A violet tunic, shot with gold and aqua threads, hung from a wooden hanger at the front of the stall. Olivia kept her eyes on it as she made her way along the row, the hanger turning in the gentle breeze.

She was fingering the supple yarn and admiring the fine handiwork when the vendor approached her. "That matches your eyes perfectly," the woman said.

Olivia brought her hand to her mouth. "It's lovely. Did you knit this?"

"I did. It's my favorite piece in the booth."

Olivia kept her free hand on the garment.

"I think it'll fit you perfectly," the woman said, stepping back to appraise Olivia. "Would you like to try it on?"

Olivia hesitated. The woman removed it from the hanger and held it out for Olivia to put her head through the neck opening. Olivia smiled, set her purse at her feet, and slipped into the garment.

The woman exhaled softly. "It looks like it was made for you. That color is gorgeous on you."

Olivia raised her eyebrows. The woman put her arm around Olivia's shoulders and turned her to the mirror hanging in the front of the booth.

"See for yourself. You look beautiful."

Olivia gazed at her reflection and blinked hard. Had anyone ever—other than her grandmother—said she looked beautiful? Was it possible that this woman was right?

"I don't know," Olivia said, turning to the side to view her profile in the mirror.

The woman regarded her thoughtfully. "Do you usually wear what you have on today? Gray and black?"

Olivia nodded.

"You're a lovely young woman with remarkable eyes. Violet—like Elizabeth Taylor's, you know? Most women would kill to have your eyes. You should show them off."

Olivia breathed in slowly through her nose. She dropped her hand and stared at her image in the mirror.

"Would you like to wear it out of here?" the woman asked.

Olivia hesitated. The words from her grandmother's letter reverberated in her mind: I think you'll be lovely in violet, so buy yourself something to match those remarkable eyes of yours. She reached for her purse and paid the woman.

Olivia stood at her grandmother's grave and swung her head in each direction. She was alone in this section of the cemetery. She took a step forward and twirled, her arms stretched wide.

"See, Grams? I bought this sweater today at the flea market. I went looking for toasters but I came home with this." She smoothed her hand down the front of the garment. "It's that color you told me to buy. It's hand-knit and the woman who made it said it's the perfect color for me."

She stood, silently looking at the headstone. "She said I look beautiful in it. I think so, too," she said in a small voice. She closed her eyes and inhaled deeply, drinking in the sweet pungency of newly-mown grass.

"Is that you, Olivia?" came a voice from her right.

Olivia jumped and took a step back.

"I didn't mean to startle you, dear." Mrs. Marshall reached out and put a hand on Olivia's back. "I almost didn't recognize you in that lovely sweater. I wanted to tell you how wonderful you look. Your eyes pop when you wear that color."

"Thank you," Olivia said, coughing lightly to cover her embarrassment. "I didn't hear you come up." She looked at her friend.

"I'm afraid I don't have your mixer with me today. It's done but I forgot it at home."

Mrs. Marshall waved her hand in a dismissive gesture. "No worries. I'm in no hurry. I just wanted to say hello."

The two women walked toward the parking lot.

"I've been meaning to ask you something," Olivia said.

Mrs. Marshall stopped and looked at Olivia. "Anything, dear."

"Do you know the other women who come to visit graves? The other regulars, like us?"

"My husband died six years ago and I've been coming here almost daily since then, so I've become friendly—at least in passing—with most of the women who visit loved ones in this part of the cemetery."

Olivia nodded encouragingly.

"We just wave or say 'hello.' I've talked to you more than the others. Most of us are elderly, so people often quit coming. Whether due to death or infirmity, I don't know. We're a transitory lot, we cemetery visitors."

"Did you know Cheryl Robinson?" Olivia pointed over her right shoulder to a grave in the next row. "Her husband is buried over there."

"Funny you should mention Cheryl. She came to mind when I just mentioned about people coming and going."

Olivia's pulse quickened.

Mrs. Marshall continued. "Cheryl's one of the ones I know a bit better. She was visibly upset one day—crying uncontrollably—and I approached her out of concern."

"Did she say what was the matter?"

"She did. Her husband had left her comfortably well off and she'd done something unwise with the money and was afraid she'd lost it. She was apologizing to her husband over and over. Inconsolable, she was."

"Did she say how she lost it?"

Mrs. Marshall shook her head. "I think I embarrassed her by coming up to her."

"Have you seen her since then?" Olivia held her breath, waiting for the reply.

"Not once. I don't know if she's trying to avoid me so she's coming at different times or if she's sick. I'm a bit worried about her." Mrs. Marshall looked into Olivia's eyes. "Do you know what's happened to her?"

Olivia paused, debating whether to bring the older woman into her confidence. *What do I really know for sure? Is there any reason to upset this kind woman when I'm not sure what happened? Even the police didn't believe me.*

Olivia shook her head. "I haven't seen her here recently, either. I was just wondering.

CHAPTER 20

Olivia pulled out of the cemetery parking lot and turned in the opposite direction of her house. The afternoon remained clear and sunny and the only thing she had on her agenda was to review the packet of information Mrs. Walters had sent her about the science fair. She had no plans that evening—it was a Saturday night, after all—so she could put on the Hallmark Channel and go through the papers later.

She came to a turnoff onto a rural road that wound past picturesque farms and would take her to the Marquette Country Club. She loved this drive and made it often when she had a lot on her mind. Driving always relaxed her and helped her think.

The police—or at least Detective Novak—didn't believe that there had ever been a dead body in the parking garage. She didn't know what Officer Tucker thought about it. He seemed more sympathetic to her, but maybe he just pitied her.

She inhaled deeply. Cheryl Robinson was the woman in the garage, she felt sure of it. After talking to Mrs. Marshall, she now knew that Mrs. Robinson had been deeply upset by her financial situation. How did the man in the ski mask figure into all of this?

Detective Novak wasn't going to do anything with the new information she'd brought him. *Where does that leave me? There've been transients in our woods from time to time over the years, but it's too coincidental that I saw a man watching me so soon after the tragedy in the parking garage.* She shivered involuntarily. He hadn't been a transient—he had to have been the masked man from the garage. She needed to convince the police that Cheryl Robinson had been murdered. *I'm not a detective. How am I supposed to do this?*

Olivia slowed at a familiar curve in the road and noticed the name on the old metal mailbox as she was coming out of the curve: Robinson. Her pulse quickened. Could this be where Cheryl Robinson lived? She thought she remembered that Cheryl lived outside of town.

Olivia pulled to the shoulder of the road a quarter mile further along and logged into the county assessor's website on her phone. She typed in "Cheryl Robinson" and waited impatiently while the search engine wheel spun. She was debating whether she should go home to retrieve the address from her notes when the record she'd been seeking flashed on her screen. The mailbox she'd just passed had, indeed, been Cheryl Robinson's.

She checked for oncoming traffic and swung her car into a U-turn. Finding Cheryl Robinson's mailbox from this direction was harder and she sailed by it before she could slow to make the turn. She doubled back and pulled into the driveway, proceeding slowly toward the house.

Olivia bit her lip as she stopped in front of the modest home. The house slumped on its foundation, its open shutters and windows reflecting the cloudless sky and giving it a vacant look.

She surveyed the scene in front of her. No newspapers littered the front walk and a neatly coiled hose peeked out from under a hedge. A few dead leaves littered the front steps but the place didn't look unkempt.

What in the world am I hoping to find? She knew what she was hoping— that Cheryl Robinson would open the front door and ask Olivia what she wanted.

Olivia clutched the steering wheel. She wanted this woman to be alive; she wanted the police to be right and the whole nightmarish scene to have been a figment of her imagination.

I didn't make this up. I have to find out about Cheryl Robinson.

Olivia got out of the car and forced herself up the steps to Cheryl Robinson's front door, rehearsing what she would say to the woman if she answered. I'm from Hilton Mortuary and I'm paying a call to see if you were happy with our services. Our survey to you got returned undeliverable. Even to her own ears, this sounded feeble.

She pressed the doorbell and heard the chime ring somewhere inside the house. She shifted from one foot to the other and waited for the woman to appear.

No sounds emanated from within the house; there was no movement at any window. Cheryl Robinson wasn't there.

Olivia returned to her car and was about to get in when she decided to walk to the bottom of the drive to check the mailbox. If mail had been piling up, that might tell her something—either Cheryl Robinson didn't care about her mail or that Cheryl Robinson was beyond caring.

Olivia quickened her pace as she walked down the driveway. If Cheryl had been murdered, as she believed, would this be tampering with evidence? *I'm not going to take anything—I'm just going to see if anything's in her box. I won't touch a thing.*

Olivia tugged at the stiff latch and finally managed to open the box. She was bent over the empty mailbox when the man from the parking garage drove past on his way home. She missed seeing him turn his head in her direction; missed the wave of surprise cross his face that turned to malice.

Olivia straightened and closed the box. Either she was wrong about Cheryl or someone—the masked man?—was collecting her mail. A shiver ran down her spine. If it were the latter, he might stop by and find her here. She turned and ran back to her car. Her hand shook as she put her key in the ignition and pressed the door lock button, clicking it twice to be sure. She proceeded back down the driveway as quickly as she dared and was relieved that there were no cars in sight on the road. She turned right and picked up speed, leaving Cheryl Robinson's residence behind her.

The man turned sharply into the next driveway, a quarter mile down the road. *What in the hell is she doing there? Was it even Olivia?* He brought his palms to the sides of his head. He was sure it was. *Wasn't he?*

He turned off the ignition and leaned over the back of his seat to get a good view through the rear window. He'd been traveling in the direction of Olivia's house. If it was Olivia, her car should pass by him on her way home.

His blood pounded in his temples. He checked his watch. How long had he been there? No more than a minute, surely. It felt like hours.

He was about to pull back onto the road when a white Corolla sped by him. He couldn't clearly see the face of the driver, but he could tell it was a woman. *Olivia. It has to be Olivia.* If she was nosing around his latest victim's house, it might be time to eliminate Olivia.

He started the ignition. He'd need to be very careful with this one. People would be looking for her. She couldn't go missing. He'd make it look like a suicide. Everyone knew what a miserable loner she was. The police even thought she was crazy. They'd believe a suicide.

He smiled as he turned onto the road. An overdose would do the trick nicely. He'd have to bide his time and wait for the perfect opportunity. He pushed himself back into his seat and began to whistle as he drove in the opposite direction.

CHAPTER 21

Olivia stood in the hallway outside Mrs. Walters' sixth-grade classroom. She placed her hand on the door knob, then pulled it back. She knew she'd enjoy coaching the sixth-grade science fair team, but dreaded meeting her students for the first time. Introductions were always painful, as surprise, and sometimes pity, registered on people's faces when they recognized her disability.

She breathed in slowly through her nose. She'd promised to do this. She opened the door and entered the classroom.

Mrs. Walters smiled and motioned to the young woman in the black turtleneck and gray cardigan to join her. She addressed the three boys and one girl seated at desks in the front row.

"This is Ms. Osgoode, everyone. She worked with our sixth-grade team last year and they took fifth in the state."

Olivia brushed an imaginary strand of hair off of her face and gave the students a quick wave.

"We're thrilled that she's agreed to work with us again this year. If you give her your full attention and cooperation, I think you've got a good shot at winning this." She leaned against her desk and crossed her ankles. "You're the most gifted students I've had in my thirty years of teaching. You're smart, creative, and hardworking. With Ms. Osgoode's help, I can't wait to see what you can do." Mrs. Walters gestured to Olivia to take control.

"Hello, everyone. I'm excited to be here today. Mrs. Walters has told me all about you and I know we can put together a formidable project. A real contender for a prize. And along the way, we're going to learn a lot and have a ton of fun."

Missie Tucker turned wide eyes to Olivia.

"The key to our success will be teamwork. Our first step is to get to know each other. I'm a graduate of this middle school and I went to Marquette High. I'm currently working at Hilton Mortuary as a bookkeeper. My hobby is collecting and restoring vintage toasters. I plan to go back to school to get my degree in electrical engineering." Olivia paused and drew a sharp breath. *Where in the world did that last statement come from?*

"I'm sure you know each other, but why don't you tell me who you are and what you're most interested in? Let's start with you." Olivia pointed to the boy on her far right.

"I'm Eric Lowe. I want to be a veterinarian and I'm interested in animals and biology."

"Excellent," Olivia said. "Do you have animals at home?"

Eric nodded. "Two dogs, three cats, a hamster, and a snake. My mom says 'no more'."

Olivia laughed. "I can see why. That's a full house." She pointed to the boy next to Eric.

"My name is Todd Graham. I'm into chemistry. I have the giant Thames and Kosmos Chemistry Set and I've done most of the experiments."

"That's awesome," Olivia said.

"I'm Missie Tucker," the girl said. "I'm interested in lots of things. I think your hobby sounds cool. Can you bring one in to show us?"

"Thank you, Missie. I'd love to."

The girl tilted her chin to her desk as a closed-mouth smile spread across her face. Olivia's heart lurched—she knew better than anybody the telltale signs of someone who was afraid to open their mouth in a smile.

"I'm interested in space," the last boy said. "I want to work at NASA."

"That's very cool." Olivia forced her attention away from Missie. "What's your name?"

"Larry Clark."

"Okay, everybody. Looks like we've got a wide variety of interests represented." She gestured to the teacher. "Mrs. Walters will help you research ideas for your project. I'd like each of you to come with two suggestions when we get together next week. We'll meet right here, after school. Just like we did today. We'll discuss everyone's proposals and we'll decide on our project."

The four earnest faces in front of her nodded in unison.

"As I said, teamwork is the key to winning. Picking our project is our first opportunity to demonstrate the exceptional teamwork that we'll need to win this thing." Olivia smiled, keeping her lips firmly shut. "I can't wait to see what you come up with.

CHAPTER 22

Sam forced his features into a pleasant expression. His insides felt like molten lava, ready to burst and destroy everything in its path. The last thing he needed was for his banker to sense the panic he was feeling.

"My bookkeeper didn't bring any of this to my attention," he lied. "We've been quite busy and a bit short-staffed with vacations and all. I've been preoccupied with the renovations and haven't been watching the finances like I usually do."

"I'm sorry to have to pay you a personal visit, but the president of the bank told me that I should meet with you in person." The man shifted uncomfortably in his chair. "We went to school together, Sam. Hilton's handled the services for both of my parents."

"I'm sorry you've had to come, Rudy," Sam said. "We'll get this straightened out." Sam extended his hand and began to rise from his desk.

"There's more," Rudy said, remaining in his chair. "If you don't get all caught up by Wednesday, we're going to start foreclosure proceedings." The man looked aside as he said this.

"After forty years of our business, you're going to foreclose at the first hiccup?" Sam exploded.

"This isn't the first hiccup. You've been behind for months and haven't reached out to us once to discuss it; we always have to come to you."

"You've come to Olivia, right? I assure you, she's not bringing any of this to me. Now that I know, I can do something about it."

Rudy and Sam stared at each other across the desk.

"Can you give me a week to get the money together? Liquidate some other investments."

Rudy regarded him carefully, then nodded slowly. "We can give you a week. But that'll be the end of it. No more extensions."

"You'll have your money." Sam rose stiffly and walked the banker to the door. He watched until the man was backing out of his parking spot before he stormed down the hall to Olivia's office.

"What the hell do you think you're doing?" Sam exploded.

Olivia swung her chair around to the door where Sam now stood. She stared at him, mouth agape.

"Well?" he shouted.

Kathy came out of her office and stood in the hallway.

"What are you talking about?" Olivia stammered.

"The loan." Sam jerked his head toward the door. "Rudy just left. We're on the brink of foreclosure. How did you let this happen?"

Olivia's color rose. "I've been trying to tell you this for weeks. We can't make our payments and payroll. Mechanic's liens have been filed and subcontractors call me every day, looking for their payments." She gestured to her phone. "I just got off the phone with the plumber. Every time I tried to tell you, you said you didn't have time and rushed out of here."

"She's right, Sam," Kathy squeezed past him and stood next to Olivia. "This isn't Olivia's fault and you shouldn't blame her."

A heavy silence fell over the office. Olivia got to her feet. Sam glowered at the two women.

"Whatever's going on with you, Sam, you've got to fix it. We need you back here, paying attention to the funeral home," Kathy said.

Sam nodded mutely. "Don't worry about a thing. I'll take care of this." He turned away without meeting their eyes.

Tom restrained himself from slamming the receiver down on his phone. His assistant sounded irritated when he'd told her to inform his brother that he was on a call and he'd see him in half an hour. What business is it of hers if I want to keep my brother waiting?

Sam could always tell when he was high and Tom was definitely feeling the effects of his pills now. He'd been so strung out by the time he'd paid his dealer and gotten more that he'd broken his unwritten rule and gotten high at work. He pulled a large bottle of water out of the mini fridge behind his desk and drained it as fast as he could. He rose from his desk and circled his office, scissoring his arms in front of him.

He stopped in front of the framed diploma on the wall and looked at his reflection in the glass. Tom ran a hand through his neatly trimmed hair and straightened his tie. He checked his watch. This would have to do. He stepped to his desk and lifted the receiver.

"You can send him in now," he said to his assistant.

"Sorry to keep you waiting, Sam," Tom said, rising slightly and indicating the chair in front of him.

Sam sat and focused on his hands, folded in his lap.

"What's up?" Tom asked, unnerved by the uncharacteristically dejected posture of his composed and collected brother.

"I'm in financial trouble, Tom," Sam said so quietly that Tom leaned across his desk to hear his brother. "I've got to make an eighty-eight-thousand-dollar payment to the bank within the week or they are going to start foreclosure on the mortuary." He looked up at his brother and his eyes telegraphed fear. "If the foreclosure doesn't bring enough, they'll take my house. Nancy and I have guaranteed the bank."

"How in the hell did it get to this point?"

"Cost overruns from the very beginning," Sam twisted his hands. "I should have come to you earlier. I liquidated all of the mortuary's reserve funds and cashed in all of my retirement funds and personal investments. I thought I'd be able to handle this."

Tom sank against the back of his chair. "I don't know what to say."

"There's more," Sam continued. "Ben's been accepted into that elite food science program at Cornell and I need to put down a deposit. I don't have the money for it, either."

"Surely you can put that on a credit card," Tom said.

Sam shook his head and locked eyes with his twin brother. "I maxed out all my cards weeks ago." He inhaled slowly. "You've always talked about how well you're doing. You offered to put my kids through college. Hell—you even bought me a Rolex for our fiftieth birthday just two months ago."

Sam paused and they sat in silence. "I've never asked you for a cent until recently."

Tom turned his gaze away from Sam.

"You're a minority owner in the mortuary and I have a right to make a capital call on you for your share of the debt payment," Sam said coldly.

"Understood. As I've said, I'm strapped right now, too."

"You were rolling in it and now you're broke in a few short months."

Tom didn't respond.

"You're using again. That's the only logical explanation," Sam said in disgust. "You're high right now, aren't you?" He came around the side of the desk and stood in front of his brother.

Tom rose and pushed Sam back. "Who the hell do you think you are?"

"I'm the brother who loves you."

Tom sucked in his breath. "I'm fine. Just cash poor at the moment." He put a tentative hand on his brother's arm. "I'll get you the money. I know what to do."

CHAPTER 23

The stress and tension were too much. He had to do something—had to get some sort of relief. He knew who it would be.

The man made the drive to his destination in record time. He stopped in front of her house but thought better of leaving his car in plain sight. He pulled around the side of the house and parked in front of the detached garage in back. He rubbed his hands together and assessed the privacy of the backyard. *Nobody'll see me carrying her body out the back door.* He got out of his car and proceeded to her front door.

Dorothy Ransom answered his knock with a delighted smile. "What a lovely surprise," she said, stepping back and beckoning him inside. "Why don't you come in? What brings you here?"

"I was driving by and decided to stop in on the spur-of-the-moment." He flashed her his most disarming smile.

"I was just heading out to the bank to deposit a check," she said, patting her purse that lay on the console table in her entryway. She looked at him and smiled. "But I'm in no rush. Tomorrow will be fine, too. Would you like a cup of tea?"

"Only if you'll join me in one," the man said as he followed his victim into her kitchen.

The man consulted the app on his phone that displayed the times for sunup and sundown each day of the week for Marquette. He knew Steve always did everything by the book and would shut off the ovens by sundown, as required by law. He checked his watch; sundown was in twelve minutes. With any luck, he could get into the crematorium promptly, perform his ghoulish task, and be home before the eleven o'clock news.

He eased his car into the parking lot of a vacant building down the block and parked in the shadows along one side. From this vantage point, he'd be able to see Steve's car pass by when he left for the day. He switched off his ignition and settled back into the seat to wait.

Sundown came and went. The man yawned and shifted in his seat. This was no time to fall asleep. Fifteen minutes passed, then thirty, and forty-five, and there was still no sign of Steve's car. He rubbed his hand over his eyes. Could he have missed the car? He didn't think so.

When it was a full hour past sundown, the man started his engine. Steve must have slipped by him. He couldn't sit in his car all night with a dead body in the trunk. He pulled onto the street and turned toward the crematorium as a set of headlights appeared in the crematorium driveway. He could just make out the tall figure that got out of his car and stepped to the gate to padlock it.

The man quickly pulled into an alley and cut his ignition. He slid down in his seat and watched Steve's car drive by in his driver's side mirror. He released the breath he didn't realize he'd been holding. He hoped Steve hadn't noticed his distinctive car.

The man sat up in his seat and watched for Steve to come back around the block. When he was satisfied that Steve was not returning to the scene, he proceeded to the crematorium.

The man unlocked the gate, pulled his car into the yard, and closed the gate. The long wait for Steve to leave work and his near encounter with the man left him on edge. The cantankerous lock on the old overhead door to the oven room wouldn't yield. His heart hammered in his chest. Had they changed the locks?

He stepped to the door to the office and his key fit. The door swung open. He wiped the sweat from his brow with his hand and proceeded through the dark building, cursing when he banged his shin on a metal cart.

He opened the overhead door from the inside and stepped into the chill night. The man debated bringing the cart to his car to transport the body but decided against it. The wheels would clang and clatter on the uneven concrete of the yard. The quietest way to transport the now deceased Dorothy Ransom to her destination would be to carry her. She was a tiny woman. *Surely I'm in good enough shape to handle her.*

The man paused and filled his lungs with the crisp night air. He opened his trunk and clamped the body to his. He used his chin to close the trunk.

He placed the body onto a trolley at the entrance to the old oven and closed the overhead door. With the outside world shut out, he felt his way along the wall until he found the switch for the powerful overhead fluorescents. He turned on the lights and winced as the room jumped into illumination.

He squinted as he walked swiftly to the old oven. Was he letting his imagination run away with himself, or did the area by the oven seem warm? He flipped on the controls and waited as the gears clicked and the door to the oven rose slowly.

The man stared at the opening and blinked. A skeleton lay inside the old oven, it's bones stark white and brittle, it's teeth still in place. He cursed and his words reverberated in the concrete room.

He switched on the controls to the newer oven and opened the door. He was greeted by a similar sight of cremains.

Steve must have run both ovens all day. He would come in the next morning to sweep the bones out of the ovens through the open troughs on the bottom and into the metal trays inserted in the slots below the ovens. The trays transported each person's individual ashes and bones to the giant processors that pulverized the bones and turned them into the cremains that would be returned to the deceased's loved ones.

The man raked his fingers through his hair. Now what was he going to do? He took his phone out of his pocket and began snapping photos of the remains in the old oven. He'd have to remove them and replace them exactly the same way. Steve must have decided to allow them to cool down overnight before sweeping them through the trough and into the trays, but he would have checked to make sure that cremation was complete before he left for the night. Will Steve notice if a skeleton has been moved slightly? As detail oriented as Steve was, he knew that he would. He'd have to take his time and replace the skeleton perfectly.

The man found a large piece of cardboard standing against the wall and retrieved an empty cart from the walk-in cooler. He'd move the skeleton to the cardboard and meticulously reposition it in the oven after Dorothy's cremation was completed.

He picked up the ten-foot metal rake used for sweeping remains down the trough and slid it toward the skull. A cloud of ash rose in its wake, coating the skull. He cursed and quickly discarded the rake. He wouldn't be able to keep everything intact using it. He'd have to reach in and remove the remains by hand. There was no other way.

The brick was still hot to the touch. The man reached for Steve's work gloves perched on top of the control box but stopped. He'd retrieve his gloves from the car.

The man returned to the oven and placed his gloved hands on the opening as he rocked back and forth on his heels. *How in the hell has my life come to this?* There was no going back now.

He inhaled sharply and reached both hands into the oven, being careful to keep his arms away from the brick walls. He carefully grasped the skull and began to pull it toward him. He had moved it no more than an inch when the jaw bone disengaged on one side and the top vertebrae separated.

The man froze. *Shit! This isn't going to work!*

It would be impossible to remove the skeleton, use the oven to cremate Dorothy, and replace the skeleton in a condition that would go unnoticed by Steve. He could not risk it. *I may have done enough damage already.*

The man carefully settled the skull back into place. He leaned in to reposition the vertebra but couldn't quite reach it. He tried again, stretching as far as he could, his face millimeters from the oven floor. Heat radiating from the bricks singed his cheek. He got two fingers under the vertebra and lifted it gingerly to the right. It would have to do. He slowly withdrew his hand, stirring up a cloud of ash. He pulled himself out of the oven as he choked on the ash clinging to his mouth and filling his nostrils.

The man tore off his gloves and wiped the ash from his face. He consulted the photo of the skeleton that he'd taken with his phone and compared it to the image in front of him. With any luck, Steve wouldn't notice that it had been disturbed.

He closed the oven door. He'd have to deal with Dorothy Ransom another time. He would store her in the outside chest freezer in their garage. He'd get rid of the meat that they kept there. They rarely remembered to use it. Most of the meat was full of freezer burn and would have to be thrown out anyway. That's what he'd tell his wife if she asked. They'd kept the freezer locked ever since the garage had been broken into years ago. He'd make sure he had the key on him until he got rid of the body. He shuddered at the prospect. *What else can I do?*

The man returned the cardboard to the wall and replaced the cart. He went into Steve's office and found the clipboard with the cremation schedule hanging in its usual spot on the wall. He carefully turned the pages and saw that both ovens were scheduled for use every day for the next week.

He slammed his fist against the wall. He'd have to wait it out; there was nothing else he could do.

The man checked his watch. It was almost ten. He'd better replace Dorothy in his trunk before rigor mortis made her hard to handle. The sooner he got her to the freezer, the better. He shut off the light in the office and returned to Dorothy.

CHAPTER 24

Olivia kept an eye peeled for Mrs. Marshall as she told her grandmother about the new group of science fair contestants she would be coaching. "There's even a girl in the group this year. Reminds me of myself at her age. She's self-conscious about her horrible buck teeth. I'll bet braces will cure her problem." Olivia glanced up and was relieved to see Mrs. Marshall heading to her husband's grave.

Olivia put her hand to her lips and pressed a kiss into her grandmother's headstone. "Gotta go. Love you, Grams."

Mrs. Marshall turned to Olivia as she approached. "How are you today, dear?"

"Fine. I've got your mixer for you."

"Thank you so much. I was hoping you would. I want to make a cake to take to my Bible study group. It's my turn to bring refreshments. I could mix it by hand, but it's been years since I've done that."

"No need. I've got it in my car."

"I want to leave my friend his dinner." Mrs. Marshall held up a tinfoil-wrapped package. "Have you seen him again?"

Olivia shook her head no.

"Me either. I almost didn't bring food today, but then I thought about how cruel that would be if the poor creature was still out there and was counting on me."

Olivia walked with her to the break in the fence. Yesterday's tinfoil wrapper lay on the ground, licked clean. "Whether it's him or not, some creature is enjoying what you bring."

Mrs. Marshall nodded and laid out her offering. She and Olivia stepped back and waited, but the dog didn't appear.

"This is like watching the kettle boil," Mrs. Marshall said. "No point in it—it'll happen when it's supposed to. Let's go get my mixer. I'm sure you have things to do and I want to get home to bake that cake."

The two women started for their cars.

"Have you seen Cheryl Robinson recently?" Olivia asked.

"You mean since we talked?"

"Yes. I'm still wondering about her."

"I haven't. You're worried, aren't you?"

Olivia nodded.

"I was, too, but I think we're being silly. People come and go all the time. Maybe she's away visiting family or she's helping a friend." Mrs. Marshall put her arm around Olivia's shoulder. "Don't go looking for bad news around every corner."

"I suppose you're right," Olivia said half-heartedly.

"I know I'm right. If I tried to track down every person that I saw one day and didn't the next, I'd have a full-time job. For example, there's a woman in our Bible study who has suddenly stopped coming. It happens. People make other plans."

They reached Olivia's car and Olivia lifted the mixer off of the passenger seat. "Here you go, good as new. I'll carry it to your car for you."

"I'm right over there on the next row," Mrs. Marshall said, pointing to a small white sedan.

Olivia stowed it in the trunk. "Do you need help bringing it inside? I can follow you home."

"Nonsense. It's not that heavy. I'll be fine. Thank you so much for doing this. How much do I owe you?"

Olivia waved away the offer of money. "Nothing. I didn't have to replace anything except a bit of wire and I had fun doing it."

"That's so sweet of you, dear. I'm going to make you some of my famous pound cake." She squeezed Olivia's hand. "Your grandmother would be very proud of the kind, smart young woman you've become."

Olivia brushed her hand across her eyes. "I'll see you tomorrow," she stammered, turning toward her car. She had only taken a few steps when she turned back to Mrs. Marshall. "I'm just curious. What is the name of the woman from your Bible study that suddenly stopped coming?"

"Dorothy Ransom. Why do you ask?"

Olivia shook her head. "No reason. Let me know if you have any problems with your mixer."

CHAPTER 25

Olivia double-checked the amount of the electronic payment with the amount on the bank's payment demand and pushed the Pay Now button. She circled the amount paid, made a notation of the date, and slipped the paper into a folder in her desk drawer. She stood and started toward Sam's office. Did she really want to risk disturbing her erratic boss?

Sam asked her to let him know the minute she'd sent the payment to the bank. Olivia sighed heavily and made her way down the hall to his office.

"The payment's been made, Sam," Olivia said. He looked up from the blueprint spread out on his desk.

"That's a day earlier than I expected."

"Tom's check cleared overnight and the funds were available to us so I decided to make the construction loan payment today. I hope that was okay?"

"Perfect." Sam relaxed back into his chair and ran his hand through his hair. He regarded her intently and pushed himself to his feet.

"I've behaved badly these last few weeks. I've been frustrated and have taken it out on you."

Olivia turned her face aside. "I understand," she mumbled. "It's okay."

"It's not okay, Olivia. I'm sorry." He looked at his watch. "It's almost eleven. Why don't you take the afternoon off? You deserve it."

"That's not necessary," she began, but Sam cut her off.

"An afternoon off hardly covers it, but it's all I can afford right now." He gave her a wry smile. "Whatever you're working on can wait."

"Alright. There's something I'd like to research online—it's personal—so if you don't mind, I'll do that and then take the rest of the day off."

"Be my guest," Sam said. "We can relax the rules about personal use of our computers this time."

Olivia returned to her desk and found Dorothy Ransom's address in the local telephone directory. She scribbled it on a scrap of paper. The current phone book listed only Dorothy. Olivia went to the work room and pulled down a cache of old telephone directories stacked on top of a row of dusty lateral files. She hit pay dirt on the third directory she consulted from four years earlier. The listing in the older directory was for Derek and Dorothy Ransom at the same address and phone number.

She returned to her desk and searched the mortuary's records. There was no entry for Derek Ransom. Hilton's hadn't handled his services. She located his obituary online and confirmed that he died after a lengthy illness and his body had been interred in a family plot in Pennsylvania. She found no obituary for a Dorothy Ransom.

Olivia released the breath she had been holding. Dorothy Ransom was not one of the widows associated with the cemetery. Maybe Mrs. Marshall was right and she was imagining things. She jumped when Sam called her name from behind her.

"Are you still here? What's an employer got to do to get an employee to play hooky?"

Olivia snatched her cardigan off the back of her chair. "I was just leaving."

"Have fun this afternoon," Sam said.

Olivia gave her boss a fleeting smile as she stepped past him. It was nice to have the *kind* Sam Hilton back—she hoped his good mood would last.

Olivia brought her mug of tea to the trestle table and spread out the materials Mrs. Walters had given her. There were hundreds of ideas for science fair projects available on the internet. She was scheduled to meet with her group of students after school to go over the ideas they had come up with. It would be helpful if she had some ideas of her own, too.

She poured over the papers in front of her and was surprised to see that it was almost two o'clock when she looked up. She hadn't made herself anything for lunch and knew she should grab a quick sandwich now. A mug of tea wouldn't hold her. But she wasn't hungry and, try as she might, she couldn't get Dorothy Ransom off her mind. If she left now, she'd have time to drive by the address scribbled onto the paper in her purse on her way to school to meet with her students.

Olivia quickly gathered the papers into a stack and shoved them in her satchel. She placed her mug in the sink and set out.

Dorothy Ransom's neat bungalow sat at the end of a cul-de-sac on a quiet residential street. An overgrown rambling rose blocked the view of the front door. *What am I trying to prove? Just because she hasn't been at Bible study, I think this woman's been murdered? Maybe I'm as crazy as Detective Novak thinks I am.*

Olivia parked at the curb and stared at the house. *I really should drive on.* She switched off the engine and got out of the car, looking from right to left. None of the neighbors came to their doors or looked out their windows. The street was deserted.

She proceeded up the driveway to the door. The front stoop was littered with more than a week's worth of newspapers and a tradesman's flyer, offering bids on gutter cleaning, was stuck into the security screen. From the weathered look of the flyer, it had been there for some time. A package from Amazon was sticking out from under the doormat. It appeared that Dorothy Ransom wasn't home. And that her absence hadn't been planned. She'd ordered a package and she hadn't stopped her newspaper—or asked a neighbor to collect them.

Olivia used the side of her hand to wipe away the grime in a six-inch circle on the frosted glass panel that flanked the door. She pressed her face to the spot and tried to see inside, but couldn't make out anything beyond the wavy glass. Maybe there would be a window on the back of the house that she'd be able to peer in?

Olivia followed the driveway around the side of the house to the garage. She paused and glanced about her. *What in the world am I doing? I think someone may have murdered this woman and I'm poking around back here? By myself?*

She was turning to leave when she noticed the muddy footprints leading from the back door of the house to an area by the garage. Olivia forced herself to take a closer look. Next to the footprints was a solid muddy swath—as if someone had been dragging a muddy blanket with them. A heavy, muddy blanket—with Dorothy's body in it?

Olivia's strangled cry broke the silence. She ran down the driveway and flung herself into her car. Was she letting her imagination run away with her? She didn't think so.

She sat, contemplating the house, while her labored breathing returned to normal. She pushed a loose strand of hair off of her face with a shaking hand. Her discovery could mean that Dorothy Ransom was the masked man's latest victim. Or it could mean nothing. She'd have to figure out which one it was.

CHAPTER 26

Olivia burst through the door to the classroom to find her science fair students seated at desks in the front row. "Sorry I'm late," she said in a rush as she stumbled and dropped her purse. The contents scattered on the tile floor.

Mrs. Walters knelt beside her, helping her retrieve the items. "I was getting worried about you."

"I got caught up in something." Olivia shoved her wallet into her purse. "I should have called."

"You seem a bit frazzled, dear. Are you sure you want to do this today?"

"Yes. Quite sure. We need to get started. There's no time to lose." Olivia forced herself to smile reassuringly at Mrs. Walters. "Let's put your ideas on the board." She took a deep breath and repeated herself, talking slowly and concentrating on forming her words.

"We understood you the first time, Ms. O," Missie said quietly. "We understand you."

"Thank you," Olivia replied in a husky voice. "Eric—we'll start with you." She stepped to the whiteboard and began writing.

"These are all terrific ideas," Olivia said. "I'd be interested in working on all of these, wouldn't you?"

The four faces turned to hers nodded in unison.

Mrs. Walters moved to a filing cabinet in the back of the room.

"Let's recap." Olivia said. "We've got 'Does Chewing Gum Make You Smarter?' suggested by Todd, 'How to Make a Solar Powered Radio' from Larry, 'Do Dogs Understand English?' proposed by Eric, and 'The Mechanics of Carnival Games' contributed by Missie. They all appear to be of the same difficulty." She turned to Mrs. Walters. "Have any of these been done in prior years?"

"I was just checking my records," she said, holding up a folder that she'd removed from the filing cabinet. "The solar powered radio project was a finalist from another school last year."

"We shouldn't do it again this year," Larry said.

"Can we cross it off our list?" Olivia asked him.

Larry nodded.

"One of our groups tried the dog project several years ago and it proved harder than it looked. The data we collected was too subjective and we all got frustrated," Mrs. Walters continued.

"We can cross that one off, too," Eric said. "I want a project that can win."

"Thank you, Eric," Olivia said. "That leaves chewing gum making you smarter and the mechanics of carnival games. Let's take a closer look at each," Olivia began as Todd's hand shot up.

"I'd like to work on the carnival game one," he said. "We go to the state fair every year and my dad gives us spending money. I use all of mine on carnival games. I've never won anything. I'd like to learn how."

"My dad says they're rigged," Larry chimed in. "That should be illegal."

"Or they're relying on scientific principles to make it harder," Missie said. "Maybe if we knew about them, we could win."

"Let's do that one," Eric said. He turned to Missie. "Good going."

The girl lowered her face to her desk and smiled.

"We've reached a consensus, then," Olivia said. "We're going to explain how carnival games work. I have to admit—I've always wondered. How did you come up with the idea, Missie?"

"My dad won me a humongous stuffed bear a couple of years ago at the fair," Missie said. "When I saw this topic online, I was surprised that it's difficult to win these games. I asked him how he did it and he said that I should do the project and find out for myself."

Olivia nodded. "Then that's just what we'll do." She gestured to Mrs. Walters. "Can you make copies of these materials?" she said, pointing to the papers that Missie had turned in.

"Of course," Mrs. Walters replied. "You kids can get them from me after class tomorrow. I'll drop your set off at the mortuary on my way home."

"I don't want to put you out."

"I drive right by," Mrs. Walters insisted.

"Thank you. Each of you should read about the project and come prepared to discuss how we're going to acquire the necessary materials and which tasks you'd like to volunteer for." Olivia stepped to the whiteboard and erased the list of projects. She wrote Mechanics of Carnival Games at the top of the board and the date of the science fair. "This is when we compete. We'll create a timeline of what needs to be done, working backwards from the date of the fair." She glanced over her shoulder and was met with blank stares.

"Have any of you worked on a schedule?"

Four heads shook no.

"Sure you have—you just don't know it. Every time you have an assignment with a due date, you have a schedule."

Missie nodded.

"This schedule is a bit more complex." She put her marker in the tray and faced them. "We're not going to be successful if we don't give ourselves deadlines associated with the steps that we need to accomplish. Your assignment is to come up with a written schedule of the activities to complete our project and the dates that we should have each activity done. I'll work up a form for you to use." She turned to Mrs. Walters. "If I email it to you tonight, can you give it to the kids with their packets?"

"I most certainly can," Mrs. Walters said. "Learning to break a big project into smaller tasks is an important skill. It may be the most valuable thing you learn from this project."

Olivia looked at the large clock on the wall at the back of the room. "We're out of time for today. Thank you for your great ideas. I'm excited about the project you've chosen and I think we're going to have a lot of fun with it. I'll see you next week."

Olivia gathered up her papers and stashed them in her satchel. "I'll email that form to you tonight." She glanced at Mrs. Walters. "This

134

group of kids is really nice and smart. I think we've got a good shot at winning."

"I agree," said the older woman. "I'm especially pleased that they picked Missie Tucker's idea. She's a nice girl and has had such a hard time of it."

Olivia raised an eyebrow quizzically.

"Since her mother died," Mrs. Walters replied. "About two years ago. That drunk driver?"

Olivia nodded. "I remember now. Hilton's handled her services." She paused and looked away. "It's always sad when a child loses a parent."

"You know that pain, don't you?"

Olivia nodded again.

"That's one of the reasons I was thrilled that you agreed to mentor the science fair participants again this year. You and Missie have a lot in common. She really likes you already—you're going to be a terrific role model for her."

"I have to confess; I do feel a special connection with her. And I certainly know what it feels like to lose your mother at a young age. Is she being raised by her grandmother, too?"

"Her dad's raising her. He's a super guy."

"I'm glad. I never knew my father." Olivia hoisted her satchel onto her shoulder. "I'm not complaining. My grandmother gave me the happiest childhood you could ask for."

Mrs. Walters sighed. "Pearl Osgoode was one of the finest people I've ever known. I miss her every single day."

"Me too." Olivia swallowed the lump in her throat. "See you next week."

Olivia cut across the school parking lot to her car. She placed her satchel on the back seat and was opening the driver's side door when she noticed Missie, sitting by the sidewalk with her back against a tree and her knees bent in front of her.

Olivia hesitated, then approached the girl. "Are you waiting for someone?" she called.

Missie scrambled to her feet and smiled, abandoning her habitual self-consciousness. "Yeah. My aunt picks me up after school when I stay late like this and miss the bus. My cousin has a ballet lesson today so they won't be here for another ten minutes."

"That's nice of your aunt." She glanced to the west, where the sun was getting low in the sky. "Mind if I wait with you? It'll be getting dark soon."

"That'd be cool, but you don't have to. She always comes."

"I'd like to get to know you better, anyway." Olivia smiled at the girl who was now staring at her with rapt attention. "Us 'science gals' are still few and far between. Tell me how you got interested in science."

Olivia sat cross-legged on the ground under the tree and Missie joined her.

"I've always been into science. Even as a little kid. I wasn't much for dolls or crayons—I wanted Legos and models and stuff like that. You should have seen my ant farm—it was huge. We just got rid of it last year," Missie said.

"Sounds like me. I found a bunch of discarded appliances in a junk pile behind my grandfather's workshop and spent hours taking them apart and putting them back together."

"That sounds cool," Missie said, giving Olivia her full attention. "It's neat that your grandmother let you do that."

"My grandmother taught me to follow my passions." Olivia gazed at a beetle making its way slowly to a hole under the sidewalk. "Grams was amazed when I was able to put an old toaster from the 1940s back together and it worked. I guess that's what got me interested in them."

"And now you fix them for a hobby?"

"I do. Old toasters are very collectible and some of them are quite valuable. They've been around for over a hundred years—even before sliced bread." She looked at Missie thoughtfully and realized the girl was genuinely interested in what she had to say. "The original models only toasted one side of the bread. Modern-day toasters are more efficient, but the old toasters were beautiful. That's why people collect them. And they're so much more valuable when they're cleaned up and in working order."

"Is that what you do—clean them up and fix them?"

"Exactly. I go to flea markets and yard sales and buy them really cheap. Sometimes I have to do research on them and it can be hard to find parts. But usually, I can get almost everything I need on the internet."

"Do you sell them when you're done?"

"No. I probably should, but I keep them. I have rows and rows of them in my workshop and they're beautiful. Sometimes I just go in there to look at them."

Missie nodded. "I'd love to see them," she said shyly.

"I think we can arrange that," Olivia said slowly, thinking. "I'd like to have all four of you out to my place to see them. Maybe we can do that as a celebration after the science fair."

Missie's eyes grew wide. "That would be so cool. I know the boys would think so, too."

"I'll talk to Mrs. Walters about it."

A minivan turned into the parking lot and made its way to them.

"That's my aunt," Missie said, hopping to her feet and hoisting her backpack onto her shoulder.

Olivia stood, brushing grass from the back of her jeans.

"Thanks for waiting with me," Missie said.

"It was my pleasure. I had fun talking with you." Olivia waved to Missie's aunt behind the wheel and made her way to her car.

"Who was that?" the woman asked her niece.

"That's Ms. Osgoode," Missie replied. "She's helping us with our science fair project and she's the coolest person ever. Wait until you hear about her hobby…"

The minivan pulled from the curb as Missie recounted what she'd learned about her new mentor.

CHAPTER 27

Sam handed his keys to the valet and skirted the imposing stone columns of the main entrance to the Marquette Country Club. The Watering Hole restaurant ran along the back side of the building, overlooking the eighteenth green. Tom had called the night before to suggest meeting for breakfast at the country club. He couldn't remember the last time he and Tom had shared a private meal. He also couldn't help wondering what his brother had up his sleeve.

Sam approached the hostess and was annoyed when she informed him that Tom had called to say he was running fifteen minutes late. In *Tom time*, that meant thirty minutes at least. He sighed heavily and told the hostess that he'd like to be seated. What he'd really like to do was leave, sending Tom a message that Sam's time was valuable too.

Sam took a chair overlooking the golf course. It was a beautiful morning and it would be nice to spend a few minutes relaxing over his coffee. He could use the time to gather his thoughts.

Sam took his phone out of his pocket and logged onto the bank's website to check his bank balance. He'd done this at least a dozen times in the last twenty-four hours. It remained unchanged. No miraculous deposit had appeared. He'd brought the loan payments current and covered payroll, but he didn't have enough to pay himself back so he could make even half of the required deposit for Cornell.

Sam glanced around at the quietly expensive furniture and fixtures. If Tom could afford a membership here, he could afford the capital call for the funeral home.

Sam started when he felt the familiar hand squeeze his shoulder. "How's my older brother this morning?" Tom asked, sliding into the chair opposite Sam.

"Older by less than a minute. I'm good, thank you," Sam lied.

"Beautiful day," Tom remarked, shaking out his napkin and placing it in his lap. "Too bad you never took the game up; we could be out

138

there right now." He jabbed his thumb over his shoulder at the golf course.

"Maybe when I retire," Sam said. "You know how much work the funeral home is."

Tom bristled. "Like my clients don't keep me busy? You think I have more leisure time than you do?"

Sam put up a hand. "I didn't mean that. Don't take offense."

Tom glared at his brother.

"I don't want to fight," Sam said. "It's a beautiful morning. Why did you invite me here?"

Tom withdrew an envelope from the breast pocket of his jacket and slid it across the table to his brother. "Here's my capital contribution. As requested."

Sam picked up the envelope.

"Go on; look at it. It's all there."

"I don't need to check it. I trust you." Sam exhaled slowly. Now he'd have the money to pay off the mechanic's liens.

The waitress came to take their orders. "Coffee's fine for me," Sam said, holding up his cup.

"You've got to eat, Sam," Tom said. "Order the buttermilk pancakes—they're the best in town." Without waiting for his brother's assent, Tom ordered two plates of pancakes and bacon. "Our favorite as kids, as I remember."

Sam allowed himself to smile. "Mom couldn't make them fast enough to keep us fed."

Tom took a swig of his coffee. "How's that bookkeeper of yours doing? Olivia Osgoode?"

"Fine, I guess. Why do you ask?"

"I helped her call the police after she reported seeing a dead woman in that parking garage, remember?"

Sam nodded. "I almost forgot. The police never found a body and I haven't heard any more about it."

"I'm not sure that they believed her," Tom said.

"I guess not," Sam agreed. "Frankly, I'm not too sure either. She's still struggling with her grandmother's death."

"Isn't she in counseling or something? Or in one of your support groups? What do they say about her story?"

"Not to my knowledge," Sam replied. "Olivia has always been a very private person. She didn't even tell me about the incident. Whatever she's thinking, she's keeping it to herself."

"Poor kid. If the whole story is a figment of her imagination, she's a very disturbed person. And with that botched cleft lip of hers, it doesn't seem like she can catch a break."

"I wouldn't say she's entirely unlucky," Sam said. "Her grandmother left her the house they lived in and almost five hundred thousand dollars in cash and stocks."

Tom fumbled his coffee cup as he brought it to his lips, sloshing the dark liquid onto the crisp linen tablecloth. "How'd you hear that?"

"The one gal in the office that Olivia's close to told me."

"That's a nice chunk of change for a young woman her age. Hell— that's a nice chunk of change for anyone."

"It sure is," Sam agreed. "And I'll bet she has no idea how to invest it." He looked at his brother. "Maybe that's got her scared, too. Would you come by the office to talk to her? Offer to help her with her investments?"

Tom furrowed his brow and shrugged.

"I know that you usually deal with military widows and wealthy business owners, but I'd be very grateful if you'd come see Olivia."

"She's part of the 'Hilton family' since she works for the mortuary. I'd be happy to see if I can help." Tom smiled inwardly. The fees for handling that much money would be very welcome right now.

CHAPTER 28

Ashley flung open the front door and raced across the columned porch and down the curved walkway to the driveway, waving a large black envelope over her head. "Tom… wait," she called as he backed his car out of the garage.

Tom stopped, rolling down his window as she caught up with him. She grabbed at the front of her thin bathrobe to hold it shut.

"What in the world are you doing?" he asked. "I'm late for an appointment."

"You promised to drop this invitation off at the mortuary yesterday and then you walked off and left it on the kitchen counter. You did the same thing this morning." She handed him the envelope through the open window. "It's almost as if you don't want us to have this party for Ben."

Tom sat in stony silence.

"That kid's done really well for himself and I promised Nancy that we'd host this party to celebrate his getting into Cornell. It's the least we can do—especially since they were so supportive of the silent auction for the hospital. Their bid pushed us way over goal."

"Are you done? I need to go."

Ashley stepped back from the car.

"The party is four weeks from Saturday."

"How much is this going to cost me?"

"I'm doing all the cooking myself. It'll be reasonable, I promise. It's a barbecue and we have most of the meat in our freezer anyway." She pointed to the envelope. "Will you take this to Sam at the mortuary today?"

Tom stared past his wife, deep in thought.

"Are you alright? You look like you've seen a ghost."

Tom forced his attention back to his wife. "I'll drop this off on my way to the office. I'm fine. I'm under a lot of pressure at work."

"You're always under a lot of pressure at work." Ashley leaned into the open car window and placed a light kiss on his cheek. "Don't forget," she said, pointing to the envelope, and retreated to the front door.

Tom pulled into the section designated Hilton Mortuary Employees Only and parked next to a white Corolla. He picked up the invitation from the passenger seat.

Tom made his way through the back door and into Sam's office. He knocked on the door frame as he stepped to the desk where his brother was hunched over his laptop. He extended the invitation to Sam. "Ashley wanted you to have a copy."

"Thanks for hosting Ben's party. Our house isn't big enough—we would have had to rent out somewhere." He gave his brother a knowing look. "That's an expense I don't need right now."

"No problem," Tom said, looking past his brother and down the hall. "Is Olivia here today? I'd like to say 'hello' to her if she is."

"I think I heard her come in." Sam pointed down the hall. "See for yourself."

"Great. I'll see myself out."

Sam nodded and returned his attention to his laptop as Tom approached Olivia's door and knocked lightly on the doorframe.

Olivia finished placing her purse in her bottom drawer and turned to the doorway. "Tom," she exclaimed. "What are you doing here?"

Tom shot her his close-the-sale smile. "I had something to drop off for Sam so I thought I'd check on you. See how you're doing. You've been on my mind."

Olivia felt a flush creep up her neck. "I'm fine."

"Have you heard from the police?"

Olivia shook her head. "Not a word."

"These things take time," Tom said. "And some crimes are never solved. Just be patient." He crossed the room and stood behind the desk next to her. He put one hand on her shoulder.

Olivia leaned back.

She likes this. He had enough experience with women to know when he was having an effect on one. *I'll bet she's never had a boyfriend.* He began to massage her shoulders gently. He'd build her trust and she'd sign her investments over to him.

"I also know that you've been grieving." He bent toward her, gauging her reaction. "How are you doing with all of that?"

"I'm coping. It's starting to get better." He felt the tension leave her shoulders.

"Glad to hear it." Tom paused, willing her to continue. She remained silent.

"I understand your grandmother left you her house and some money. It can be hard to know who to trust for advice. As you know, I'm a financial planner."

Olivia inclined her head slightly.

He smiled at her. "Since you work for the family business, you're like family to me. I'd be more than happy to look at your inheritance and advise you on how to invest it. I don't want you to worry about that."

Olivia raised her eyes to his.

"Has that been troubling you?"

She nodded slowly.

"Then why don't you come see me tonight after work?"

"Aren't you busy?"

"I'll always make time for you, Olivia." His smile took on an added luster. *She's falling for me.* "I'll see you about five thirty?"

"Alright. I'd be grateful. I've got my papers in my purse." She wondered if Sam had asked his brother to help her. "Thank you."

"Good. See you soon." Tom made a beeline for the back door and his car. With any luck, he'd be managing Olivia Osgoode's inheritance before the day was out.

CHAPTER 29

Sam Hilton pulled up to a parking meter at the curb outside Marquette's most reputable pawn shop. He placed his right hand on top of the Rolex watch on his wrist and rocked it back and forth. He'd never dreamed he'd own a luxury watch. When Tom presented the Rolex to him on their fiftieth birthday, he'd been unexpectedly pleased. It matched the Rolex he'd admired on his brother for years and Sam was touched that his brother had noticed and remembered.

The thought of pawning it now—less than six months after he'd received it—sickened him. Ben's college deposit, however, was only the beginning. He'd have tuition payments to make soon enough and all of their savings were gone. Meeting his obligations to his family was more important than his pride.

Sam gripped the car door handle but couldn't make himself open it. He'd never been inside a pawn shop. The news would spread through town like wildfire that he'd pawned the Rolex watch that his brother had given him. He flushed with the shame of it. It would be a stain on the reputation of the funeral home, too. He couldn't allow that.

Sam brought his hand back to the steering wheel and started the engine. He needed to do this—pawn the watch—he had no other choice. But he wouldn't do it here in Marquette. He'd make the long drive into Nashville where the act could be cloaked in anonymity.

Sam gassed up on his way out of town and checked his watch as he entered the highway. With any luck, he'd be back in Marquette before five. He made good time on the clear roads and exited into the downtown area. A Google search on his phone showed that he had a number of establishments to choose from.

He parked and walked the street, past pawnshop windows that showcased guitars of every make and model. He guessed that was to be expected in this town. He stopped at one establishment where the lettering on the window boasted Nashville's best selection of diamonds and prestige watches.

Sam opened the glass door and stepped into the crowded store. Guitars hung from the ceiling and along every wall. Glass display cases ran around the perimeter and down the center in two rows.

A man seated on a high stool behind the counter at the back of the shop called, "Can I help you?"

Sam nodded and approached the man. "I'd like to pawn my watch," he said, pointing to his wrist.

The man rose quickly and extended his open palm. "Let me take a look."

Sam unhooked the metal clasp and slipped the watch off his wrist, giving it one last look before he placed it in the man's hand. "It's a Rolex. Almost new; I've only had it for six months."

The man nodded but didn't reply. He turned the watch over in his hands, then opened a drawer below the counter and removed a jeweler's loop. He examined the watch thoroughly. When he was done, he placed the watch back into Sam's hand and brought his eyes to meet Sam's.

"Where did you purchase this watch?"

"My brother gave it to me for my fiftieth birthday," Sam said, unable to conceal the note of pride in his voice.

The man nodded. "I'm sorry to be the one to tell you this," he said slowly, "but this watch is not a genuine Rolex."

Sam stared. "What do you mean?"

"It's a fake."

Sam recoiled as if he'd been slapped in the face.

"I'm sorry," the man said. "I know this must come as quite a shock."

"How do you know it's a fake? Are you sure?"

"I've been doing this for more than forty years, and I know real from fake. We see knockoffs all the time. This is one of the best I've seen."

"My brother wouldn't have given me a fake," Sam said, knowing the instant he said it that it wasn't true. Tom would cut any corner he could and it wouldn't matter who got screwed in the process.

"I'm not saying that your brother knew it was a fake. He could have been duped. You may want to tell him about this so he can try to get his money back."

Sam nodded mutely.

"Did you have an insurance appraisal for this?" the man asked.

Sam reached into the breast pocket of his overcoat and pulled out a paper and unfolded it on the counter.

The man bent over and examined the document. He looked over the rims of his reading glasses at Sam. "This is a forgery too."

Sam scooped up the document and the watch and stuffed them unceremoniously into his pocket. It took him a moment to collect himself.

"I'm sorry to have troubled you," he said to the man.

"No trouble at all, sir. I'm sorry that what you've got isn't a real Rolex."

Sam turned on his heel and made his way to the door.

"It's a nice looking fake. Maybe you should just wear it and enjoy it," the man called after him.

Sam pushed through the door and stood on the sidewalk while he tried to make sense of what he'd just learned. The sun that had been shining when he'd entered the pawn shop was now hidden behind a swath of dark clouds. The wind had picked up and bit into his exposed face and hands.

He buttoned his overcoat and set off for his car. *Why in the hell does Tom always have to play the part of the successful businessman? Why does he live beyond his means?*

Sam couldn't have cared less if his brother had given him nothing for their birthday. Why this big, fake, ostentatious show? He knew why: Tom had never gotten over needing to feel better than Sam.

For that matter, why didn't Tom have the money for a Rolex? His lifestyle certainly indicated that he could afford gifts like this. But all of his recent conversations with Tom about money told a different story.

He knew why Tom didn't have any money. He brought his hand up and rubbed his forehead. It made so much sense. Despite his protestations to the contrary, Tom was using again. Whether it was cocaine or opiates—or something else—didn't matter. His brother was no longer clean and had slid into the abyss of addiction.

CHAPTER 30

Missie checked the time on the large wall clock over the classroom door. She sighed heavily and began gathering the notecards arranged in neat rows on her desk. Ms. O wasn't coming. Now she'd have to practice her presentation about their group's science fair project at home, on her own.

She hated speaking in class and the presentation would be ten times worse. Mrs. Walters had insisted that she be the one to present it to the class, even though Eric and Todd had both volunteered. She drew in a deep breath. She'd really wanted Ms. O to help her with it.

She unzipped the front pouch of her backpack and was shoving the notecards inside when the classroom door swept open. A chill wind and funnel of dried leaves preceded Olivia through the door.

"You're still here," Olivia said breathlessly, stopping in front of Missie's desk. "I was afraid you would have left already. I'm so sorry to be late. I got hung up at work." Olivia ran her eyes over the young girl.

"You're upset." Olivia lowered herself into the seat next to Missie. "Did you think I forgot about you?"

Missie brought her eyes to her desktop and nodded.

Olivia leaned over and put a hand on the girl's back. "I would never forget about you. I've been looking forward to this all day." She inhaled deeply and leaned back.

"Would you like to practice with me now? I know you'll be fabulous. You've been remarkably thorough in your preparation but it's always good to practice."

Missie slowly withdrew her notes from her backpack. "I wish I could just turn in a report. I hate to talk in front of people."

"I know the fear of public speaking," Olivia said. "I was even scared to come talk to you kids when we started working together."

Missie's brows shot up.

"My speech impediment," Olivia said, amazed that she was able to articulate her fear to this young girl. "You sound like everyone else when you talk. I don't."

"I sound okay but I still hate my mouth," Missie said. "I don't like anyone to see my teeth. The boys in our group don't tease me but the other kids do."

Olivia leaned toward Missie. "Will braces fix them?"

Missie nodded. "They say they will. I was supposed to get them last summer."

"Why didn't you? I know they're very expensive."

Missie turned her face away. "It's not the money. My dad says we have insurance. It's just that," her voice cracked, "I'm so afraid. I'm a coward."

Olivia's mouth felt dry. "I know how that feels. I was born with something called a cleft palate and had surgery to correct it when I was a baby." She pointed self-consciously to her mouth. "The surgery didn't go well."

"That's not being a coward. You didn't have anything to do with that."

Olivia shook her head. "They can fix the surgery. I'll be able to look and speak normally and I have the money to pay for it. I haven't made an appointment with the surgeon because I've been afraid."

Missie and Olivia stared at each other.

Olivia sat up straighter. "I'll make the appointment with the surgeon if you go home tonight and tell your dad that you're ready for braces. There's no reason either of us should delay. We can support each other in this. Would you like that?

A smile spread across Missie's face. "I would." She took a deep breath. "I'll talk to my dad tonight."

"Good. We'll report back about our appointments the next time we get together." She checked her watch. "We've got time to run through your presentation several times before you get picked up. Are you ready?"

Missie picked up her notecards, walked to the front of the room, and began.

"You're awfully cheerful tonight," Byron said, placing the rotisserie chicken and side dishes he'd picked up at the supermarket on the kitchen table. It might not be a home-cooked meal, but it was the best this working single parent could do. "What got you out of that funk you were in when I dropped you off this morning?"

Missie retrieved plates and silverware and brought them to the table. "I went through my presentation for our science fair project with Ms. O. She said it was 'exceptionally well done.' That's exactly what she said." Missie beamed. "She said that it was at the high school level."

Byron stopped thumbing through the mail and approached his daughter. "High five," he said, raising his hand.

Missie slapped his palm with hers.

"I'm not the least surprised."

Missie looked at him quizzically.

"I overheard you practicing it in your room last night."

"You eavesdropped?" Missie made a show of being upset but was secretly pleased.

"I most certainly did. And I thought you did great."

"Ms. O helped me make some improvements to it this afternoon. Wait until you hear it at the science fair."

"That's day after tomorrow, right?"

Missie nodded. "And you'll get to meet Ms. O, too. You'll really like her, dad. She's so smart." Missie gave her father a sly smile. "I think you should ask her out."

"Not you, too," he said. "I don't need anyone fixing me up."

"You never go out on dates."

"That's because there's no one I want to go out with." He fixed his daughter with a stern glance. "I'll find someone when I'm ready." Olivia Osgoode flashed through his mind.

Missie turned her face away from his. "Okay, okay. But at least say 'hello' to her."

"Of course I will," he replied. "She's been so helpful to you. I want to thank her."

Missie cleared her throat. "And I'm ready to get my braces on."

Byron's head snapped up.

Missie smiled triumphantly.

"That's wonderful, sweetheart! I'll make the appointment tomorrow. What changed your mind?"

"Just something Ms. O and I talked about."

Byron took a deep breath. He hadn't been able to convince Missie to get the braces she so clearly needed. If her mother hadn't been killed in that car accident, she would have talked her daughter into it. Byron always felt like he'd failed in his deathbed promise to be both mother and father to Missie. He swept his daughter into a hug. He really wanted to meet this Ms. O.

CHAPTER 31

Byron blew on his cupped hands as he milled about in the throng of parents, grandparents, siblings, and teachers waiting for the gymnasium doors to open. He'd dropped Missie and her teammate Larry off at the gym an hour earlier. They insisted that they needed to make sure their display board and interactive tablet were set up and ready to go. The two kids whispered in the back seat the entire way there and he knew that they had something up their sleeves. He had his suspicions but didn't want to spoil their fun.

He checked his watch. There was still more than twenty-five minutes to go. The sun was obscured by thick clouds and a brisk breeze whipped around the corner of the building. He was considering waiting in the warmth of his truck when he heard a familiar voice call his name.

He turned to see his well-meaning but overly intrusive neighbor bearing down on him, a harried-looking woman following in her wake.

"Hello," she called. "I thought that was you. What perfect timing." She turned to the woman behind her. "Have you met Connie Strom?" she asked, making the introduction.

Byron extended his hand and they shook.

"Connie manages the main branch of the credit union," the woman said. "She likes to bike and do outdoorsy things, just like you do. I knew the two of you had to meet."

Connie blinked behind her large glasses.

"Do you have someone participating in the science fair?" Byron asked.

"Four of my children are in it," she replied.

Byron shot his neighbor a quizzical look. "How many children do you have?"

"Seven."

"They must keep you very busy," he said, staring pointedly at his neighbor.

"They most certainly do." She put her fingers in her mouth and whistled at two boys tussling in the grass at the edge of the field surrounding the gym. "I've gotta go. Nice meeting you," she trailed off as she hurried toward the boys.

Byron stepped aside to let her pass. "I don't think that one'll work out," he said, smiling down at his neighbor.

She returned his smile. "I'll find someone wonderful for you yet," she replied.

A loud clank reverberated through the silence as the doors were flung open.

They moved forward with the crowd. "I'll consider myself warned," he said playfully when they stepped inside the gymnasium. She turned right and he headed left.

Byron skimmed over the displays lining both sides of the gym. He found Missie's stall in the corner spot at the far end. He wove his way through the crowd and smiled broadly when he caught his first view of her team's display.

He'd been right. They'd been able to borrow actual carnival games for their station. Three groupings of milk bottles filled with water were stacked in different configurations on a long table, a bucket of baseballs adjacent to each one. A starting line of yellow tape had been placed on the floor. People were already lining up to try their hand at the popular carnival game.

He stood back and observed the four students explaining their findings to a young man that Byron guessed was a senior in high school.

"Cool," the boy said. "I'll remember this next year at the state fair. Instead of losing money every year, maybe I'll score one of those giant stuffed animals for my girlfriend. Thanks, guys." He stepped away, then turned back. "I hope you win."

Byron caught Missie's eye and approached the table. "Congratulations. You've done a remarkable job." He swept his hand across the display board and toward the games. Larry and Todd were busy resetting the milk bottles as a long line of people waited to try out their newly acquired knowledge of the physics of carnival games.

Missie grinned. "It's really good, isn't it?"

"It sure is. The four of you worked extremely hard. You deserve all of this success. I'd like to thank your Ms. O," he said, turning his head to search for her. "Is she here?"

"One of the judges came and got her right after the fair opened," Missie said. "She'll be back."

A small boy who had been politely waiting for Missie's attention raised his hand.

Byron smiled at the boy. "I think this gentleman has a question for you," he said.

"I want to try the game but the sign says that you have to be forty-eight inches tall. That's not fair."

"I'm sorry," Missie said, "but that's the school's rule."

"It's still not fair," the boy dug in his heels.

Missie lifted her eyes to her dad and shrugged. "I can't make any exceptions."

"How about if we play together?" Byron asked the boy. "Would that be alright with you? You can stand on my shoes. That'll make you tall enough, I'm sure."

The boy nodded vigorously. He and Byron stepped to the back of the line, the little boy talking a blue streak. Byron bent over to listen to him.

Olivia watched the scene play out in front of her as she made her way back through the crowd to her group. The tall, muscular figure of the man talking to Missie and the little boy seemed so familiar. It wasn't until he turned in profile that she realized he was Officer Byron Tucker. She hung back and observed him as he placed the boy on his shoes and held him steady while the boy tossed the ball at the milk bottles. She grinned when the boy's efforts were successful and Byron ceremoniously shook his hand.

Olivia closed the gap to her group and called to Byron. "Officer Tucker," she said. "Who's your friend?" She smiled at the boy.

"We don't know each other," Byron said. He was pleased that she'd seen him being nice to the boy. "He just needed a little bit of assistance."

Olivia cocked her head to one side and regarded him thoughtfully. What a kind man he was.

"Congratulations," she said to the boy. "Did you read the display?" The boy nodded.

"And you applied what you learned. Good for you," Olivia said.

"Thanks," the boy said and shot away.

"Olivia," Byron said. "What brings you to the science fair?"

"I'm the mentor for this group," Olivia replied, pointing.

"*You're* the Ms. O that's been helping my daughter?" Byron brought his hand to his forehead. "I never guessed."

"I am," said Olivia. "This is my second year working with science fair contestants. This group is terrific. Is Missie your daughter?"

Byron nodded.

"She's very bright. And she's been a joy to work with."

"Missie's been raving about you." Byron smiled at her and she felt like she was standing in a sunbeam. " 'Ms. O this and Ms. O that.' You've spent a lot of time with these kids and I know they've all learned a ton." His expression turned serious. "You've had a huge impact on Missie. I understand you convinced her to get braces."

Olivia shrugged.

"I'm very grateful."

Olivia hoped she wasn't blushing. "Can you keep a secret?" She moved close to Byron.

"You bet I can," he whispered, leaning toward her.

"They won't announce it until the end of the day, but our team won the school science fair. We'll be moving on to the state championship in two weeks."

"That's terrific. And so well deserved, from what I can see." He looked into her eyes. "This calls for a celebration. The science fair is over at two? Why don't I take the three of us for ice cream at that new place by the mall that freezes it for you while you wait?"

Olivia's heart caught in her throat. Was that attraction she saw behind his eyes? For her? Was he asking her out? She hesitated. *Of course, he's not interested in me. Why would he be? Get hold of yourself.* She opened her mouth but couldn't find words.

"You must be busy," he replied hastily. "You've already spent most of your day here. I'm sure you've got things to do."

Olivia stood, rooted to the spot, unable to speak.

"I'd better go check out the competition," Byron said. "Thank you, again, for all you've done for these kids."

Olivia watched him walk away until he was lost in the crowd. *Why in the world didn't I accept? Why was I tongue-tied?* She liked this man—she liked him a lot. *Who am I kidding?* His invitation was surely just a casual one to his daughter's teacher. She shook her head. She shouldn't allow herself to entertain thoughts of a romance she'd never have.

CHAPTER 32

Olivia sat cross-legged in the grass next to her grandmother's grave. The sunny afternoon softened the chill air.

"The science fair was a huge success. My group won first place in our district and is going on to the state competition. They're a neat group of kids and our project is very interesting." She drew a deep breath.

"Remember the girl I told you about in my group? The one who needs braces? Her dad invited me to go for ice cream with them after the fair." Olivia cradled her head in her hands. "I wanted to go with them, Grams. It was just ice cream and there would have been other people there, too. It wasn't like it was a date or anything." She rocked slowly back and forth. "I couldn't make myself say anything when he asked me. He's really a nice man and he's very cute. Now I think I've offended him and I'll never get another chance."

Olivia brushed her hand across her eyes. "I know what you'd say. You'd say that I need to have that surgery and get this behind me. And you'd be right." She drew a deep breath, then exhaled slowly. "I've got an appointment with that specialist you found. I'm not going to chicken out this time. I made a promise to this girl that if she got braces, I'd have the surgery."

Olivia pressed her fingers to her lips and touched the headstone. She began uncrossing her legs to stand when a furry brown dog streaked across her path, knocking her back. She looked up to see Mrs. Marshall approaching her, the stray dog trailing close behind.

"Are you alright?" Mrs. Marshall called. "I've been feeding him every day at this time and he's waiting for me."

Olivia stood and dusted the grass from the back of her pants. "I'm fine." She pointed to the animal as Mrs. Marshall placed a plastic bowl full of kibble in front of him. "He's back and he's not timid anymore."

"He sure isn't."

"Why don't you take him home?"

"I've tried to lure him to my car but he won't come with me."

"So you feed him every day?"

Mrs. Marshall nodded. "Ridiculous, I know. I'm just hoping that he'll come with me soon." She glanced at Olivia. "Is something the matter, dear? It seems like you've been crying."

Olivia looked into the kind eyes of the older woman. "I was too scared to do something I really wanted to do."

Mrs. Marshall nodded encouragingly.

"I'm lonely but I keep to myself—even when people invite me out—because of this." She pointed quickly to her mouth. "But I've decided to change all that. Grams left me money to have surgery to fix my cleft palate. I've finally decided to ignore my fear and have it done."

Mrs. Marshall stepped to Olivia and put her arm around her shoulders. "That's wonderful, Olivia. I'm sure your grandmother is delighted to hear this. I've come to love you like one of my own granddaughters and I'm so pleased. I'll bet it won't be as difficult as you think. There are plenty of times in my life where I've dreaded doing something—made myself suffer—and when I've finally done it, it wasn't half bad."

"Really?"

"I'm sure of it. And if you need help with anything, you let me know."

Olivia smiled as the brown dog licked the bowl clean and streaked back into the woods. "Maybe one of these days we can work together to catch him.

CHAPTER 33

Tom stared at the remaining handful of pills in the ziplock bag that he kept hidden underneath the lining of his briefcase. He'd have to taper off on his consumption—this stash wouldn't last him through the end of the week. He opened his wallet and knew he would only find a five and two ones. He was broke and his credit at his dealers had run out.

Olivia Osgoode could be his salvation. If the amount his brother said she had inherited was true—and he could convince her to allow him to manage her money—he might even be able to syphon off some of the interest and no one would ever be the wiser. At the very least, he could churn the portfolio and rack up impressive fees. She wasn't savvy enough to know any better.

Tom flung the briefcase into the far corner of his office. Damn her. She'd left him a polite voice mail message apologizing for cancelling their appointment. She was sorry—she just wasn't ready to think about her grandmother's estate yet. She'd contact him when she was. He didn't have time to wait for her to get ready.

Tom pushed himself out of his desk chair and retrieved his briefcase. He removed one of the tablets, put it on the back of his tongue, and swallowed. Come hell or high water, he'd get his hands on Olivia's money.

Tom checked his appearance in his rearview mirror. The pill had delivered its desired effect and he was feeling cocky and sure of himself. He straightened his tie and pulled a comb out of the glove box to run through his hair. Satisfied that he now looked the part of the successful financial planner, he got out of his car and pushed through the double glass doors of the Hilton Mortuary.

"Tom," Flora said, looking up from the computer. "Sam just left."

"I'm here to see Olivia."

Flora's brows shot up as he strode past her. "She's…" Flora began, but he was out of earshot. He returned to the reception station a moment later.

"Olivia's door is locked," he said.

"I tried to tell you," Flora said. "She and Sam went out to the crematorium."

Tom swallowed his irritation and kept a smile fixed on his lips. "Why in the world did they go out there?"

Flora shrugged. "No one tells me anything. Steve's been in a bit of a snit. But then he's always harping about something."

"Is that so?"

"Oh, yes," Flora said, warming to her subject. "But this time, it must be more serious. I can't remember the last time anyone went out to the crematorium."

"Why would Olivia go? She doesn't have anything to do with the operations side of the business."

"That's what I thought. It must be something financial." Flora turned away to answer the phone. "Good afternoon. Hilton Mortuary. How may I help you?"

She didn't notice Tom catch his toe on the carpet and stumble as he stepped away from her. *What in the hell is going on at the crematorium?* More importantly, when would he be able to talk to Olivia?

CHAPTER 34

Sam drummed his thumbs on the steering wheel as he waited for the traffic light to turn green. The light changed and the line of traffic inched forward.

Olivia stared out of the passenger seat window and was thrown forward into her seatbelt when Sam stomped on the brakes. The siren of an emergency vehicle grew steadily louder.

Sam cursed under his breath. "I don't have time for this shit today."

Olivia pressed herself into her seat. Sam never used curse words—until recently. "You didn't need to come out here with me," she said.

"And leave you to deal with Steve's paranoid theories on your own? I wasn't going to let that happen."

"Maybe he just needs attention from someone from the main office. Face time, you know?" Olivia glanced at an ambulance that sailed past. The line of traffic began to move forward again. "His brother is sick and he's been very stressed."

"I didn't know the two of you were close." Sam glanced at her.

"We talk on the phone most days. I wouldn't say we're close." Olivia shrugged. "He lives alone and works by himself. I thought it might be nice if I came out here to listen to his concerns in person."

"You don't think there's any truth to his cockamamie theories, do you?"

Olivia hesitated. What did she think about Steve's suspicions that someone was using the crematorium at night? Steve was the most fastidious person she'd ever met. If he thought something was amiss, it might just be. "I... I don't know. It doesn't seem likely."

"Doesn't seem likely? It's completely crazy," Sam hissed as he pulled up to the gate at the crematorium. He was unbuckling his seatbelt to get out of the car to deal with the gate when it slid open.

Steve stood at the entrance and motioned them into the parking lot.

"I didn't know you were both coming out." Steve ushered Sam and Olivia into his office. "I thought it would just be Olivia," he said as he absentmindedly straightened the pens on his desk.

"I wanted to hear what you had to say," Sam said.

"Let me get another chair." Steve turned to the workroom beyond his office.

"I'll stand," Sam said, motioning Olivia toward the sole chair across from Steve's desk. "We don't have much time."

"Alright, then," Steve said, fumbling with a legal pad on his desk. "I've done some calculations. We've used between two and four percent more gas during each of the last six months than I believe we should have." He looked at his visitors expectantly.

Olivia shifted her gaze to Sam.

"That's it? We've had an insignificant increase in our utilities and you think something fishy is going on?" Sam struggled to keep his tone low. He turned to Olivia. "Do our utilities vary from month to month?"

Olivia nodded slowly.

"So you don't detect an alarming pattern?" Sam addressed the question to Olivia.

"No."

Sam pushed away from the wall that he'd been leaning against. "You see—everything's fine. No need to worry."

Steve sucked in a deep breath. "Our utility usage is consistent, based upon the number of bodies we've handled. I track all of that. We haven't been off for just one month—it's been the last six months."

"I seem to remember the same thing happened four years ago." Sam held Steve's gaze. "It was nothing then and it's nothing now."

"It's not just the utility usage." Steve cleared his throat. "Things were disturbed in the workroom a couple of weeks ago. In the morning when I came in."

Sam took a step back. "What do you mean—disturbed?"

"The stack of cardboard caskets along the wall had been touched and the cremains in the old oven had been moved."

"Show us," Sam said, striding into the work room as Steve and Olivia followed behind.

"Here," Steve said, pointing to the caskets.

"That's where you always keep them," Sam said. "Were they somewhere else in the morning? Along one of the other walls?"

"No. They were still here, but…"

"Were any of them missing?"

Steve shook his head. "They were all still there but I could tell that someone had gone through them." He straightened the precisely stacked boxes. "The top one was out of alignment." He glanced at Olivia, then looked away. "I'm very… tidy."

Sam huffed impatiently. "What else? What were you saying about the cremains?"

Steve stepped to the old oven and punched the button to open it. The door slid up to reveal a skeleton and cremains, waiting to be swept into the trough and taken to the processor. "I'd been running both ovens all day long. I'd finished the last cremations just before sunset and they hadn't cooled down by the time I needed to leave for the day."

"And?"

"I rarely leave cremains in the ovens at the end of the day. I like to have everything finished up, but I had choir practice and couldn't be late."

Sam narrowed his eyes and stared coldly at the man.

Steve cleared his throat and continued. "I opened both ovens and checked to make sure that the process was complete before I left for the day. When I came in the next morning, the skull in the old oven had been moved."

"Moved how?" Sam hissed. "Was it out here somewhere?" He gestured to the room around him.

Olivia frowned. Steve's story seemed farfetched to her, too, but there was no need to belittle him.

"No… of course not. I would have called the police if that had been the case." He turned toward Olivia. "The skull had been dislodged

163

from the spine and it looked like the ash at the base of the skull had been smeared."

Sam spun on Steve.

Olivia took a step forward. "Could the skull have settled overnight?"

"I suppose so. That happens once in a great while."

Sam released the breath he'd been holding. "There you have it. That must be what happened. Thank you, Olivia."

Olivia raised her eyebrows quizzically at Steve.

Steve shrugged and lowered his gaze to the floor.

"I have a meeting back at the mortuary." Sam said. He made his way to the front door and Olivia followed. Sam stopped in the doorway and turned to Steve. "Thank you for bringing this to our attention. You've always been a very conscientious employee and I appreciate how hard you've been working. I think you agree that there's nothing to worry about. If you notice anything else, please call me."

Olivia nodded her agreement. She patted his arm as they walked by Steve on the way to Sam's car.

Steve stood in the doorway and watched in stony silence as they pulled out of the lot.

"That was a complete waste of time," Sam said as he sped back to town. He settled into his seat and slowed down. "I don't need to make matters worse by getting a speeding ticket."

"Maybe we made Steve feel better."

"You think?"

"I'm not sure. I hope so."

"You're satisfied that there's nothing to his fears, aren't you?"

Am I satisfied? Elderly widows are disappearing. Could this be why their bodies aren't being found? Olivia turned to observe his profile as he drove. The only two people with keys to the crematorium were Sam and Steve. *Is one of them killing these women and disposing of their bodies? Why would they be*

164

doing that? I know these men—I've worked with them for years. Could one of them be a killer? A chill ran down her spine and she shivered involuntarily. *Am I as paranoid as Steve?*

Olivia cleared her throat. "I am. I don't think anything untoward is going on at the crematorium at night."

Sam relaxed into his seat. "Maybe he needs to take some time off."

"I've suggested that. He keeps saying we're too busy. There's no one else to run the crematorium."

"I know how to run it," Sam said.

"I didn't know that."

"Tom and I both learned how in high school. Dad made sure we both learned how to run the ovens.

CHAPTER 35

"You had a message for me?" Olivia asked.

"Not a message, exactly. I just wanted to tell you that Tom Hilton stopped by shortly after you and Sam left." She stared at Olivia over the top of her half-moon glasses. "He said he came to see you."

"Okay. Thanks for telling me."

Flora cleared her throat. "I didn't know the two of you were friends."

Olivia felt her face grow hot. "We're not. He offered to help me with something but I'm not ready yet."

Flora's expression softened. "I'm just glad that's all it is."

"What do you mean?"

Flora stood and leaned in close to Olivia. "Tom's not like Sam. He's got quite a reputation about town as a ladies' man." She shot Olivia a knowing look.

Olivia's cheeks burned.

"If he's paying extra attention to you, you need to be very careful. He's broken many a heart."

"Thank you," Olivia said, looking at Flora, then turning away. "I'm sure it's nothing like that," and as she said it, she felt a frisson of disappointment.

"I've got other news," Olivia continued.

"Oh?"

"I'm having surgery to correct my cleft palate," she said in a rush.

Flora came from behind the reception station to hug Olivia. "That's wonderful. I'm so glad to hear it. I know this is a big step for you but it'll be a wonderful thing. Your grandmother would be pleased. That's why she left you that money."

"You know about the money? Did Kathy tell you?"

Flora flushed. "It's hard to keep a secret around here. Don't be mad at her. She loved your grandmother and she loves you. We all do."

Olivia sighed. "I know. You're all like family to me."

"When is your surgery?"

"I'm waiting for them to call me with the date. I've already met with the doctor. He said it would be sometime next month."

"I'm so pleased. Have you told Kathy?"

Olivia shook her head. "I was waiting to get the date and check with Sam to make sure I can have the time off."

"Sam won't say 'no' to that. If he gives you any guff, you come to Kathy and me. We'll take care of him."

Olivia smiled at her coworker.

"So, what had Steve in such an uproar?" Flora asked.

"He thinks the utilities are too high for the crematorium."

Flora cocked her head to one side.

"You know how fastidious he is with everything. There's not a nickel spent at the crematorium that isn't accounted for." She rolled her eyes. "He keeps detailed lists of everything. He says our gas usage is two percent above what it should be."

"And he dragged both of you out there for that?"

"Yep. Sam reminded him that he'd said our utilities were too high four years ago—tried to make the point that our utilities fluctuate from time to time."

"Did that placate Steve?" Flora asked.

"Not a bit. Steve also thinks the old oven may have been used one night several weeks ago. Said that cremains in the old oven had been moved slightly overnight."

"Doesn't that beat all," Flora said. "His imagination must be running wild. He's worked that job too long, that's what I think."

"He's stressed, that's for sure. Sam thanked him for being so conscientious but that everything seemed to be within normal ranges. Told him to let him know if anything else seemed out of place."

Flora snorted. "I think Steve needs to take a vacation. Get away and decompress a bit."

"You may be right." Then again, he may be on to something, Olivia thought.

CHAPTER 36

Olivia lingered at her grandmother's grave in the growing dusk. She'd told her grandmother the date of her surgery when she'd visited her grave on Monday and had been looking forward to sharing the good news with Mrs. Marshall. She'd visited at the usual time when she would run into the older woman and hadn't worried the first few days when their paths hadn't crossed. It was now Sunday and she hadn't seen the woman all week.

Olivia arrived at the cemetery early and brought a book and her lunch. The day had been fair and mild, but storm clouds began to gather midafternoon. The wind had picked up and tore through her thin jacket. She turned up her collar. A growing sense of unease enveloped her. Had Mrs. Marshall joined the other missing widows from the cemetery?

She stepped to Walter Marshall's grave. Was it her imagination, or did it look unkempt? Olivia headed to the parking lot when a plaintive howl rose from the woods at the perimeter. The mutt Mrs. Marshall had been feeding stood at the break in the fence.

She walked slowly to where he waited and stretched out her hand. He whimpered. "Are you hungry?"

The dog wagged his tail in response.

Olivia opened her satchel and took out the sandwich that she hadn't had the appetite to eat. She removed it from the ziplock bag and laid it on the ground in front of him.

The animal consumed it in six gulps, licked his lips, and looked at her expectantly. She handed him the apple she'd also brought. "I'm afraid this is all I've got," she said. "Isn't Mrs. Marshall feeding you?" As she said this, a cold chill ran down her spine.

"I'll be back tomorrow," Olivia cooed to the animal. He finished the apple and retreated into the darkening woods before being lost to sight.

Olivia glanced nervously around her in the deserted area. Women who visited this cemetery were disappearing. She was sure of it.

The sun sank low on the horizon. She put her head down into the wind and made her way quickly to the safety of her car.

"Good morning, Olivia. Did you have a nice weekend?" Kathy replaced the coffee pot on the burner. "It was lovely. Did you get to spend some time outside?"

"I was at the cemetery all day yesterday."

Kathy drew up short. "All day? Whatever for? I know it's beautiful and peaceful out there, but…"

"I went out in the morning to tell grandma that I'm going to have the surgery."

"That's wonderful news! I'm so happy to hear it. When?"

"Two weeks from Thursday."

"Will you stay in the hospital?"

Olivia shook her head. "It's outpatient, unless things don't go as planned and they need to keep me overnight. I'm taking Friday off, too. I should be back at work the following week—hopefully on Monday."

"You never take time off, so if it takes longer to heal, you just stay home and don't worry about this place. In fact, why don't you come to my house to recuperate? I've got a spare bedroom and I could help you if you need anything."

Olivia patted her coworker on the shoulder. "That's very kind of you, but I like being in my own bed. And there's Tinker and Bell to consider."

"I can go by and feed them every day. If you're up to it, you could come with me. At least spend Thursday night with me."

"I don't think that'll be necessary. But if you wouldn't mind driving me there and picking me up, I'd be grateful."

"Of course I will."

169

Kathy ran her eyes over Olivia's face. "You look worn out, dear. Are you worrying about this surgery?"

"I'm trying not to. The surgeon thinks it'll be no big deal. He says the results will be 'transformative'. That's the word he used." She smiled at Kathy. "I'm upset because another widow from the cemetery is missing."

Kathy took a step back. "What do you mean?"

"You know that I've become friends with some of the other women who visit their husband's graves at the cemetery?"

Kathy nodded.

"I've gotten close to a woman named Mrs. Marshall. She knew my grandmother. And she used to be there every day when I was there. You and Mrs. Marshall were the ones who always encouraged me to have the surgery."

It was Kathy's turn to smile.

"Anyway—I wanted to tell her that I've scheduled the surgery but she hasn't been at the cemetery all week. That's why I spent all day there yesterday. I was trying to catch her."

"Maybe she's sick or on vacation?"

"She would have told me if she was going on vacation. She feeds a stray dog that lives in the woods by the cemetery and she would have asked me to feed him for her. And she was in perfect health the last time I saw her."

"People can get sick pretty fast."

"I suppose," Olivia replied. "I called the hospital and she hasn't been admitted."

"You really are worried, aren't you?"

"I am. She would be the third woman that's disappeared in the last six months."

"What do you mean?"

"First there's the dead woman I saw in the garage. Cheryl Robinson."

"They've never found her body, have they?"

"That's my point. Or Dorothy Ransom's."

"Don't you think you're taking this a little too far? It's hard to believe that someone is killing elderly widows in this city."

"The police don't believe me and now you don't either." Olivia turned sharply and coffee sloshed out of her mug onto the tile floor. She set her mug onto the counter and both women reached for a paper towel. "I've got it," Olivia snapped.

"I don't mean to upset you," Kathy said. "Just give it some time. I'm sure Mrs. Marshall will be back."

Olivia bent to wipe up the spill. "I hope you're right, but I don't think so."

CHAPTER 37

Sam looked up from his desk. Kathy was hovering in his doorway.

"Can I talk to you for a sec?" she asked.

He sighed heavily. "Sure."

Kathy entered his office and carefully shut the door behind her to muffle the click of the lock.

Sam raised his eyebrows.

"I don't want Olivia to know I'm in here with you, behind closed doors."

"What's up with Olivia?"

Kathy sank into one of the chairs in front of his desk and leaned toward him. "She's going on about someone killing widows again," she whispered.

Sam rocked back in his chair. "I thought she'd gotten over all that nonsense."

"I did too, but then she started up again this morning."

"What did she say?"

"There's a woman that she saw at the cemetery every day who hasn't been there for a week. She's afraid she's been killed."

"That's it? She's away for a week so she must be murdered?"

Kathy shrugged and looked at her hands.

"This is nuts. The police never found any evidence to support the dead body in the garage, did they?"

Kathy shook her head. "I'm worried about her."

"Do you think we should insist she get counseling?" he asked.

"That's what I'm wondering. She's finally having surgery to fix her cleft palate, so I don't think we should do anything before she has that done."

"I agree. When is that?"

"A couple of weeks."

"Let's see how that plays out. In the meantime, please keep me posted if she comes up with anything else."

Kathy rose from her chair. "Thanks, Sam. Will do."

"Who is this latest supposed victim? Did Olivia give you a name?"

"Mrs. Marshall."

Sam looked up. "A Mrs. Marshall just came into our care from the hospital. She'd been undergoing tests when she'd had a heart attack and died on Friday."

"That's got to be the same woman," Kathy said. "I'm relieved there's an innocent answer but I'm sorry Olivia's lost someone else she cares about."

"Do you want to tell her before she sees the name on the roster?"

Kathy twisted the hem of her cardigan. "You're so much better at this sort of thing than I am, Sam. Would you do it?"

Sam nodded slowly as he rose from his chair.

Sam pushed open the door to the supply room and quietly shut it behind him. Olivia was bending over a box of office supplies, her back to the door. Her earbuds were in place and she was listening to one of her favorite true crime podcasts, unaware of Sam's presence in the small space.

He paused, unsure how to get her attention, then reached out and touched her shoulder.

Olivia stumbled, dropping the boxes of binder clips she'd been holding which sent them scattering across the floor. One of the boxes broke open, discharging the shiny black clips around her feet. She tore the earbuds out of her ears and gasped. "I didn't hear you, Sam. You scared me to death."

"I'm sorry. I didn't mean to."

Olivia wound her earbuds into a coil and shoved them into the pocket of her cardigan.

"Can I speak with you for a moment?" Sam asked.

Olivia nodded and bent to pick up the clips.

Sam cleared his throat. "Kathy tells me you've been worried about your friend, Mrs. Marshall?"

Olivia nodded again. "I saw her name on the roster." Olivia's voice was barely a whisper.

"She'd been in the hospital undergoing tests and died of a massive heart attack on Friday." Sam took one of the boxes of tissues from the tall stack along the wall and handed it to Olivia. "She was eighty-eight and healthy until the last week of her life. The paperwork says she was very active in her church and we're expecting a large crowd for her service." He bent to catch her eye. "We'd all like to end our days that way."

Olivia sniffed. She pulled a tissue from the box and blew her nose. "You're absolutely right. She had a lot of friends—including me. I'll miss her."

"God took her in His time. Nothing untoward happened to her."

Olivia cut her eyes to his. "I know. Maybe I've been letting my imagination run away with me these last few months."

"That's very possible. You've been under a lot of stress."

"I saw that body in the parking garage—I didn't make that up." She faced him. "I can't get her out of my mind. And the police don't believe me. The killer is out there. He's seen me. He could be after me and the police aren't doing a thing. There are others, too. I'm sure of it. Or at least I thought I was sure of it. Until today. I don't know what to think anymore." She lowered her face into her hands. "At least Mrs. Marshall wasn't one of his victims."

"No, she wasn't." He cleared his throat. "Why don't you give it a rest for a while? I understand you're taking time off to have surgery?"

Olivia nodded in acknowledgement.

"I'm glad to hear it, Olivia. Take all the time you need. You've earned it. We'll keep things going here until you get back. Don't worry.

CHAPTER 38

Tom pushed through the double doors of Hilton Mortuary. "The sidewalk is a mess," he said. He stamped his feet on the mat inside the door, knocking chunks of dirt off of his expensive shoes.

Flora furrowed her brow. "It's all the construction. I'll call maintenance…"

"Sam in his office?" Tom interrupted her.

Flora nodded and Tom started down the hall. "Don't worry about the mess," she called after him. "I'll sweep it up."

Tom knocked on Sam's closed door and pushed it open without waiting for a reply.

Sam spun around in his chair and cupped his hand over the telephone receiver. He motioned for his brother to take a seat in one of the chairs in front of his desk. "Be right with you," he mouthed at Tom.

"We can't give you thirty days' terms anymore, Stan. I know we're both family funeral homes and we've been doing your cremations for decades, but your account is seriously overdue. We're going to have to insist on weekly payments until you get caught up." He paused to listen. "I understand and I'm really sorry, but I just can't. That's my final word."

Sam hung up the phone and turned to his brother.

"Sounds like you're doing what you should have done a long time ago."

"That's easy for you to say, Tom. You haven't worked with these people your entire adult life. We've always been there for each other—in good times and bad."

"It's just business, Sam. You're doing the right thing."

"It sure doesn't feel right."

The brothers stared at each other across the desk. "This isn't why you came here."

Tom shook his head. "I came by the other day to check on Olivia and you were both out at the crematorium. Seems Steve had some problems? I wanted to see if everything was alright."

"Oh, that," Sam said. "Steve is always dreaming up some crisis or other. It was nothing."

"Ah… well, that's good then. And how's Olivia?"

"The same. She hasn't given up on her story about the dead woman in the parking garage. In fact, she's got a theory that other elderly widows have disappeared."

Tom whistled softly. "That seems far-fetched. Why does she think that?"

"Because she hasn't seen them at the cemetery."

Tom's brows shot up. "That's hardly definitive. What do the police think?"

"They're not giving it any credence."

"I can understand that." Tom steepled his fingers. "She's certainly not reliable. She blew off our appointment to discuss her investments."

"I'm not surprised. Maybe it's because she's focused on her surgery to fix her cleft palate. She's using some of her inheritance for that."

Tom squelched his irritation. How much of her portfolio is she spending on this procedure? He took a deep breath. By all accounts, she had a lot more where that came from.

"She's in her office. Why don't you go see her? I'm sure she'd like that."

Tom nodded. "If you think it will help."

"Can't hurt," Sam said. "By the way, I'll still need money from you for construction cost overruns."

Tom nodded. "Just let me know. I'm about to land a big new client."

Olivia stretched her arms over her head. She'd been working on the analysis of utility expenses for the best part of the afternoon. Steve was right—gas and electricity usage were slightly up at the crematorium—

but were within expected ranges. Maybe his precise records of body weights and oven times weren't completely accurate. After all, his eyesight wasn't what it used to be. Perhaps he'd misread the timers when he'd set them. The smallest variation could account for these overages.

She really should finish putting the supplies away in the storage room. The break would do her good. She scanned the items on her desktop. She shouldn't leave her list of names and addresses of the women she believed were missing out in plain view. She picked up the stenographer's pad where she'd written them and stuck it in a side pocket of her purse.

She checked her watch. She'd have more than enough time to finish the spreadsheets before the end of the day. Olivia refilled her coffee cup and didn't hear the front door open as Tom entered the lobby. She shut the door of the storage room behind her and popped her earbuds back into place.

Tom found Olivia's door open and spreadsheets strewn across her desk. She, however, was nowhere to be seen.

Tom stopped and listened in the doorway for the sound of voices nearby. Everything was silent. If Olivia was in the break room, he would have heard something. He stepped into her office and leaned over her desk. Maybe some of these papers had to do with her inheritance. He still didn't know exactly how much money she'd gotten or where it was currently invested.

He couldn't make out any of the numbers, but he could read the textual entries down the sides of the columns. Even scrutinizing them upside down, he could see she was working on the expenses of the business. On the far corner of her desk, partially obscured by a calculator, was a stack of invoices bearing a logo he recognized as belonging to the gas company. What had Flora told him? Something was out of line with the crematorium's expenses?

He straightened and was about to step back when he noted the stenographer's pad sticking out of Olivia's purse on the floor by her desk. It was open to what looked like a list of names. He went to the hallway. There was no sign of anyone about. He moved swiftly toward her purse and leaned over the stenographer's pad. Olivia's scrawl was too small to read from this distance. He fumbled in the pocket of his coat for his reading glasses.

"Tom," Olivia said as she entered her office. "What are you doing?"

He spun around sharply at the sound of his name. "I... I just wanted to check on you. See how you're doing." He forced his lips into a smile.

Olivia moved past him and came around to her side of the desk.

"I stopped in last week, but you and Sam were out at the crematorium, dealing with Steve." He looked at her closely. "Ridiculous, really," he said, trying to shift her focus off of his obvious snooping.

"Sam told you about it? Steve is so incredibly precise. He noticed that we've used a smidgeon more gas and electricity out there and he thinks something fishy is going on."

"Seriously? How could that be?"

"Beats me. No one but Steve and Sam have keys to the place, anyway. I just know that Steve wasn't entirely satisfied with our explanation."

Tom remained silent.

"I'm doing all this work to prove to him that there isn't a problem," she said, sweeping her hand across the papers on her desk. "I'm working on the month-end reports and I'm already behind. I shouldn't be spending time on this."

He came around her desk to stand next to her and leaned over the spreadsheets. "Looks like you're doing an excellent job. This should put Steve's mind at ease. Everything seems within normal tolerances." He smiled reassuringly. "Speaking of putting one's mind at ease, what have you heard from the police about the missing woman?"

"That's another thing," Olivia said. "I'm convinced they still don't believe me and aren't doing anything to look for the killer."

"I'm sure they're devoting whatever resources they can to the case," he said.

"It's not just this one woman, either," Olivia said indignantly. "I've got evidence that at least one other woman is missing. And I suspect a third. I've got their names and addresses right here." She pointed to the stenographer's pad sticking out of her purse.

Tom stepped back. "What do the police say?"

"I haven't told them, yet. After the way they treated me about the first victim, I wanted to gather more information."

"You know best." He clasped his hands in front of him. "Have you had any more thoughts about your investments? I'm more than willing to help you. Maybe we should reschedule that appointment and I can give you some preliminary ideas to think about?"

"I'd like that," Olivia said.

Tom's countenance brightened.

"I'm having surgery in a couple weeks so let's plan to get together after I recover."

"When do you anticipate that will be?"

"Can I come in after the New Year? I know you and Mrs. Hilton are always very busy during the holidays."

"It'll be no trouble to meet with you before then," he said. "It'll put your mind at ease that your finances are taken care of. Many of my clients come to see me before they have surgery. They tell me it helps them heal, knowing everything is squared away."

Olivia hesitated and tapped the end of her pencil against her teeth. "That seems like a good idea."

"Tomorrow at 5:30?"

"Alright." She smiled at him. "Thanks for stopping in. I appreciate your checking on me."

"Of course, my dear," Tom said. "I'll let you get back to your spreadsheets. Don't let my brother keep you here too late. A pretty young woman like you must have better things to do in the evening." He gave her his most ingratiating smile. He couldn't be sure, but he thought she flushed with pleasure at his compliment.

He left her office and strode past the reception desk. He returned Flora's cheerful "Have a nice night" with a dismissive wave of his hand.

Tom had a lot on his mind. He needed to get his hands on Olivia's money.

CHAPTER 39

Olivia took the pen that Tom held out to her. "I need to sign everywhere there's a little yellow flag?" She glanced at Tom who sat with her at the small conference table in his office.

"That's right," he said, barely concealing his glee. "It seems like a lot, but I need all of these so I can manage your accounts."

"That's what this Power of Attorney form is for?"

"Exactly." He leaned toward her and stared at the signature line as her hand hovered over it.

"Why do you need to be able to sign for me? I'm just down the street. I can come here to sign stuff."

Tom's nostrils flared. "This is just in case something needs to be signed while you're in the hospital or recovering. I've explained that this is standard procedure when someone's having surgery, remember?"

Olivia nodded.

"You'll be signing most of the papers. This is only if you can't or it's inconvenient for you and you want me to sign." He forced himself to speak slowly and calmly. "You can revoke the Power of Attorney any time you wish," he continued.

Olivia drew a deep breath. She lowered her hand and began the familiar stroke of her signature. She stopped halfway through her mark and looked up at him. "I think it's out of ink."

Tom rose swiftly from his seat, using every ounce of willpower to restrain himself from swearing. "I can fix that in a jiffy," he said, retrieving another pen from the stand on his desk.

Olivia resumed her progress through the documentation that would give Tom Hilton access and authority to manage her entire inheritance. She hesitated over the final form.

"I'll need money for my surgery right away." She turned anxious eyes to his. "How can I get it?"

"I'm sure those bills won't come in for months after your surgery. They'll need to submit to insurance first and you know how long all that takes. You'll have plenty of time before you need to pay them."

Olivia shook her head. "They've already figured all that out with my insurance carrier. My deductible and co-pay amount to $6,650. I'll need to take that out of this money." She laid the pen on the table. "I think we should finish this up after I've recovered."

Tom pushed down his rising panic. "We talked about that, didn't we? Best to get all of these details taken care of now. That way I can keep an eye on things when you can't."

Olivia shifted in her chair. "I won't be out that long…"

"When we talked earlier, you were relieved to think you'd have this taken care of. If it'll make you feel any better, why don't I give you a check right now, out of my brokerage account, for the $6,650. If for any reason—and I don't think this will happen—you can't get the money out of your accounts in time, you can use my check."

Olivia's countenance lightened. "You'd do that for me? That would make me feel much better."

"Of course I would. You're part of the Hilton Mortuary family." He stepped to his desk and pulled out his checkbook. "I'm happy to do anything that'll make you feel better."

He wrote out the check with a flourish and handed it to her.

"Thank you," Olivia said. She carefully folded the check Tom had just written and zipped it safely in an inner pocket in her purse.

Tom handed her the pen. She took it from him and signed the final document.

"Now that I've worked up the nerve to have this surgery, I don't want anything to stand in the way." She pointed to her purse. "Your check makes me feel much better."

"I'm so glad it does." If she only knew that there was little more than fifty dollars in that account. The check would bounce sky high if she ever tried to use it. "I won't keep you. You must have a million things to do before your surgery." Now that he had her signature, he was anxious to be rid of her.

"I'm ready," she replied. "But I'm pretty nervous."

Tom ushered her to the door. "I'm sure it'll all go fine." He was shutting the door behind her when a thought struck him. With any luck, the surgery wouldn't go well and she'd be one of the miniscule percentage of people who didn't survive. He'd heard about people dying from freak heart attacks or allergies to anesthesia. Surely these things occasionally happened. Who would her next of kin be? It could take years to find them. By the time they were found, he could have syphoned off the bulk of her portfolio in ways they'd never be able to trace. Tom's eyes glittered with malice as he gathered up the papers that gave him unfettered access to Olivia's money.

CHAPTER 40

Olivia finished loading her groceries in the trunk of her car. She'd stocked up on popsicles, pudding, Jell-O, and yogurt—all the foods recommended after her surgery. She'd taken an armload of books out of the library yesterday and had a stack of magazines that Kathy and Flora had given her. She was prepared to recuperate at home after the operation.

The state science fair would be over on Sunday and she'd have her procedure on Thursday. With any luck, she'd be back at work the following week.

She was returning her cart to the cart barn when movement by the dumpster at the side of the supermarket drew her attention. There was something familiar about the shaggy brown creature routing through a cardboard box that had fallen from the dumpster.

Olivia smiled. It was the dog from the cemetery—the one Mrs. Marshall had been feeding. She was sure of it. After Mrs. Marshall's death, Olivia brought food to the cemetery in case she found him, but he never appeared. She'd worried about the poor creature and now here he was.

Olivia reopened her trunk and fished around in her grocery sacks until she found the package of deli turkey she'd planned to eat for her lunch the next two days. She opened the package and approached the animal slowly.

He stopped ripping at the cardboard and eyed her cautiously as she placed a thin slice of turkey on the pavement between them.

He leaned toward the treat, his nose twitching.

"Go on," she cooed. "You know me. I'm not going to hurt you."

The dog tentatively wagged his tail.

Olivia sat on her haunches and waited.

The dog picked up the turkey with his teeth and swallowed it in one gulp. He raised his soft brown eyes to hers and wagged his tail more enthusiastically.

Olivia held out another piece of turkey. "Here you go, boy. Come on."

The dog took a step closer to Olivia and leaned over as far as he was able to take the food from her outstretched hand. By the time she'd fed him the entire package, he was close enough to allow her to pet him.

"Stay right here," Olivia said. "I'm going to get some more and be right back."

Olivia was hurrying toward the supermarket entrance when the automatic doors opened and Missie emerged, followed by Byron pushing a loaded shopping cart.

"Ms. O," Missie cried. "This is where we shop, too."

"Hello, you two. I'm in a bit of a hurry," Olivia said, moving past them.

"I was going to email you," Missie called. "I have some questions about the science fair. But since you're here, can I ask you now?"

Olivia looked over her shoulder at the dumpster.

"It'll only take a minute..." Missie said.

"Ms. O said that she's in a hurry right now, honey," Byron said. "You can email her. She's very busy."

Missie turned away. "Okay. Sorry." She pushed her hair behind her ears.

Olivia smiled at the girl. "It's just that I'm trying to capture that dog by the dumpster." She pointed over her shoulder. "I used to see him at the cemetery. I've been feeding him lunch meat. He let me touch him for the first time. I ran out of lunch meat and was running back in to get more."

"We've got some ham in here," Byron said. "We wouldn't mind giving it to him, would we, Missie?" He reached into their shopping cart.

"Yes!" Missie cried. "Our dog was a stray that my dad got. He's like a dog whisperer." She beamed at her father. "Can we help you with him?" Missie asked, pointing at the dog who was still next to the dumpster, staring in their direction.

"I hate to put you out," Olivia turned to Byron. "But it's supposed to get very cold this week and I hate the thought of him being outside."

"What will you do with him?" Byron asked.

Olivia shrugged. "I'm not sure. I already have two cats. If they get along with each other, I'll keep him." She sighed. "My grandmother was allergic to dogs, but I always wanted one. I'm going to be off work for about a week, so it's a good time to adopt a dog."

"Let's see if we can get him into your car," Byron said. He wheeled his cart up to his car and left it there. "We can load the groceries later. Let's see about him before he goes away."

The threesome approached the dog slowly. Byron dropped to one knee and held out a rolled-up slice of ham to the dog. Without hesitation, the animal took the offering and lay on the ground next to Byron to eat it. Byron placed his large hand on the animal's back while he ate. He gave the dog another piece of ham and examined his teeth.

"He's in desperate need of a bath and probably should be dipped for fleas. His teeth are beautiful. I'd say he's no more than two years old." He looked up at Olivia who hovered nearby. "He's seriously malnourished; you can feel his ribs." He stroked the dog. "But he's calm and friendly. I'm sure he'd turn into a wonderful companion."

"Are you going to take him?" Missie peered into Olivia's face.

Olivia nodded. "I think I will. Can you help get him into my car?" She glanced at Byron.

He handed Olivia the open package of ham. "Why don't you continue to feed him? I've got a spare leash in my car. We can use it for now."

"That's awfully nice," Olivia said. "I'd be grateful."

Byron headed for his car and Olivia fed a piece of ham to the dog.

"Can I try?" Missie asked.

"Of course," Olivia replied, handing the package to Missie.

Olivia watched as the animal gently took the piece of ham from Missie. "He's very well mannered," Olivia said. "I hope my cats like him."

"I wouldn't worry about that," Missie said. "We have cats and if they don't want to be bothered by our dog they jump to a higher perch and swat at his nose when he comes near them. Dogs learn pretty quick to leave cats alone."

Olivia laughed. "Good to know."

"Okay," Byron said, holding out the leash. "Let's see how he does."

He made a loop out of the leash and slipped it around the dog's neck, handing the leash to Olivia. The animal turned and sat at her side.

"For Pete's sake," Byron said. "It looks like he's leash trained."

Olivia looked at Byron quizzically.

"Tell him to 'heel' and start walking to your car," Byron said.

Olivia gave the command and the animal walked obediently at her side, with Byron and Missie bringing up the rear.

Olivia unlocked her car and the animal jumped into the back seat and settled himself comfortably. "Would you look at that?" Olivia gushed. "He's a smart one."

She looked at Byron and his smile made her heart skip a beat.

"I think you've found yourself a very fine dog," he commented.

"What should I do with him now?" Olivia asked.

Byron laughed. "He's eaten a pound of turkey and ham, so he should be good for a while. Why don't you give him a bath? You can feed him rice and hamburger until you get dog food. I'd take him to the vet as soon as possible. He'll need shots and the vet will tell you what to feed him."

"Sounds easy enough," Olivia said.

"It is. And if you have any questions, you can always call me."

Olivia raised her eyes to his.

He gestured toward her cell phone. "Let me give you my number."

Olivia's fingers fumbled over the numbers on the screen as she input it into her phone. "Sorry this is taking so long," she said, giving Byron a rueful smile.

"No worries. My fingers are so fat it takes me forever to type anything into my phone."

"Thank you for your help with him," Olivia said. "I don't think he would have come with me without it."

"I told you my dad is good with dogs."

"He sure is," Olivia agreed.

Missie looked between Byron and Olivia and beamed.

Olivia turned to Missie. "Did you have questions about the science fair?"

Missie flushed. "Ahh… I don't remember," she stammered. "I'll email you if I do."

CHAPTER 41

Olivia broke the seal on the new eyeshadow compact she'd bought at the drug store. It contained four shades in the purple family, from the faintest shimmer of pink to a deep purple. She'd carefully examined the diagram on the bottom of the package depicting where to place which powder and began to apply the product as directed. She finished her ministrations with the coordinating eyeliner and a coat of blackest black mascara. She put on her glasses and stood back from the mirror to study the effect and recoiled slightly. She looked like one of those "made up" girls that she'd always detested in high school.

She reached for the package of makeup remover cloths that the saleslady had recommended, with the intent of removing everything she'd just applied. She took off her glasses and returned her gaze to the mirror. She had to admit, the makeup brought out the violet color of her eyes. "Like Elizabeth Taylor's eyes," her grandmother had always told her. Olivia didn't think she looked like the legendary beauty, but she did think her eyes looked pretty. She tucked the unused cloth back into the package.

She swept her cheeks with her customary light dusting of blush and accented her lips with tinted lip gloss. Dramatic eyes were enough for her.

Olivia went to her closet and picked up the violet tunic she'd purchased at the flea market. She fingered the garment lovingly. She hadn't worn it since the day she bought it and if she didn't put it on today, she never would. She slid the sweater over her head and returned to the mirror, turning to view herself from the right and the left. If she didn't open her mouth, she looked like any other pretty girl. Maybe Byron would see her this way?

"Freddie, I've got a crush on that nice man who helped me with you." The dog was never more than five feet from her side when she was home. "In the supermarket parking lot, remember?" She bent and rubbed behind his ears.

"I knew you'd remember him," she said. "You're soooo smart. And I'm soooo dumb. He'd never be interested in me in a million years. I'd better not get my hopes up."

Olivia ran a brush through her thick mane of blond hair and turned to the curling iron that she'd plugged in to heat up while she applied her makeup. She yanked the cord out of the wall and reached for her ratty old elastic band. She twisted her hair into a knot at the nape of her neck and secured it in place with the elastic. Eye makeup and a new sweater were enough for one day. No need to encourage herself in a fantasy that would only lead to disappointment.

"We won!" Missie cried, hopping up and down.

Eric pounded the table in a drum roll and Larry and Todd bumped fists.

"Congratulations, everyone. I think you won by a country mile, too. I'm so proud of you and all of your hard work," Mrs. Walters said.

"Let's get a picture of the winners in front of their booth," said a reporter from the local newspaper. "You get in the picture, too, Mrs. Walters."

"Where's Ms. O?" Missie asked.

"Yeah," Larry said. "She deserves this as much as we do."

Olivia stood at the back of the booth, fumbling with her hair that had escaped the elastic.

"Get in here with us," Mrs. Walters commanded. "And leave that beautiful hair of yours down."

Olivia blushed as she shook her hair around her shoulders and stepped into place next to Mrs. Walters.

The reporter snapped his picture as Byron stepped forward with his camera. "Stay where you are everybody. I want one, too."

"When we're done with pictures, let's celebrate. The best burger place in the state is right around the corner," Larry's dad said. "Mrs. Walters and Ms. O, I insist you join us. My treat."

"We'd love to," Mrs. Walters said without consulting Olivia. "Don't fuss," she leaned over and whispered in Olivia's ear. "You've done a marvelous job with these kids and you're the main reason they've won. They look up to you and would be so disappointed if you didn't go. Besides, you look lovely and should be going out somewhere." She fixed Olivia with a stern gaze. "So no disappearing act, okay?"

Olivia hesitated and looked over at Byron.

"That man is sweet on you, honey," Mrs. Walters said. "And he's a good one. Don't push him away."

Olivia turned wide eyes to the older woman. "You can't be serious."

"I most certainly am. It's plain as day to me."

Olivia felt herself blush.

Mrs. Walters picked up her purse and gestured to Olivia to do the same. "We're right behind you," she called to Byron as the group headed to their cars.

"You can have a half hour to play games," Eric's dad said as the server cleared their plates. All four kids headed in the direction of the arcade.

"I think I'd like to head home, if Olivia doesn't mind cutting it short since she rode with me," Mrs. Walters said.

"That's fine." Olivia began to rise from her chair at the far end of the table.

"I'll be happy to give Olivia a ride home," Byron said. "I've been wanting to talk to her anyway." He got up from his chair and went to sit next to Olivia at the end of the table.

"You don't..." Olivia began as Mrs. Walters raised an eyebrow at her and motioned for her to remain seated.

"Goodnight, Byron, and thank you." Mrs. Walters said goodbye to the parents remaining at the table. "Thank you for treating me to dinner."

Byron turned his attention to Olivia. "First of all, thank you for all of your kindness to Missie. This science fair project has done her a world of good. Boosted her confidence. She's started to come out of her shell."

"She's a great kid. Smart as a whip. You've got a lot to be proud of."

"She'll miss you now that this is over."

Olivia twisted a lock of hair. "I'd like to keep in touch with her, if that's okay with you. She said she wants to see my collection of vintage toasters that I've repaired."

He raised an eyebrow.

"I know—it's an odd hobby. But a popular one. Collecting vintage toasters is a real thing. I was never interested in dolls, but I always liked models and working with an erector set. They're in that shed behind my house. It's my workshop."

Byron ran his eyes over her face. "You are one of the most interesting women I've ever met. Beautiful and brainy."

Olivia's breath caught in her throat and she looked away.

"How's that dog of yours? Did you end up keeping him?"

"Freddie is my new right arm. I can't imagine how we ever got along without him. Tinker and Bell, my cats, seem to agree."

Byron smiled.

"Seriously—he's wonderful. He'll be such good company while I'm recovering," she said, and instantly regretted saying it.

"Recovering? From what?"

Olivia took a deep breath. "I'm going to have surgery on Thursday… to repair my cleft palate," she said, and looked at her hands.

Byron placed his hand on her arm. "Is this a complicated surgery? Will you be in the hospital for a while?"

Olivia shook her head. "It should be straightforward. It's to fix a botched surgery I had when I was very young. I should only be in overnight."

"Do you need any help with anything?"

"That's nice of you to ask. One of my coworkers is going to drive me to the hospital and home again. She's keeping Freddie overnight while I'm in the hospital. I'm all set."

"Does Missie know?"

"Yes. I told her this afternoon."

"Maybe you'd like us to take Freddie for you until you're really feeling better? Dogs are a lot more work than cats."

"I want him with me when I'm home. I feel safer with him there." Olivia turned serious eyes to him. "The killer from the parking garage is still out there, you know."

"Are you afraid of him?"

"You bet I am. Particularly since I don't think Detective Novak is doing anything to push this investigation along."

Byron turned aside.

"And don't tell me that it's hard to go forward without a body. I think other women have gone missing, too."

Byron whipped his head around to stare at her. "Why do you think that?"

Olivia lowered her voice and leaned toward him. "I've got detailed notes at home, but let me tell you what I've found out about Cheryl Robinson and Dorothy Ransom."

When she'd finished her recitation, Byron leaned back in his chair and rubbed his hand across his chin. "I wish you'd called me when you found those footprints in back of Dorothy Ransom's house. That's the kind of physical evidence we need."

Olivia lowered her head to her hands. "I wish I had, too. Detective Novak was so dismissive of me the other times I talked to him that I never thought of it. He thinks I made up the body in the parking garage. I'm sure of it." She raised her eyes to his. "I should have called you."

Byron gave her a rueful look. "I'm sorry you don't feel you've been treated with respect by the Marquette Police Department."

"I've always felt respected by you," Olivia said softly. "So—what do you think? Honestly. Doesn't this sound suspicious?"

"It could be," Byron admitted. "Or it could be pure coincidence—as you yourself just admitted."

"I need to find out which one it is," Olivia said. "Can you help me?"

Byron nodded slowly. "Let me see what I can do."

Olivia's shoulders relaxed. Maybe she wasn't in this alone, after all.

Byron checked his watch. "I think the arcade closes in ten minutes. We'd better find Missie and head back to Marquette. Thanks for staying—I enjoyed talking to you."

Olivia forgot herself and flashed him a smile.

Later that night, after they'd dropped Olivia at her car in the school parking lot, Missie turned to her father. "Did you know that Ms. O is having surgery on her mouth on Thursday?"

"She told me."

"I think that's so brave of her. I promised her that if she had that surgery, I would get braces. That's why I'm doing it."

Byron reached across the console and squeezed her hand. "That's a wonderful decision. You'll always be glad you did. I think you're both brave."

Olivia Osgoode might have some odd theories about widows disappearing in Marquette, but one thing was certain—she was a good influence on his daughter.

CHAPTER 42

Kathy pulled her car into her driveway and turned to Olivia. "You've had a rough go with nausea from the anesthesia and you're in a lot of pain. If you hadn't insisted on going home, I think they would have kept you in the hospital a second night." She put her hand on Olivia's arm. "Why don't you stay with me a day or two while you're still so bad? I'd feel much better if I could keep an eye on you here."

Olivia shook her head, ignoring the searing pain that radiated up her throat and through her ear. "That's not necessary. I've imposed on you too much as it is."

"You've done no such thing. I promised your grandmother—"

"And you've kept that promise. All I want to do is pick up Freddie and go home and get into bed. I've got popsicles and pain meds. That's all I need."

"You're as stubborn as your grandmother, that's for sure," Kathy said. "Alright. You stay in the car and I'll get Freddie. I have to go back to work after I drop you off but I'm leaving early to come by and check on you." She fixed Olivia with a stern look. "And if I don't think you're in good enough shape to be home alone, I'm bringing you back here with me. Understood?"

Olivia nodded her assent.

Kathy soon returned with Freddie and placed him in the back seat. He tempered his enthusiastic greeting of Olivia in the intuitive way that dogs have of knowing when someone's in pain.

Kathy settled Olivia and Freddie into Olivia's house and supervised her charge eating a popsicle and taking her dose of pain medication. Olivia was more than ready to tuck herself into bed. Tinker and Bell took up residence on the foot of her bed, with Freddie on the floor at the head. Sleep enveloped them all.

"I understand the surgery was a success but she's had a hard time of it." Flora looked up at Tom from her seat behind the reception desk. "Kathy's gone to bring her home from the hospital. They kept her an extra day."

"Did she have complications?"

"I wouldn't know. You'd have to ask Kathy." Flora sighed. "We're shorthanded right now. I've got my hands full with these phones."

Tom raised his eyebrows, encouraging her to go on.

"Steve had to go out of town to be with his brother who had a heart attack over the weekend."

"That's a shame. Will he be alright?"

"They think so. Steve is going to stay there until his brother gets out of the hospital. He thinks that'll be at least a week."

"Who's running the crematorium?"

"No one. We're shutting it down until he gets back."

"Why doesn't Sam do it? Surely he still remembers how."

"He says he's too busy and it's been too many years since he's done it." Flora leaned toward Tom and lowered her voice. "I think he's never liked that part of the business. He's better with the paperwork."

"You're right about that."

"Bodies are piling up in the cooler and I'm busy calling all the other funeral homes that we service to let them know we can't take any more bodies until further notice," she continued.

"How's that going over?"

"Not well, I can tell you." She shook her head as the phones lit up. "I'll bet that's another call about it now." She moved her headset back into position and answered the call.

"Hang in there." Tom mouthed the words at her as he stepped toward the back door.

He was heading for his car behind the mortuary when Kathy pulled into her assigned parking spot. He stopped and made his way over to her. She was leaning over to pick her purse off of the passenger seat when Tom called her name.

The purse slipped out of her hand as she turned toward him and powered her window down. "You scared the life out of me. I didn't hear you come up."

"Sorry about that. I wanted to find out how Olivia's doing. She had her surgery, didn't she?"

"She did. I just dropped her at her house—against my better judgment. The surgery was a success, but she had considerable nausea and she's in a lot of pain."

"That's too bad. Is she alone?"

"She is. I told her I'd check on her later this afternoon. I'm going to leave work early. If she's not better, I'm going to bring her back to my place with me."

"That's very nice of you, I'm sure." Tom opened her car door. She rolled up the window and stepped out. "When you see her, please give her my regards."

Kathy nodded but Tom had already turned and was striding across the lot to his car. He flung himself into the driver's seat and pulled out of the lot as fast as he dared, an idea forming in his mind.

CHAPTER 43

"Sweetheart," Tom said in his most solicitous voice when Ashley answered his call. "You weren't feeling well this morning when I left. Another migraine coming on? How are you?"

"I just got home from the pharmacy," Ashley said. "I tried to call you to ask you to pick up my prescription, but you didn't answer."

"Sorry, honey. I saw that I missed a call from you," he lied. "I was in a meeting and called as soon as I got out. Do you need anything?"

"I don't need anything from you now. I'll take a pill and go to bed as soon as we get off the phone. I need to zonk out and sleep this off."

"I've got to get something from the garage. I'll be home soon."

"Please don't disturb me."

"I won't even come in the house. Why don't you take your pill now? You sound miserable." He waited while the line was silent.

"There. I just did," she said.

"Good girl. You go crawl into bed. I'll sleep in the guest room tonight."

"Thank you, Tom," she said, yawning.

"Feel better," Tom said. He grimaced as he thought of the task that awaited him in his garage. He didn't relish the thought of wrangling the frozen corpse of Dorothy Ransom into the trunk of his car. At least he didn't have to worry about the prying eyes of his wife.

Tom pulled into his garage and shut the door behind him. He was in a hurry. He needed to retrieve Dorothy's body from the freezer and capture Olivia before Kathy returned to Olivia's house. He dug the freezer key out of his glove box and made a beeline for the freezer. He unlocked it and was about to begin his grim task when he stopped abruptly. Had he heard a noise from inside the house? Was Ashley up and about?

Tom hesitated and checked his watch. He had no time to spare but he had to be sure that his wife was asleep. He slipped off his shoes and walked to the door into the house. He held his breath as he opened the door that led into the mud room and then the kitchen. Everything was silent. He crept through the kitchen and down the hall to their bedroom. The door was closed. He put his hand on the door handle and then withdrew it. He didn't want to risk disturbing her. She wasn't walking around the house. His imagination had been playing tricks on him. He needed to get back to the garage and finish what he'd started.

Tom noiselessly crossed to the freezer and opened it, recoiling at the sight of Dorothy's frostbitten stare. He pressed the button on his key fob to open his trunk and cursed as the fob's cheeping sound reverberated in the closed space.

He wrangled Dorothy's contorted body out of the freezer and pressed it to his chest as he carried her to his trunk. He was reaching up to close the trunk when the door from the house into the garage opened and Ashley stood in the door frame, one hand gripping the door handle and the other holding her sleep mask on her forehead, out of her eyes.

"Tom? What are you doing?"

Tom slammed the trunk shut. "I came home to get something, remember?"

Ashley nodded slowly and he could see that the motion was painful. She turned her head toward the freezer. "What are you doing in the freezer?"

Tom sucked in his breath. "You said that you were using meat from the freezer for Ben's party. I was checking to make sure it's okay."

Ashley was silent, considering this. "That's nice of you. I'm sure it's all fine."

"Actually, it wasn't," Tom said, warming to the subject. "It was full of freezer burn so I'm throwing it all out." He pointed to the trunk. "I'll get more. Just text me what we'll need."

"I'm sure it's fine," Ashley said. "Let me see." She dropped her hand from the door knob and stepped into the garage. Her slippered foot caught the edge of her nightgown and she stumbled, falling to her knees on the concrete floor.

Tom rushed to her and helped her to her feet. "We need to get you back into bed. You've got no business being out here. Don't worry about this. Just get some sleep and feel better."

Ashley brushed the hair out of her eyes and nodded. She leaned heavily against him as he put his arm around her and steered her to their bedroom.

"Your shirt is all cold and clammy," she murmured, resting a palm on his chest.

"I was taking meat out of the freezer," he replied.

Ashley looked at him with unfocused eyes.

"Here we are," he said. He helped her into bed and pretended he didn't hear her ask him to get her a glass of water as he shut the bedroom door.

He rushed back to the garage. Tom shut the freezer, relocked it, and pulled out of the garage as fast as he could. He had no time to lose.

CHAPTER 44

Tom steered his car into a small clearing overhung with trees behind Olivia's workshop. A strong wind sent the branches slapping the roof of his car like an angry mob. He removed the X-Acto knife from his glove box. He'd rehearsed his plan on the drive out there and decided he needed the element of surprise. He wouldn't announce his presence by pulling his car up to the house but wanted it nearby so he didn't have to carry her body very far. Although slender, Olivia was tall and outweighed his usual victims by at least thirty pounds.

He cursed as the slick leather soles of his shoes slid on the damp leaves that clung to the grass. He stuck to the trees as he circled to a protected spot where he could view her back door. He withdrew into the shade, watching for any sign of her.

He didn't have long to wait. The screen door opened and Olivia, clad in a long chenille robe and fuzzy slippers, stepped out and down the back steps with a mutt at the end of a leash. The dog attended to his business as soon as his paws hit the grass.

Tom held his breath. The dog would certainly sense Tom's presence and set up an alarm.

The animal finished, stretched, and scented the air. A throaty growl rumbled in his chest and crescendoed to a loud bark. He strained at the end of the leash.

Tom leaned back into darker shadow.

Olivia scanned the tree line and retreated a step, tugging the leash with both hands to bring the dog with her. She dragged the barking dog back to the steps. "Quiet," she finally yelled at the dog in a voice that betrayed her physical pain. The animal gave one last sharp bark in the direction of the woods and followed Olivia into the house.

Tom released the breath he had been holding and consulted his watch. He'd wait another thirty minutes to give Olivia time to go back to bed before he made his move. With any luck, she'd take pain medication and would be in an opiate-induced haze, making it easy for him to dispatch her with a pillow held over her face. It'd been so easy to kill his first victim that way. He rubbed his hands together against the cold. His plan was coming together. He'd add Olivia's body to the one in his trunk and head to the crematorium to dispose of them. If that damned dog came near him, he'd finish it off with a kick in the head and add it to the pile.

Tom remained in the shadows, observing the house. Olivia didn't reappear. The curtains were drawn. If she was awake, he'd put on an Oscar-winning performance of concern for her welfare. Then he'd lure her to his car and kill her there. He didn't dare risk creating a violent crime scene in her home. He'd watched enough television to know that the tiniest fiber or hair could convict a killer.

Olivia had identified the rest of his recent victims. They were all listed on that stenographer's pad in her purse. Too smart for her own good—that's what she was. Unfortunately, killing Olivia would take concerted effort. She was young and strong. Thank goodness she'd had this surgery and wouldn't be up to par.

Elderly widows were so easy to dispatch. Helping himself to their money after they were dead was even easier. He'd slip roofies into the cup of coffee that he'd offer them, then finish them off with a pillow over the face. Easy.

Once his victims were gone, he stopped making payments on the bogus annuities he'd sold them. Ponzi schemes were a tremendous amount of work to keep going—Bernie Madoff had certainly come to that conclusion. At least Bernie hadn't been forced to kill off clients to keep himself afloat. Is being alive and penniless in one's old age really better than being dead? He'd watched countless interviews with Madoff's clients—all insisting that Bernie had ruined their lives. His own victims repeatedly bemoaned the fact that they were still alive. They all said that they were anxious to join their husbands on the other side. He just helped them fulfill this wish.

He looked at his watch. It was time. He left the safety of the trees and flattened himself against the side of the house, ducking under her bedroom and bathroom windows until he reached the steps to the back door.

He quietly ascended the steps. The screen door was unlocked. Tom brought his hand to the doorknob of the kitchen door. It was locked. He removed the X-Acto knife from his pocket and cut along the glass of the bottom pane in the top half of the door, carefully tracing the wooden trim holding the glass in place.

He cursed under his breath as he tried to remove the pane without letting it drop and break. The winter gloves that he wore eliminated fingerprints and prevented him from cutting himself on the razor-sharp glass but they were too cumbersome to allow him to be dexterous. He inserted the tip of the X-Acto knife under one corner of the glass and managed to tilt the pane toward him. He grasped it with his gloved hand and inched the pane out of the opening. Tom reached through and turned the lock from the inside. The door opened noiselessly into the kitchen. He paused, listening for any sound. He laid the pane of glass on a stack of newspapers on the counter to the right of the door.

He sidled into the kitchen and crossed slowly to the hallway that he suspected led to the bedrooms. He stepped into the hallway and a floorboard groaned under this weight. Barking exploded from behind the closed door of the bedroom at the end of the hall.

The din penetrated Olivia's foggy brain. The pain pill she'd taken when she'd brought Freddie inside had taken full effect. She pushed herself into a sitting position with unsteady hands. She attempted to throw off her covers but they tangled around her feet. She leaned over and almost fell out of bed as she fumbled to unwind them. She snatched her glasses off her nightstand and stood, swaying slightly. Freddie thrashed and jumped wildly at her feet, knocking her off balance.

Tom froze.

Olivia lunged for her bedroom door and pulled it open. Freddie shot down the hallway, teeth bared. Olivia teetered in the doorway and put her hand on the door frame to steady herself.

Tom drew back his right leg, preparing to deliver a fatal kick to Freddie.

"Tom," Olivia cried. "What are you doing here?" She clapped her hands sharply. "Freddie, come," she commanded. The dog returned to her, keeping wary eyes on the intruder, a snarl locked in place.

Tom put his foot back on the ground and straightened. "Kathy told me you were home and not doing well, so I came by to see if you need anything." He ran his finger under the collar of his shirt and pointed to Freddie. "He's a good watchdog."

"How did you get in?" She paused and it required a concerted effort to form the next sentence. "Why didn't you ring the doorbell?"

"I did, but you must not have heard it," Tom lied. He noted that her eyes looked glassy, her expression unfocused. "I knew you were here and I got worried when you didn't answer so I tried the back door. You left it unlocked."

Olivia brought her hand to her head. "Golly—that's unlike me. I must really be doped up. I always lock my doors." She sagged into the door frame. "I'm worried that the killer from the parking garage is out to get me."

"Are you still concerned about him?"

"Of course," Olivia replied.

"Maybe you shouldn't stay here by yourself," Tom said, improvising a new plan. "Especially now. Kathy said you could stay with her. Why don't you let me drive you over to her house? You don't want to be here if you can't remember to lock your doors. Something could happen to you."

"I suppose you're right," Olivia said. "Kathy's coming by later so I can go with her."

"You shouldn't be alone here until then. Why don't you let me save her the trip?" He observed Olivia carefully and could see that he'd hit his mark. "You've inconvenienced her enough already, haven't you?"

"When you put it like that, I guess you're right." Olivia turned back to her bedroom. "Let me grab my robe and my medications. Thank you, Tom. I'll be right with you."

He waited for her in the hallway, with Freddie stationed in her bedroom door.

"I've got a meeting at my office in half an hour so please don't take too long," he called. He wanted to grab Olivia and get out of there.

Olivia came out of her room with a small satchel. She clipped a leash onto Freddie and came down the hall to Tom, handing him her satchel.

"Excellent," he said. "I'm parked around back."

Tom put his arm around Olivia's waist.

"I'm alright," Olivia said. "You don't need to help me walk."

Tom's grip tightened. "Nonsense. We don't want you to stumble."

A sense of unease rippled through her. Something was not quite right, but her mind was too foggy to think clearly. Freddie continued a low, throaty growl.

"Your dog doesn't want to come. Why don't we leave him here? He'll be fine."

"I'm not leaving him." Olivia gave Freddie's collar several short jerks. "Stop it!" she commanded. "I don't know what's gotten into him."

Tom kept Olivia positioned between himself and the animal as he steered her across the kitchen. He shifted his weight and turned her body slightly when they reached the kitchen door. He swung it open and propelled her through. "I'll make sure it's locked," he assured her.

Olivia stopped suddenly and turned back. "Wait," she said. "I need to get Freddie's food." She reached for the door and froze. "You said the door was unlocked. Why's the glass missing?" She raised her eyes to meet his.

Tom's eyes glittered.

"What's going...?" Her words were interrupted by the sound of a car coming up the driveway. Olivia pushed herself away from Tom.

Tom lunged at Olivia, clamping his hand over her mouth. She cried out in pain but the sound was drowned out by Freddie's ferocious barking. He twisted one of her hands behind her back and forced

Olivia through the kitchen and into the windowless hallway. He struck out at Freddie with his foot, landing a solid blow that silenced the dog.

Kathy rang the doorbell and knocked, calling Olivia's name with increasing volume. Olivia sank her teeth into the palm of Tom's hand. He swallowed a curse and tightened his grip. She thrashed against him, trying to break free and scream.

Tom ground his hand into Olivia's mouth. Despite the medication in her system, pain exploded up through her face until she went limp in his arms. He allowed her unconscious body to slide to the floor.

He listened to Kathy's footsteps as she walked around the side of the house to the back door. He knew he hadn't locked the screen door. If she opened it and found the missing glass pane from the door, she would call the police. She climbed the back steps and knocked firmly on the screen door as she called Olivia's name. He held his breath and waited. She didn't open the screen but returned to the front door and resumed ringing the bell.

Tom moved swiftly to the back door and secured the lock on the screen door. Freddie cowered quietly in a corner of the kitchen. Tom heard footsteps approaching and dropped to the floor.

Kathy stopped at Olivia's bedroom window and rapped on the window frame, calling her name.

He crawled across the kitchen to where Olivia remained unconscious in the hallway. Tom heard Kathy try the screen door before her footsteps receded and he heard her start her car and drive down the gravel driveway.

She'd raise a hue and cry for sure—she might even be calling the police to request a health and wellness check. He needed to collect Olivia and get out of there.

He managed to pick her up firefighter style and staggered under her weight to the back door. He was making his way through the door when Freddie recovered himself and lunged at Tom, delivering a glancing blow to his wrist. Tom flung his arm out to the side, sending the dog back into the house and the Rolex that the dog had snagged with his teeth into the yard. He pulled the door shut and locked the screen.

Tom stumbled but caught himself before he and Olivia sprawled onto the grass. He spread his stance wide and paused to catch his breath, shifting her center of gravity to balance the load. He continued to his car, unaware of the loss of his watch. He opened his trunk and recoiled at the stench of rotting flesh. He stuffed the unconscious woman into his trunk with the corpse, poking and prodding Olivia until he could slam the lid shut.

He put his car into gear and headed to the crematorium. It was time he finished with them both.

CHAPTER 45

Kathy hurried to the reception desk and motioned for Flora to put the person she was talking to on hold.

"What's the matter?" Flora asked.

"Where's Sam? His car is in the lot, but his office door is shut."

"He's in there, but said he doesn't want to be disturbed."

"Really? He never does that. Well," Kathy said, "he's going to be disturbed this time."

"He'll be annoyed," Flora warned. "Can't it wait?"

Kathy shook her head vehemently. "I think Olivia is in trouble."

"What do you mean? Weren't you just at her house?"

"I was and she never answered the door."

"Maybe she was asleep? Those painkillers can knock you out."

"I rang the doorbell over and over. I even went around the back and pounded on her bedroom window. That new dog of hers was making enough noise to wake the dead but suddenly went silent." She stifled a sob. "I'm telling you what—something's wrong."

"You're right—you need to talk to Sam. He always knows what to do in an emergency."

Kathy took a deep breath and marched to his closed office door. She knocked on the door frame and opened the door without waiting for his response.

Sam swung around in his chair. "I don't want..." he began, but stopped short when he saw the look on Kathy's face. He jumped out of his chair and came to her. "What's happened?"

Kathy recited the details of her recent trip to Olivia's house. "I never should have left her, Sam. If something's happened to her, I'll never forgive myself."

Sam steered her into a chair in front of his desk. "I understand your concern, but I'm sure Flora is right. She's just sound asleep, which is probably the best thing for her right now."

Kathy shook her head. "I don't think so."

"I was just finishing up and getting ready to leave. How about I go check on her and if she still doesn't come to the door, I'll call the police for a wellness check."

"Do you think she keeps a spare key in her desk? I have one in mine."

"She might. I'll nose around her office. If she does, that'll be much easier than calling the police."

"Okay," Kathy replied, wringing her hands.

"Try not to worry. I'll call you when I'm there. If she's still really bad I'll insist that she come with me and I'll bring her to your house. I won't take 'no' for an answer." He looked into the anxious eyes of the older woman. "Does that make you feel better?"

"It does. Maybe I let my imagination get the better of me."

"I suspect you did."

Kathy nodded and headed for her desk while Sam walked the short distance to Olivia's office. He sat in her desk chair and paused. It seemed intrusive to be rifling through her desk while she was out. Still—his motive was pure and he'd promised Kathy.

He went through the organized drawers carefully. It was only in the bottom drawer—full of neatly labeled files—that he found the folder bearing the simple title "home." The file contained copies of the new deed placing the property into her name, her paid-off mortgage, and her homeowner's insurance policy. Nestled in the stack of papers was a metal ring bearing one key.

This has to be a spare key. Sam sighed in relief. He pocketed the key and was replacing the folder in its proper alphabetical order when his eyes were drawn to a folder labeled in bright red capital letters: VICTIMS.

Sam hesitated, then pulled the folder out of the drawer and opened it. By the time he'd finished skimming the first document, he turned on her desk lamp and settled into her chair. A cold knot formed in his stomach as he began a thorough review of the contents of the folder.

CHAPTER 46

Byron pulled into the school pickup lane and spotted Missie at the front of the line. She was standing on her tiptoes, searching for his vehicle, and waved her arm over her head in a large arc when she spotted him.

"You seem anxious to get out of here today," he said as she opened the passenger door and climbed in.

"I am." His daughter turned to him, her face shining with excitement. "Ms. O texted Mrs. Walters that she's home from the hospital and everything is fine. I want to stop by her house so we can give her our present."

"I don't know if that's such a good idea, sweetie," Byron said. "She may not be up to having visitors."

"We don't have to stay. She's going to love that stuffed dog. He looks exactly like Freddie." Missie turned big eyes on her father. "You know how much I like stuffed animals when I'm sick. Besides," she said, sealing the deal, "if she isn't feeling well and Freddie is too much for her to handle right now, we can bring him home with us."

"We don't have time to go home to pick up the stuffed dog before—"

Missie held up her backpack. "Got it right here," she said proudly. "I made a get-well card and signed both of our names and everything."

Byron raised his brows. "Looks like you've been planning this for quite some time."

Missie nodded.

"I'm not about to stand in the way of an organized woman and her mission," he said, smiling.

Missie kept up an excited chatter the whole way to Olivia's house. Her eager anticipation soon turned to disappointment and then worry when Olivia did not answer the door.

"She must not have come home yet," Byron said. "Maybe Mrs. Walters was mistaken."

Missie shook her head. "Freddie's in there, barking his head off. Ms. O wouldn't have left him alone. Something's wrong."

Despite the chilly temperature, a rivulet of sweat inched its way under Byron's collar. His instincts told him his daughter was right.

"Let's walk around the back of the house. I want you to stay right here by my side, you understand?" He looked into Missie's eyes.

She nodded solemnly.

"Leave your backpack over by the car."

Missie obeyed and tucked herself next to him as they walked into the back yard. Byron tried the screen door but it was locked and concealed the broken glass in the inner door. He pounded on the windows, calling Olivia's name. The only sound was Freddie's forlorn yelping.

"You're worried, aren't you?" Missie asked.

"Maybe," Byron said. "I'm going to drop you off at Aunt Gail's for the night. Would that be okay?"

"So you can look for Ms. O?"

"Something like that."

"Let's get out of here," Missie replied.

CHAPTER 47

Searing pain radiated from her throat through her left ear and jolted Olivia back to her senses. The rigid body of Dorothy Ransom poked into her at a dozen different points. *I'm lying on top of a corpse!* The frozen flesh burned through her thin nightgown.

She cracked one eye open to the lightless interior of the trunk. She was inside something that was moving at high speed. Her right arm was pinned to her side in the confined space. She shifted her body and could feel the woman's teeth on the back of her head. Olivia shuddered. She snaked her arm free and reached up to touch the hood of the trunk. The memory of Tom Hilton, stifling her scream, came flooding back to her.

She must be in the trunk of his car. With another of his victims. Tom had to be the man she'd seen in the parking garage. He'd killed the others, too. She groaned, the guttural sound filling the small space. *He's the murderer. And now he's got me!* Why hadn't she suspected him? What had she missed?

Saliva pooled in Olivia's mouth. She swallowed hard, willing herself not to throw up. Her stitches were bleeding. The metallic-tasting liquid made her gag. She turned her head to one side and allowed the saliva to roll down her chin.

Olivia squeezed her eyes shut. Now was not the time to give in to her rising panic. What advice had she heard on the morning news show months ago if she ever found herself locked in the trunk of a car?

Olivia extended her left foot and felt along the back of the trunk until she found the driver's side tail light. She kicked at the tail light with as much force as she could muster in the confined space, breaking it free on her fourth kick. The darkness beyond the hole told her that it was after sundown.

She tried to shift her weight so she could kick out the other tail light, but the rigid corpse pinned her in place. Olivia thrust her foot through the tail light she had just broken. She waved her foot around, hoping to draw the attention of any other cars on the road.

Her hopes dimmed when the car slowed down, made a sharp right-hand turn, and came to a stop. She pulled her foot back into the vehicle.

Olivia held her breath and listened, but couldn't discern any sounds over the hammering of her heart. The car resumed its forward motion, slowly turned left, and then backed up a distance of no more than thirty feet. She felt the slight lurch as he put the car in park and turned off the ignition.

He's coming for me! This must be where he disposes of his victims. She was acutely aware of the body beneath her. He'd be planning to get rid of both of them.

Olivia's head throbbed. The mental fog induced by the pain pills had worn off. For the first time in days, she was clear-headed. *There has to be something I can do. I'm not going to let him kill me.*

Tom pulled into the parking lot of the crematorium and quickly closed and locked the gate. His luck had held—he was certain no one had seen him enter the premises. He maneuvered the trunk of his car up to the overhead door that led into the oven room.

He opened the overhead door and used the flashlight on his phone to light his way to the large walk-in cooler. He wrestled with the finicky old handle and the door swung open, engulfing him in a blast of cold air. He stepped inside and turned on the light to the left of the door. Cardboard boxes containing cadavers waiting for cremation filled the wide shelves that lined the room. A long rolling cart stood in the middle of the room, the cardboard coffin that it bore at the perfect height for transportation into the oven.

The trio of industrial sized fans along the upper wall ran at full speed, keeping the putrid odor of decaying flesh at bay.

Tom nodded slowly. This would be the perfect place to store Olivia while he prepared the oven. When Dorothy Ransom was being processed, he'd deal with Olivia.

Olivia heard the click of the trunk's release latch when Tom pressed the button on his key fob. This could be her one chance to get away. She would take him by surprise. She brought her knee to her chest and flexed her foot. She felt her blood pounding in her temples as adrenaline surged through her veins.

The trunk opened slowly and Tom bent over the still bodies. When he was within two feet of her, Olivia struck out at his face with her free foot, catching him squarely on the chin and sending him reeling backward.

Olivia grabbed the rim of the open trunk and hoisted herself out. Tom reached for her, catching the hem of her jacket with one hand. She fell to one knee and yanked the fabric out of his grasp. She rose and ran toward the closed gate, flinging herself at it. One hand caught the top of the gate. She began to pull herself up and over the gate. *Hang on! You're almost over it!*

Tom reached her as she was shifting her weight to the outside of the gate and freedom. He grabbed a handful of her hair with one hand and the back of her jacket with the other and pulled her off the gate and into a vise grip against his chest.

Olivia let out a piercing cry as he clamped his hand over her nose and mouth. She sank her teeth into his hand, tearing her stitches. Tom cursed and forced her teeth apart with the side of his hand, ramming it to the back of her mouth and gagging her. Pain shot through her body. He picked her up and she flailed at his shins with her feet. Tom staggered but regained his footing. He tightened his grip until she could barely breathe and lugged her to the cooler.

Tom thrust her against the back wall of the cooler with such force that it knocked the wind out of her. She bent double, sure that he'd broken a rib.

"You bastard," Olivia gasped. "You're the man from the parking garage. You killed that woman and you've killed others. All old ladies."

"Until now." His eyes glittered.

Olivia's blood ran cold. "You're a monster."

"I just escorted them to a destination they were headed to shortly anyway. Most of them were longing to get there." He shook his head slowly and wagged his finger at her. "But you—you wouldn't be in this predicament if you hadn't started sticking your nose in where it didn't belong." He put his hand on the door handle. "This is really all your own fault. I didn't want to kill you, but you made it necessary."

"They're going to catch you, you know." She tilted her chin to look at him. "You got away with the others, but you won't get away with killing me." Could she reason with this madman? "Turn yourself in. Now." Olivia held out her arms in supplication. "Sparing me would be a mitigating factor that will work in your favor."

Tom stared past her with bright eyes. "It's too late for that. My only hope is to finish this. I'll take care of her." He jerked his head toward the room behind him. "Then I'll be back for you. If you behave yourself, I'll be merciful and kill you before I put you in the oven."

He stepped back and the door shut with a resounding clank, leaving Olivia shrouded in darkness broken only by the scant red glow of the power switch.

CHAPTER 48

Tom leaned against the closed door of the cooler and caught his breath. Olivia had more fight in her than he'd anticipated. With any luck, hypothermia would set in and finish her off before he had to attend to her.

He turned his attention to his ghoulish task and set the controls on the oven. He needed to act fast. No one would be looking for Dorothy Ransom, but Olivia was another story. This had to be his last one. He was at the end of the line. If he could just get this mess handled, he'd quit. Maybe he'd even stage his own death and disappear. A smile played at the corners of his lips.

He opened the oven door and released the breath he'd been holding. Unlike the last time, the chamber was empty. He knew Steve wouldn't have left town with unfinished work.

Tom approached the open trunk. The full moon swathed Dorothy's body in grotesque shadows. He was breathing heavily when he bent to lift her body out of the trunk. The struggle with Olivia had taken its toll and his right hand, still tender from weeks ago in the parking garage, throbbed. He manhandled the stiff body onto the trolley at the end of the oven. He closed his trunk and the overhead door. The dial on the temperature gauge told him the oven wouldn't be ready for another twenty minutes. By the time he had cremated both bodies and collected their ashes, it would be close to dawn. He needed to let his wife know that he wouldn't be home.

Tom pulled back the sleeve of his jacket to check the time on his watch. He gasped: his Rolex was missing.

He swayed and put out his hand to catch himself on the trolley. Dorothy's body pitched forward and dangled off the edge.

Where in the hell could I have lost it? He threw his head back, trying to remember the last time he remembered seeing it.

It must have come loose when he was struggling with Olivia. *That watch will place me at the scene where I lost it.* He strode to the cooler and wrenched the door open, shutting it again just as quickly as he'd opened it. The girl had shown him she had a surprising amount of fight in her. He'd need a weapon to finish her off before he approached her again. The watch would most likely be out here or in the parking lot.

He searched the area around him, then opened the overhead door. He used the flashlight on his phone and made a thorough search of the lot and the area by the gate. His watch was nowhere to be found.

Tom cursed and made his way back through the overhead door, once more sequestering himself inside the crematorium. If his watch wasn't in the cooler with Olivia, it must be at her house. There could be no worse place for it to be found. Damn it! If he had to go back there to look for it, he'd kill Olivia now and cremate her and Dorothy together. The two bodies would equal the size of one large man; surely the old oven could manage that without emitting a noticeable plume of smoke and ash. Even if it did, the industrial businesses surrounding the crematorium were vacant at this time of night. He'd have to risk it. He needed to find his watch.

CHAPTER 49

Olivia slumped against the back wall of the cooler. She was acutely aware of her full bladder. She put her elbow up to her nose and took short, shallow breaths into her sleeve. Bile rose in the back of her throat and this time she was powerless to control it. She leaned forward and vomited on the floor.

She worked around the dead every day of her life; she wasn't ready to join their ranks. She took a shuddering breath and gagged again. *I'm not going into that oven. There has to be something I can do.*

Olivia brought her fingertips to her temples and forced herself to focus. Although she didn't come to the crematorium often, she knew what the inside of the cooler looked like. Olivia could hear the three industrial fans that serviced the refrigeration unit whirring to her left. The switches for the overhead light and the fans were located along the wall to the left of the door.

Olivia took one tentative step forward, then another, in the direction of the door. On her third step, she banged her shin against the rolling metal cart that held a cardboard casket containing the next body waiting for the oven. She bent over and placed a hand on the cart and followed it along until she reached the end, where she dropped to her knees. Feeling in front of her with her hands, she located the metal door. Olivia groped her way up the wall and flipped on the light switch, sending the room into a sterile brightness.

She blinked rapidly. There's got to be something in here that I can use as a weapon. The cooler was devoid of anything other than shelves, coffins, and the rolling cart. Olivia rested her head against the wall. *Think!*

People were often cremated with their personal effects—maybe one of these coffins contained a gun or a knife. She should go through them. A wave of revulsion washed over her. *I have to do this.*

Olivia forced herself away from the wall and stiffened her spine. A dull ache radiated from her jaw. She turned to the cardboard casket on the cart and attacked the closures with shaking hands. She struggled and finally wrenched them free. She drew a deep breath and lifted the lid. *You've seen hundreds of bodies—this is no different.*

The elderly man in the casket was clothed in what must have been his Sunday suit. He held a simple wooden cross in his hands. The calluses on his hands told her that he had been a manual laborer. Probably a decent, hardworking man. She paused, looking into the face of the man that was beyond caring. "I'm so sorry," she whispered. "I've got to do this."

Olivia pried his arms from his chest and went systematically through his pockets. She found an old black-and-white wedding photograph and an embroidered handkerchief. She glanced at the photo. He'd been handsome when he'd been young, with the promise of a happy future with the petite brunette on his arm. She groaned and placed the photograph and handkerchief back into the top breast pocket of the jacket. There was nothing she could use. *I'll search every coffin in here. I'm not giving up.*

Her teeth began to chatter as she reached for the lid of the casket. She stopped suddenly and stared at the cadaver. He won't care. With considerable effort, Olivia rolled the man onto one side and began the laborious process of removing his jacket. "I'm sorry," she breathed, "but I'm not going to let him kill me and I'm not going to freeze to death, either." She wrestled the jacket free of the man, shoved her arms into the sleeves, and drew the jacket around her, buttoning the top two buttons.

She was beginning to close the lid when she felt a slight weight in an inside pocket. Hadn't she already checked there? Olivia thrust her hand into the pocket, forcing it to the bottom. Her fingers hit a small, almost cylindrical object. She pulled out a Swiss Army knife. Could one of its tools be useful?

Olivia removed the photograph and handkerchief from the breast pocket and placed them in the coffin. She picked up the Swiss Army knife and unfolded each utensil. She choked back a sob when she reached the knife. The two-inch blade wouldn't do her any good.

Damn it! She raised her arm in frustration and attempted to hurl the knife into the opposite wall but the corkscrew caught on the hem of her sleeve. She yanked it free and her eyes fell on the screwdriver. She stopped short. Could it possibly be? She hesitated, then picked up the wooden cross. With a final glance at the serene expression of the man who was now clad in his white shirt and striped tie, she closed the casket.

Olivia crossed to the switch plate to the right of the door. It housed the switches for both the light and the fans. The fans ran on 220 volt commercial electrical current. She only needed to use one of the live wires. It would be enough.

She clutched the small screwdriver and carefully began to unscrew the first of four screws that secured the switch plate to the junction box. Both the switch plate and the junction box were metal—ideal for conducting electricity. The first few turns were laborious as the miniscule screwdriver repeatedly slipped off the head of the screw. As soon as she could turn the screw with her fingertips, she abandoned the screwdriver and twirled the screw with practiced hands, removing it and placing it between her teeth. How long had it taken to remove that one screw? Three minutes? She didn't know how much time she'd have to put her plan into place before Tom came back for her. She'd have to be quicker with the other screws.

Olivia proceeded to remove the three remaining screws, cursing under her breath each time the screwdriver skidded off the head of the screw. Clamping down firmly on the four screws between her teeth, Olivia removed the switch plate and placed it in the pocket of the cadaver's coat.

She stared at the wires and connections in front of her. The ground wire would be the one coated with green insulation and was located on the bottom left side of the switch. Even with the fans turned off, she'd still be working with live wires. She only had to rewire one of them, but she'd have to be extremely careful. An anguished moan escaped her lips. *It's my only hope.*

Olivia swallowed hard, taking care not to dislodge the screws. *I can't make a mistake.* She shook her head to dispel her fear and rehearsed the steps in her mind. This wasn't so very different from rewiring a toaster.

You can do this, she told herself. Handle the wires by their insulation. Keep the wooden cross in your hand so that the live wires only touch the wood. *Focus. Focus!*

Olivia shut off the switch on the right side of the plate and the fans fell silent. *That's the one I need to work on.* She mentally ran through her plan one more time and began.

Olivia brought the screwdriver to the top screw and forced herself to slow down. She couldn't afford to fumble and drop a screw or—worse—the screwdriver. Tom could return for her at any moment. She proceeded cautiously and removed the screws that secured the switch to the box, positioning them in her teeth with the other screws.

She pulled on the switch but the stiff wires that were crammed into the junction box behind the switch prevented her from drawing it out of the box. She used her left hand to carefully free the switch from the jumble of wires and moved the switch out of the box.

Olivia focused on the ground screw on the lower left side. She brought her screwdriver to the head of the screw and used her strength attempting to loosen it. The screwdriver glanced off the metal screw head and she lost her grip. The screwdriver clattered onto the metal floor of the cooler.

She froze, an epithet on her lips. A wave of panic washed over her. She had to loosen these screws and complete the rewiring. *My life depends on it.*

She peered at the screw head: it was a Phillips-head screw. *Damn!* She should have checked—she'd just assumed that all the screws were the same kind. *What now? None of these corpses is going to have a Phillips-head screwdriver.*

How long had she been working at this already? Olivia knew she had to hurry. She'd have to make this screwdriver work. It could be done; she'd used a straight screwdriver on a Phillips-head screw before. It would just take more time. *Time I may not have.*

When she didn't see the screwdriver, Olivia dropped to her knees and felt under the edge of the cart. The tool was nowhere to be found. She leaned into the cart, pressing her cheek into the cold metal and sending a sharp jab of pain along her jaw. She moaned involuntarily as she stretched her right hand as far as it would go underneath the cart. She was about to withdraw it in defeat when her fingertips connected with a small object. Olivia clenched her teeth and pressed her hand further. She could just reach it. She hooked a fingernail over the Swiss army knife and slid it toward her knees.

She grabbed the tool so hard her nails dug into the soft flesh. She wasn't going to drop it again. She got clumsily to her feet and inserted the tip of the screwdriver into the "X" in the head of the screw. Olivia carefully exerted force. The screw turned. A trickle of sweat wound down the side of her face. She turned the screw four more times. Grasping the insulated wire with her thumb and index finger, she yanked it free of the loosened screw.

Olivia walked her fingers along the ground wire to the wire nut. Keeping a tight hold on the loosened ground wire with her right thumb and index finger, she unscrewed the wire nut with her left hand. The small piece of wire that had grounded the switch for the fans was now free. She removed it from the box and laid it in the palm of her right hand. It extended from the base of her palm to the middle of her index finger—probably five inches. *It's long enough.* She carefully placed the piece of wire into her pocket with the switch plate.

Olivia inhaled deeply through her nose and brought her fingers once more to the switch that she held clamped to the cross gripped in her left hand. *You don't have much time.* She fit the tip of the screwdriver into the upper right screw head and tried to turn it. The screw wouldn't budge. She exerted more force and the screwdriver glanced off of it. The tip of her thumb jammed into the sharp metal of the screw head, leaving a bloody gash in her fingertip.

Just one more step. You can do this. She had to loosen the screw enough to remove the wire connected to it. Olivia wedged the screwdriver into the screw head a second time. She drew a deep breath to steady herself and turned the screwdriver. This time, the screw moved. She clamped down on the screws in her teeth, the sharp edges digging into her lips. She loosened the screw three more rotations and removed the wire clamped to the switch.

Olivia released the breath she'd been holding. She retrieved the piece of wire from her pocket and slipped the "j" hook of the wire underneath the screw. Using the pad of her fingertip, she tightened the screw enough to hold the piece of wire in place. Olivia grasped the insulated portion of the wire and brought its free end down to touch the metal junction box.

There! This has to work. She pushed the switch back into the junction box and secured it in position with one of the screws. She pulled the switch plate out of the pocket of the corpse's coat. The rewiring had taken far longer than she'd expected.

Olivia positioned the switch plate back in place, pressing firmly against it to trap the wire against the junction box. The switch plate no longer fit flush, with the piece of wire now secured between it and the junction box, but it would have to do. All she needed was to get one screw into place to secure the switch plate in position. She removed one of the screws from her teeth and hurriedly brought it to a hole in the switch plate. She turned it with the pad of her forefinger. There, she thought, as she removed her hand. The screw fell to the ground as soon as she let go.

Olivia's hand shook as she retrieved another screw and brought it to the switch plate. It slipped out of her grasp and joined the other screw at her feet.

Damn it! Fear shot through Olivia like the electric shock she was working to engineer. The switch plate had to be back in its place. Her plan depended on it.

She hadn't come this far to fail now. Olivia furrowed her brow. *You can do this.* She took another screw out of her teeth, guided it to the top hole on the switch plate, and carefully turned it until it was securely in place.

Olivia was reaching for another screw when she heard the click. The door handle moved downward. She gasped and lost the remaining screw in her teeth. Being careful not to touch the metal parts, she swiped at the switch to turn off the light and flung herself on top of the cardboard casket on the cart, making sure that every part of her was up on the cart and away from the floor. If she'd done her job correctly, the rubber wheels of the cart would be the only thing that would save her. She held her breath, praying that she'd guessed right.

The door opened slightly, sending a sliver of light across the floor. Olivia winced and turned her head aside.

The door shut again and the latch dropped back into place. Olivia's pulse throbbed in her temples and a wave of vertigo washed over her. She clung to the sides of the casket and squeezed her eyes tightly shut as the dizziness subsided. *Have I done everything right?* Now was not the time to succumb to panic. She replayed her actions in her mind.

She got off the casket and crept back to the door. Olivia felt along the floor with both hands for the screws but found none and finally abandoned her task. One screw would have to do.

She turned the collar of the jacket up around her ears. With this extra layer of protection, the temperature in the room would be manageable for the near term. She could always pull more clothing off other corpses if she needed to.

Even though the fans had only been off a few minutes, the stagnant air was putrid. She once again put her nose in her elbow to breathe through her sleeve, but the foul smell seeped down her nose into her mouth. She forced herself to swallow rapidly and wondered how long she could endure this before she vomited uncontrollably.

Olivia was climbing back onto the casket on top of the rolling cart when she stopped suddenly. She brought her right leg back to the floor.

She felt her way back to the door. She hoisted her nightgown to her waist, squatted, and urinated on the metal floor as close to the door as possible. Fluids and electricity were a lethal combination. She resumed her perch on top of the rolling cart to wait for her would-be killer. She ran her hand over the cardboard. *I don't know who you are, but you may have saved my life.*

If her plan worked, reaching for the switch would be the killer's last act. God help her if her plan didn't work.

CHAPTER 50

Tom grasped one of the short metal rods used to push remains into the processors, wielding it in his right hand like a weapon. Her time had come. He strode to the door of the cooler. He had to know if his watch was in there with Olivia. If it wasn't, he'd kill her and cremate the two bodies together so he could return to her house to look for his watch before anyone else found it.

He opened the heavy door into the dark cooler. The smell of decaying flesh accosted him. He took a step forward onto the moistened floor.

Olivia stared at the figure, silhouetted in the opening. A shaft of light from the doorway fell onto Olivia, illuminating her as if she were on stage. His face was in darkness but she could see his chin twitching.

"This is all your fault, you nosy little bitch. If you'd just left well enough alone, we wouldn't be here. I would have invested your money well." His voice crackled. "I'm actually good at my job. These little old ladies," he jerked his head toward the oven, "were longing to be dead anyway. Now you get to join them."

Reach for the switch! she thought.

He coughed in an explosive burst and gagged. He bent over and choked, recovering himself before he vomited. He reached for the switch with his left hand as he began to raise the iron rod in his right.

Olivia shrank to the back of the casket, panic rising in her. She clung to the cart, forcing herself to stay off the ground. *Touch the switch!*

Tom brought the rod up and extended it back behind his head.

Touch the damn switch! Olivia lowered her left foot off the cart until it touched the floor. She crouched over the casket, keeping her eyes locked on Tom.

The hand holding the iron rod began its descent toward her. Olivia heard herself scream. She used her left foot to propel the cart forward, sending it into her assailant.

Tom fell forward onto his knees and dropped the iron rod. He put his hand onto the wet floor to catch his fall. "What the hell?" He coughed again.

Olivia lifted her left foot off the floor.

His outstretched left hand, moist with urine, went for the switch. The electrical circuit was complete. An unearthly wail escaped his lips and then died out.

Olivia watched in horror.

Tom's body jerked violently. The smell of burnt skin joined the odor of rotting flesh. The only sound was the crackle of a live electrical current. His eyes bulged and his mouth was set in a grotesque gash as the rush of current caused his heart to stop beating.

The room fell into silence as the circuit breaker popped and electricity ceased flowing. Tom's body pitched forward and hit the floor, his head connecting with one leg of the metal cart with a loud crack.

Olivia pressed her palms to her chest to calm her hammering heart. She unclenched her teeth and a trickle of blood escaped a corner of her mouth.

Tom was dead, she was sure of it.

Olivia slowly lowered her feet to the floor and attempted to stand. The deadly current had stopped when the circuit breaker popped. Her legs shook and her body trembled—whether from shock or the frigid temperature in the cooler, she didn't know. She grasped the iron bars at the top of the cart to steady herself and the cold metal bit into her bare hands.

She wasn't going to die in the oven but she didn't want to freeze to death, either. She needed to step over Tom's body and get to Steve's office to call for help. She lowered her chin to her chest and breathed slowly. Just a little bit more. *You can do this.*

CHAPTER 51

Byron used his flashing lights to cut through rush hour traffic on the way to Hilton Mortuary. He was afraid Olivia was in serious peril.

The funeral home parking lot was full and it was apparent that a viewing was in session. He cut the lights and pulled his vehicle to the rear of the property to the employee entrance. It was unlocked and he made an inconspicuous entrance.

Sam was coming out of Olivia's office as Byron rounded the corner into the hallway.

"Are you here to visit the family?" Sam asked, gesturing with his head to the viewing room.

"I'm here to see you, Mr. Hilton. I'm Officer Tucker."

Sam's eyebrows shot up. "On official business? With me or the funeral home?"

"Your employee, Olivia Osgoode. I'm wondering if you know her whereabouts?"

"She's supposed to be at her home, recovering from surgery. She just got out of the hospital," Sam replied.

"I know about the surgery and just came from her house. She didn't answer the door."

"One of the women here just came from Olivia's house and said the same thing. I'm on my way out there to check on her." He held up the key. "I think this is her spare. I was going to let myself in if she doesn't answer the door."

"I'd like to come with you," Byron said.

"That might be a good idea. I just found some papers in her desk and I'm worried about her, for other reasons." Sam took the folder from under his arm and waved it in front of him. "Olivia's got evidence that there may be other missing women, besides the one she saw in the parking garage. I know this sounds silly, but I'm afraid she's in grave danger."

Byron motioned for Sam to follow him. "I'll drive. I'd like to review that folder but you can tell me about it on the way to Olivia's. We've been stymied since we haven't found a single body. Hard to prove there's been a murder without a body. Eventually, they always turn up."

"Unless they've been cremated," Sam said.

Byron motioned him to the passenger side of the patrol car. "What do you mean?"

"The manager of our crematorium thinks that our utilities are too high out there—that either our meter is malfunctioning or someone is using the facility after hours."

"Would that be possible?"

Sam nodded slowly. "It's possible but highly improbable. Very few people know how to operate the equipment and only a few of us have a key to the facility."

Byron exited the parking lot and activated the flashing red lights. He listened without comment while Sam summarized the information that Olivia had gathered about Cheryl Robinson and Dorothy Ransom. It was dusk when the two men arrived at Olivia's home.

They left the engine running and doors open as they sprinted up the front steps. The flashing lights sent slashes of red across the white siding. Freddie sent up a ferocious din.

Byron rang the doorbell and pounded on the door, calling Olivia's name. Without waiting for her answer, Sam inserted the key into the front door. It wouldn't turn.

"There's a back door," Byron said, grabbing the key and racing toward the rear of the house.

The key opened the screen door and Byron cursed when he saw that a window pane on the door had been removed. He pushed the door open and both men rushed inside.

Freddie cowered in a corner of the kitchen while Byron and Sam quickly searched the small house, calling Olivia's name.

"She's not here," Sam said.

"Looks like she was planning to go somewhere," Byron said, lifting up the satchel that contained her medications that lay in the kitchen where Tom had dropped it. "But she never got to go there."

Sam moaned. "This isn't good, is it?"

"I'm going to call this in," Byron said. "Go wait in my car."

Sam headed out the back door. He was about to step around the side of the house when something metallic on the gravel caught his eye. He hesitated, then walked to the item and bent to pick it up. His blood ran cold the minute he touched it. He didn't need to turn it over to check for the engraved initials. This was his brother's watch. He choked as he gasped for breath. This could mean only one thing. He ran back into the house.

"I've found something," he said, his voice cracking as he placed the watch in the palm of Byron's hand. Their eyes met.

"This is my brother Tom's watch," Sam said, turning it over and pointing to the engraved initials "TH" on the back. "Thomas Hilton. Tom is one of the only people who has a key to the crematorium and knows how to operate the equipment."

Both men began to run toward Byron's car. "What's the fastest way to get to the crematorium?" Byron asked.

Sam jumped out of the car before Byron brought it to a complete stop. The padlock for the gate lay on the ground and he thrust the gate open with shaky hands. A loud groan escaped his lips when he recognized his brother's car, backed up to the overhead door to the oven room.

Byron placed his hand over his service revolver and caught up with Sam. "Tom's car?"

Sam nodded. He was already throwing the overhead door open. "Where's the light switch?"

"Inside the doorway, on the right-hand side."

"Wait here," Byron ordered, blocking Sam's progress with an outstretched arm.

Sam nodded slowly and stepped back.

Byron flipped the switch on the wall, to no avail. "Get my flashlight out of the glove box," he ordered.

Sam complied.

Byron switched on his flashlight and shone it around the room. The light threw eerie shadows in its path. He took a step back when it came to rest on the tangled mass that was Dorothy Ransom's body.

Olivia heard the clank of the overhead door as it was thrown open. She turned toward the door and saw the arc of the flashlight tracing across the room outside the cooler—beyond the body of the man she'd just killed. She drew air into her lungs and tried to open her mouth to call out. Pain exploded behind her eyeballs.

Byron stepped further into the room and could make out the faint glow of the lights on the oven's control panel. "OLIVIA," he shouted. "POLICE."

Olivia released her grip on the cart and took a step toward the voice. She faltered and went down on one knee. She spat out saliva and blood that had pooled in her mouth. The flashlight came closer.

She heard his footsteps and released a guttural moan.

"Olivia!" Byron appeared in the doorway.

She held up her hand to shield her eyes as he swept the light across the scene. "Olivia!"

"He's… he's dead," she gasped.

Byron lowered the beam of his flashlight to the floor. Tom's body lay in the center of its bright circle. He leaned over, placed two fingers on Tom's neck, and confirmed what he knew to be true from looking at the body.

"Are you alright?" He stepped over the body and squatted next to Olivia, drawing her to him.

"Yes," she replied in a small voice, leaning into his embrace.

"What happened to him?"

"I hot-wired the switch so he would be electrocuted when he came to get me." A sob caught in her throat. "He was going to kill me—kill me and cremate me with that poor woman out there."

Byron let out a low whistle.

"I was trying to work up the nerve to crawl over him and call the police. The circuit popped when he…" Her voice stuck in her throat.

"Is everyone okay?" Sam's voice came from the area just inside the overhead door.

"I'll need you to stay back," Byron called. "Don't come any further."

"Is Olivia here? Is Tom?"

"Olivia's here," he shouted, turning back to her. "You're really something, you know that?" He stood and pulled her with him. He lifted her over the corpse and set her down on the outside of the cooler. "I'm going to bring her to you. She's suffered trauma and needs to go to the hospital."

Olivia shook her head in disagreement as Byron led her to Sam. "This isn't up for debate," he told Olivia firmly. "Call an ambulance," he ordered Sam. "Take her out to my car and put her in the back seat. You can call from there. Stay with her."

Sam nodded and put his arm around Olivia's waist. "What about Tom?" he asked, turning over his shoulder to Byron. "Is he here too?"

"I'm sorry, Sam." Byron said. "Your brother is dead."

Sam stopped abruptly and glanced away, then resumed his progress. "I'm so sorry," he said into the still night air. He looked into Olivia's tear-rimmed eyes. "I'm so sorry this happened to you."

CHAPTER 52

Olivia put her hand to her heart as the nurse brought in yet another bouquet of flowers. "I don't know where we're going to put all of these," the woman said. "I've never seen anyone get so many flowers."

"That's because Olivia is a local hero—solving a case that the police didn't even know was a case in the first place." Kathy patted the covers next to Olivia's leg.

"I don't need all of these," Olivia said, sweeping her arm around the room. "Why don't you give them to other patients who need cheering up?"

"That's a great idea," the nurse said. "One of the aides will get right on it. But we'll leave some for you to take home."

"I've got two inquisitive cats at my house, so I won't be bringing any of them with me."

"You're not going home, young lady." Kathy placed her hands on her hips and faced Olivia. "Freddie and your cats are at my house and you'll be staying with me until you're fully recovered." She held up a hand to silence Olivia's protests. "Not another word. Your grandmother would never forgive me if I allowed you to go home."

Olivia sank back against her pillow. "I think I'd like the company right now." She smiled at Kathy. "Thank you."

Both women turned their attention to the door as Byron knocked softly on the door frame. Missie stood in the doorway, smiling from ear to ear.

"Hey Ms. O," she said. "Can we come in?"

"Of course you can," Kathy said. "You stand right here next to her." She stepped aside. "I want to get myself a cup of coffee, anyway." She winked at Byron as she passed him. "Officer Tucker has been checking on you every day since you've been in here," Kathy said over her shoulder.

Olivia felt herself flush. "That's nice of you but unnecessary. I'm fine."

"We've got something for you," Missie said. "We were going to give it to you when we went to your house and found that you weren't there."

Missie thrust a gift bag into Olivia's hands. Olivia removed the stuffed dog from the bag.

"He looks just like Freddie, don't you think?" Missie gushed.

"He sure does," Olivia said, smiling and hugging the toy to her chest. "He's adorable. Thank you so much." She leaned forward and drew Missie into a hug.

"That's not all we've got for you," Missie said, swaying from side to side. She looked up at her father. "Tell her, Dad."

"Detective Novak will be contacting you to arrange a formal installation ceremony, but he authorized me to tell you that the Marquette Police Department is awarding you its Medal of Honor and naming you an honorary member of our department for your bravery and heroism."

Olivia's breath caught in her throat. "That's ridiculous. I didn't do anything..."

"You most certainly did. Your ingenuity and calm under pressure are an inspiration to us all."

Missie said, "The mayor is going to have a day in your honor and you get to be the Grand Marshall of the Founder's Day parade this year. You can even invite a friend to ride with you in the back of that fancy convertible. If you wanted to—you wouldn't have to."

Olivia laughed. "I wouldn't want to be by myself. Would you ride with me?"

Missie nodded vigorously.

Byron pressed her hand into his. "Looks like good things are happening to a deserving person."

Olivia smiled and squeezed his hand.

"If you have time when you get out of here, I'd like to take you to dinner."

"I'll definitely have time," she said, smiling up at him. This might just be the best news of all.

THANK YOU FOR READING!

If you enjoyed FINAL CIRCUIT, I'd be grateful if you wrote a review.

Just a few lines would be great. Reviews are the best gift an author can receive. They encourage us when they're good, help us improve our next book when they're not, and help other readers make informed choices when purchasing books. Reviews keep the Amazon algorithms humming and are the most helpful aid in selling books! Thank you.

To post a review on Amazon or for Kindle:

1. Go to the product detail page for FINAL CIRCUIT on Amazon.com.
2. Click "Write a customer review" in the Customer Reviews section.
3. Write your review and click Submit.

In gratitude,
Barbara Hinske

ACKNOWLEDGEMENTS

I'm blessed with the wisdom and support of many kind and generous people. I want to thank the most supportive and delightful group of champions an author could hope for:

My insightful and supportive assistant Lisa Coleman who keeps all the plates spinning;

My life coach Mat Boggs for your wisdom and guidance;

My kind and generous legal team, Kenneth Kleinberg, Esq. and Michael McCarthy—thank you for believing in my vision;

The professional "dream team" of my editors Linden Gross, Kelly Byrd, and proofreader Dana Lee;

Ardra Hansen and Rachel Brown for so generously sharing your knowledge about funeral homes and the cremation process;

Electrical engineer Paul R. Bzdak for your exceedingly careful review and extremely helpful editorial suggestions;

My favorite electrician on the planet Tony Boyer for patiently explaining to me—and showing me—how electrical wiring works!;

Electrical engineers Kim Humphry and Christopher Hanks for their technical review and comments; and

Elizabeth Mackey for a beautiful cover.

ABOUT THE AUTHOR

BARBARA HINSKE recently left the practice of law to pursue her writing career full time. Her novella *The Christmas Club* has been made into a Hallmark Channel Christmas movie of the same name (2019), and she feels like she's living the dream. She is extremely grateful to her readers! She inherited the writing gene from her father who wrote mysteries when he retired and told her a story every night of her childhood. She and her husband are slaves to their two adorable and spoiled dogs. They live in a historic home that keeps her husband busy with repair projects and her happily decorating, entertaining, and gardening. She also spends a lot of time baking and—as a result—dieting. Together they have four grown children.

Please enjoy this excerpt from **DEADLY PARCEL**,
the first installment in the "Who's There?!" Collection:

CHAPTER 1

The knife blade, honed to a professional sharpness, traced the orbital bone and along the ridge of the nose, slicing open a neat fissure. The dead man was beyond caring. It circled the lips, bluish-purple in the early stages of lividity. The tip of the knife sank easily into the ridge between lip and chin. One swift motion and the lower lip swung free.

The knife moved upward and hovered over the body, laid prone on the floor. A slim shaft of moonlight glinted on the blade.

The tip moved down and found the knot on the lace of the right shoe. It sliced the knot open and worked its way along the loops, breaking the laces. The shoe came off.

The blade probed the ankle, poking and pressing until it found the indentation between the ankle bone and the fibula. The blade pressed until it encountered the tendon, rigid and tough. A small trickle of blood, aided by gravity rather than the pumping of the now-still heart, trickled onto the floor.

The knife carved through the tendon and sliced through the tissues until it separated the tibia from the calcaneus. The foot dropped into the blood below.

The tip plunged into the fleshy underside of the foot, skewering it and lifting it up and into the Ziploc bag that was its intended destination.

The blade wiped across the corpse's shirt as it made its way to the dead man's right hand. Once more, the tip poked the bruised flesh until the wrist joint was penetrated. The tendons proved less dense than those of the foot. A series of precise cuts yielded the desired result. The severed hand was removed to another Ziploc bag.

The corpse's face was the next target. The handle pressed into the left cheek. Rigor mortis had set in. Considerable force was needed to turn the face to the side, exposing the left ear.

The blade meticulously outlined the soft fleshy junction between the skull and the ear. This final prize was the easiest yet. The ear came off with one expert cut and plopped into its own Ziploc bag. An oozing hole gaped in its wake.

The three bags—with their heinous contents—were now ready.

Available at Amazon in Print, Audio, and for Kindle

Guiding Emily

The "Who's There?!" Collection

DEADLY PARCEL

FINAL CIRCUIT

The Rosemont Series

Coming to Rosemont

Weaving the Strands

Uncovering Secrets

Drawing Close

Bringing Them Home

Shelving Doubts

Novellas

The Night Train

The Christmas Club (adapted for The Hallmark Channel, 2019)

UPCOMING IN 2020

The seventh novel in the Rosemont Series

I'd love to hear from you! Connect with me online:

Sign up for my newsletter at
BarbaraHinske.com to receive your Free Gift,
plus Inside Scoops and Bedtime Stories.

Search for **Barbara Hinske on YouTube**
for tours inside my own historic home plus tips
and tricks for busy women!

Find photos of fictional Rosemont and Westbury,
adorable dogs, and things related to her books at
Pinterest.com/BarbaraHinske.

Email me at **bhinske@gmail.com** or find me at
Instagram/barbarahinskeauthor
Facebook.com/BHinske
Twitter.com/BarbaraHinske